Alice

at heart

Deborah Smith

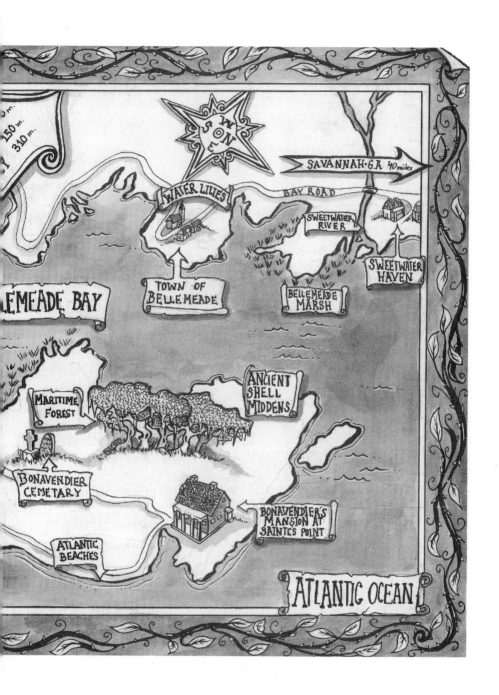

ALICE AT HEART

BY

DEBORAH SMITH

www.authordeborahsmith.com

ISBN 0-9673035-2-4

ALICE AT HEART

First Printing: January 2002
Copyright 2002 Deborah Smith
ISBN: 0-9673035-2-4
All rights reserved. No part of this book may be reproduced or transmitted by any means without the written permission of the publisher.

BelleBooks
P.O. Box 67 Smyrna, GA 30081
www.bellebooks.com

Cover Art: "Stars" by Maxfield Parrish
Cover Design: Martha Shields
Map and Bonavendier Family Crest: Dino Fritz

Author's Note

Without the friendship and assistance of a number of fine people, this book and the books to follow it in the WaterLilies series would not exist. My deepest gratitude goes to my wonderful partners in BelleBooks—Debra Dixon, Sandra Chastain, Virginia Ellis, Martha Shields, and Nancy Knight. No doubt, we'll sit in our company-owned beach house some day and toast our success with tall mint juleps. In the meantime, it continues to be a pleasure and an honor to work our way up the sand dunes together. Thanks also to Maureen Hardegree and Ellen Taber, whose skillful copyediting found all my lost commas, split infinitives, and transposed letters, except the ones probably lurking in this author's note, which was written after their inspection. For that, dear readers, they deserve no blame.

Regarding the lovely Maxfield Parrish painting ("Stars,") which is used on the cover of this book, I wish to thank Alma Gilbert, curator of the Parrish Museum in New Hampshire, for allowing BelleBooks to reproduce the artist's fantastic work. From the first moment I saw a print of "Stars," I knew it conveyed the tone of my story perfectly. The work of Maxfield Parrish evokes the sweetest fantasies, and I am now a devoted fan.

Finally, I'd like to thank the unusual and intriguing couple I met while strolling on the secluded beach of a Georgia island a few years ago. I have no doubt that you both dived into the surf as soon as I was out of sight beyond the next dune. I hope you don't mind that I've used you as inspiration. Sometimes, in my dreams, I imagine I hear you singing.

So, maybe, just maybe, you're still out there beyond the soft shore.

Dedication:

This book is for Hank, Mother, and Alba
(aka "She Who Lives By The Sea.")
And for Oscar, my dear old friend.

Water is life, water is love, water is the womb.

—Lilith Bonavendier
Fables of the Water People

The Old Ones are all wayward women with tales behind them, you might say—luring ordinary men to mate and meander and occasionally drown. Those Old Ones give us, their halfling descendents, a lurid reputation but also great charm, and we had best remember to use both wisely. By nature, you see, we are very hard to believe in, but very easy to love.
—*Lilith*

One
~

We are all bodies of water, guarding the mystery of our depths, but some of us have more to guard than others. I've never known quite who I am, but worse than that, I've never known quite *what* I am.

This morning I stood naked beside the icy waters of Lake Riley, high in the Appalachians of north Georgia, above the fall line where the tame Atlanta winters end and the freezing wild mountain winters begin. A mile away, in my dead mother's hometown, Riley, people were just breaking the ice on their gravel roads and barnyards and church lots and sidewalks, stomping the mountain bedrock before little stores with mom-and-pop names, most of which belong to heavy-footed Rileys. But there I was, alone as always, Odd Alice, the daughter of a reckless young mother and an unknown father who passed along some very strange traits. I had slipped out to the lake from my secluded cabin for my morning swim. Doing the impossible.

I should freeze to death, but I don't. It is February, with a high of about twenty-five degrees, and the lake has an apron of ice like the white iris on a dark eye, narrowing my peculiar view of the deep world beneath. I should fear its dangers, but I don't. Water is the only element in my life I trust fully and completely. I stood there in the cold dawn as usual, not even shivering.

As I stretched and filled my body with frigid air, I looked out over the icy mountain world and heard a thin trickle of sound. It stroked the frosty branches of tall fir trees so far around a bend in the lake my ears shouldn't be able to recognize it if I were like anyone else. The sound was a child screaming. And then I heard a splash.

I dived into the cold, safe water, deep into the heart of the lake, faster than anyone imagines a person can maneuver, fluting the currents with the iridescent webbing between my bare toes, able to go farther, deeper, quicker, and for much, much longer in that netherworld than any human being possibly can. Across the lake, down twenty feet, then thirty, then forty. Into the darkness of a world I love.

I've never had a vision before and never wanted to. But suddenly there he was—not the child whose scream I had heard, but a man, or the illusion of one. He was so vivid in my mind's eye, floating in front of me as if he were flesh and blood. He was clothed in a diver's wet suit, torn and bloody. His dark eyes, half-open and dreaming of death, were set in a handsome, determined face. He gagged and fought. I felt his pain, his fear, his confusion. Yet I knew he could live if he wanted to. The oxygen had not failed in his lungs; he had failed to believe in it.

No, no, no, I sang out. *Breathe.*

He looked straight at me, and a kind of wonder appeared on his face, infusing him. He understood. He breathed.

And for the first time in my life, I wasn't alone.

∾∾∾

Griffin Randolph had not been prepared to be rescued by a vision. A few minutes earlier, in the vast, dark ocean off the coast of a Spanish fishing village, he had touched one hand to a small tattoo on his left forearm, where a naked woman held a dolphin in her arms. *Now I'll find out which one owns my soul.*

As a scuba tank hissed its last minutes of oxygen into his lungs, he once again aimed a cutting torch at the shelving that had collapsed around the legs of his nervous diver, an Italian nicknamed Riz. Griffin and the diver were deep inside the cavernous hold of a sunken American cargo ship, the *Excalibur*. During World War II, the *Excalibur* had ferried ammunition to allied warships off the coast of North Africa until a German submarine torpedoed it. Alongside Griffin and the trapped diver were stacked hundreds of gunnery shells, each as thick as a man's forearm, all nearly a half-century old, threatening to tumble to the bottom of the ship's hull.

No problemo, Griffin's head diver, Enrique, had proclaimed when they first surveyed the ammunition. *Old and wet. Not going to cause us any trouble.* Griffin had agreed until the storage shelving collapsed on Riz. As the crew worked methodically to free him, Griffin discreetly picked up one of the precariously balanced shells.

The old missile spoke to him, just as he feared it would.

Death.

The sensation—which he often felt in the water, but never revealed to anyone— became a silent song. Sound waves vibrated in his brain, and waves of energy shimmered along his skin. In every instance where some object spoke to him, Griffin felt an almost orgasmic shiver, the stroking of an unseen and dangerous hand. Along with that sensation always came knowledge. And this time that knowledge made Griffin's blood freeze.

Riz's dazed eyes begged him to hurry. The rest of Griffin's six-man team huddled on the surface aboard the deck of the *Sea She*, Griffin's massive boat, whose high-tech, state-of-the-art computers and dredges and sonar and satellite tracking systems had helped locate some of the world's most famous undersea treasure wrecks. *All of it is absolutely goddamned worthless for saving a man's life right now*, Griffin thought.

He strained to see through the fierce light spewing from his cutting torch in the dark Mediterranean water. The torch finally burned through a thick steel cable, and he hurriedly pried the tangled shelving apart with hands too large and brutal for the bourbon-and-magnolias Southern aristocracy that had birthed him.

Riz kicked and struggled. Griffin's gaze went back to the shells, hundreds of them, ready to fall. All it would take was the right one, just one. Finally, he eased Riz free. The diver's face relaxed into smiling eyes. Griffin squeezed his shoulder, tugged on the guideline attached to a harness, and instantly Riz began to float upwards through the water, pulled by a powerful electric wench. As he disappeared above Griffin the shelving shuddered and gave a soft, wrenching groan. A half-century after men had died inside its steel sanctuary, the *Excalibur* wanted to close like a flower over what remained.

Griffin eased out of the tomblike hull, *feeling* the ship's sinister memories, the hum of its ghosts inside him, the hum of his own ghosts, too. The *Excalibur* was just waiting for him to move. No, it wasn't the ship waiting. It was the ocean. Always waiting for him to make one *wrong* move.

Test me, Griffin told the invisible forces. He surged upward, exiting the hull with a speed and grace that always astonished people when they saw him swim, even hampered by scuba gear. He shrugged off his tank, spit out the mouthpiece, then ripped the mask from his eyes. He propelled himself toward the light, dozens of feet above him.

Inside the depths of the *Excalibur*, one shell tumbled from the shelving. It pirouetted downward through the dark water, almost beautiful in its heavy grace. It struck the hull's bottom with a muted clang, its voice the last ringing of any bell for the lost ship.

And it exploded.

The world erupted in billowing, churning chaos. Griffin felt a giant hand slap him from below, then sweep around him, squeezing him between invisible forces. The ocean, which had always been a living monster to him, pressed him in its jaws. Pain shot through his body; his eardrums ruptured. His wet suit tore and then his skin as fragments of the *Excalibur's* hull sliced him. The explosive concussion slammed into his brain. He went limp and floated, filling the water with his blood.

He opened his eyes, dreaming of death.

No, no, no! Breathe. A voice. Feminine, urgent, strong. She sang to him silently in a stunning vibration of emotion that conveyed meaning.

Griffin struggled. *Can't. No one can. Impossible. Can't breathe.*

You can. Try.

Suddenly his lungs expanded, he expelled the water from his throat, and somehow, life bloomed into blood-red oxygen inside him. A mystery. A miracle.

Who are you? he begged.

Just Alice.

Then, she was gone. He made himself remember, as darkness filled his brain, that he was alive because of an extraordinary illusion named *Alice,* singing to him beneath the bloody water.

~~~

I blinked and the man was gone. I was alone again in the freezing, black water at the bottom of the Lake Riley dam. My hand closed around a little girl's soft arm. She had sunk, unconscious, into a grotesque underwater landscape of junked cars and appliances and huge, tickling catfish. The temperature slowed her heart and respiration, making her as quiet as a hibernating animal, prolonging her life, saving her. The water can be so kind.

She did not know she was drowning, I think. I carried her to the shallows. Her parents screamed when they saw us. Two local paramedics and several of our county sheriff's deputies began yelling.

At me.

"I found her—" I started nervously, but

then they were all over me. The men snatched the child away and threw a blanket around her as I huddled in the lake with my arms crossed over my breasts. Then they dragged me out and covered me, too.

"What the hell are you doing out here, Alice?" yelled one of the deputies, a Riley cousin of mine.

How could I possibly explain? I lay there on the ground, hugging the blanket over me, and said nothing. In the water, I came alive. On land, I tried very hard to be invisible.

At the moment, I wished I were dead.

Water People say the earth formed as an afterthought inside the glorious depths of great seas, hardening like the dull, dry pit of a luscious fruit.
—Lilith

Two
~

Two hundred miles southeast of Lake Riley, the Bonavendier sisters of Sainte's Point Island, Georgia, were already as much legend as fact. They were rarely seen outside the ethereal borders of their moss-draped barrier island or the beautiful little coastal village, Bellemeade, across from it. It was said that all three were older than sixty, yet all resembled beautiful young women. It was said when they were truly young they'd suffered terrible tragedies out in the world and had returned to the island, vowing never to leave again. It was said they'd secluded themselves even more after murdering Undiline McEvers Randolph—their own distant cousin from Scotland—and her blue-blooded Georgia husband, Porter Randolph, of the Randolph Shipping dynasty. But that had been nearly thirty-five years ago, and who knew what was truth and what was gossip anymore?

The accepted facts were these: The

Bonavendier sisters owned Sainte's Point Island and most of Bellemeade, culturing the tiny village like a pearl: the shops exquisite, the bay front inn, WaterLilies, a place of true charm, the marina across from main street a perfect combination of hardworking fishing boats and exotic little yachts. People swore a kind of enchantment came over them when they visited the town. They gazed across Bellemeade Bay with wistful envy at the island, which made a faint strip of wooded magic on the horizon of the Atlantic Ocean. *Look toward the other side of the world*, people said, *and you'll see Bonavendiers.*

Sainte's Point Island, enclave of the Bonavendier family since Revolutionary War times, was glamorous, notorious, alluring, and haunted by gossip even stranger than murder. It was said every Bonavendier for two centuries had been born with webbed feet, always swam naked, could seduce anyone at will, was beloved by dolphins, and drank like a fish. Vodka, preferably.

Most of the rumors, if people could have believed them, were quite true.

That night Lilith Bonavendier dreamed of lost children, again. A cold dawn breeze slid through the open French doors of her bedroom. She turned restlessly, naked, her hair streaming over her body. *Oh, Griffin, that I could have saved your dear mother, at least.* The eldest of the three Bonavendier sisters sighed as the drowning, black-haired boy cried out to her and her sisters to save his parents, too. Other souls came and went in the mists behind her eyes. Lost chances, lost futures, terrible secrets. Lovers, children. Her only son. All the Bonavendiers who would never be born. Bonavendiers who floated between land and water, lost.

Suddenly a little girl appeared in Lilith's dreams. Like Griffin Randolph, this child was outside the realm of the womb. This mystery girl with auburn hair and haunted green eyes floated in an endless void just beyond Lilith's reach.

Lilith woke with a jerk and sat up in a massive, canopied bed of teak wood and Asian silk. She rose and hurried toward the morning light at her open doors, throwing a turquoise robe around her slender body and stroking aside hair that hung in wavy tangles to her knees.

Be calm. It was only a dream.

The soft blast of a small boat's horn sent Lilith hurrying down a hallway filled with antiques and antiquities, the shells of giant sea turtles, the skulls of small whales, a Picasso portrait of her grandmother, a Van Gogh of her great-grandfather, a bust of a caesar filched from a Roman wreck. *An ancestor of ours,* some Bonavendier wag had written on the bottom.

Lilith descended the mansion's curving gothic staircase. She swept past her younger sisters' bedroom suites and then the mansion's front parlors warm with fine lounges, exquisite works of art, well-played musical instruments, and exotic books. Several luxurious cats and a fluttering white cockatiel joined her, screeching at the chilly sub-tropical winter. Lilith padded barefoot onto a deep veranda strewn with heavy wicker, plush cushions, and several ancient Grecian urns of suspiciously authentic conformation. She stood for a second, gathering her senses in the pink light, her webbed toes curling on a floor of smooth ballast stones her ancestors had plucked, along with gold, from a wrecked Portuguese merchant ship in the late 1700s. A large lawn and massive oaks dripping moss stood before her. Below them was a pretty cove where boathouses and docks housed the island's vessels. Beyond that, the Atlantic burst in frothy tides on the beaches at the edge of the continent.

Several small commercial fishing boats bobbed in the cove, waiting for Lilith.

She followed a path down a terraced slope, composing her regal face by the time she arrived at the docks. The rough men and women who captained the small fleet stood on the bows of their boats with respectful patience. The steam of their breaths rose around them. They fought the chilled air in heavy sweaters and lined slickers, while Lilith stood there wearing only sheer silk, unfazed.

"Good morning, ma'am," each said in a languid drawl.

"Good morning, ladies and gentlemen. The grouper are running out beyond the reef, and you'll have good luck with them until nearly noon." She went on, detailing other prime catches and fishing sites for the day and telling them the weather would begin to warm by midweek.

"Thank you, ma'am," each said.

This ritual was as old as the Bonavendier legacy on Sainte's Point. For over two hundred years, the mainland villagers had relied on Bonavendier guidance regarding fish and fowl, weather and tides. As a result, the small town of Bellemeade was one of the most prosperous fishing burgs in coastal Georgia, and no citizen had ever been caught unawares by a hurricane.

"Your newspapers, ma'am," a captain said and stepped off his boat just long enough to present Lilith with a canvas bag stuffed with local, state, national, and even several international editions of newspapers. She knew she should buy a computer and gather her news from the Internet, but that would disrupt the ritual.

"Thank you for the news of the world," she said, as always.

The boats motored away, their engines fading into the slow lap of the surf on the cove's sandy rim. Lilith spread the papers across a low marble table taken from an English ship in 1822. A chorus of soft whistles and clicks signaled the arrival of a dozen dolphins in the cove, their bulbous, blue-gray heads protruding just above the dark water as they spoke to her. She acknowledged their agitated greetings with a low keen of welcome.

"Be calm," she called out. The cockatiel settled on the tabletop, still shrieking. "Be calm, Anatole," she said to the moody bird. "Be calm," she said to the cats, which paced the pebbled ground around her feet. All felt her mood. *Be calm*, she said to herself, again.

Lilith unwrapped the *Savannah Morning News* first. The front page fell open as if commanded, and she saw the day's headlines.

Savannah native Griffin Randolph critically injured in explosion. Relatives rush to side of controversial treasure hunter in Spain

Lilith pulled the paper closer, urgently seeking more information about him. *This was why I dreamed about him.* He was her cousin Undiline's son. As a child he'd been caught up in a tragedy from which Lilith's family had never recovered. *Oh, Griffin, Griffin.* But as she tried to concentrate on the details of his accident her gaze was drawn to another large headline above a story and photograph.

Suspicions taint rescue of governor's grand-daughter from icy lake
"Impossible circumstances," authorities say.

Lilith had no time to recover from the shock of Griffin's circumstances. She raised a hand to her throat. A photograph taken outside the doors of a small hospital in the mountains of northern Georgia showed a pale, slender young woman in obvious distress. She stared out at the world with stunning green eyes beneath a scruffy cap of auburn hair. Her body was swamped in pajama-like blue scrubs the hospital must have loaned her, and she clutched a white hospital blanket around her like a shield. A crowd of frowning, yelling paramedics, police officers, reporters, TV cameramen, and others seemed to be on the verge of rushing her back through the doors or attacking her. The young woman's horrified expression and humiliated eyes leapt out at Lilith like a scream. Lilith read about her quickly.

Alice Riley of Riley, Georgia.

Alice Riley.

She had to be Joan Riley's daughter. Lilith took one look at her and saw the resemblance, but more than that, she *felt* it. So Alice Riley hadn't died as a baby. *She's alive,* Lilith thought, reeling. *And Griffin is alive but hurt—and somehow, his fate has crossed Alice's. That's what my dreams have meant.*

Lilith threw her arms wide to the pink and magenta glow on the horizon. She had not sung in more than thirty years. The music, the flow, the vibration, had been lost in tragedy and regret, though she'd tried in vain to recall it so many times. Now, suddenly, welling in Lilith's soul, stunning her, came a vibrato symphony. She caressed the world with waves of emotion, as much a beacon as the lighthouse that could be glimpsed above the pines far down at the island's southern tip. Tears slid from her green eyes.

There is hope for this family, this place, our kind.

Inside the mansion, her sister, Mara, sat up in her bed. Mara put her hands to her throat. "No, no, no," she whispered to herself. "Whatever it is, let's leave well enough alone. We're safer that way."

In another suite of the huge house, Pearl Bonavendier turned to her lover, Barret, and began to cry with joy. "Lilith is singing again." She and the aging German held each other tightly.

"It's a miracle," he said.

Up and down the southern coast, in clapboard farmhouses and antebellum mansions, in shabby trailer camps and suburban bungalows, sleeping mothers nuzzled their babies like dolphins, and women making love turned their faces from their men, yearning for the ocean. Out on that ocean, fishermen smiled in their bunks on huge tankers and factory ships, or paused at their nets on family shrimp boats that had worked the cold winter night, or turned from their fishing reels and first mugs of hot coffee on deep-sea yachts. All stiffened with arousal, warm and puzzled, trying to hear what they couldn't fathom, mysteries that ultimately made them both eager and a little afraid. There was so much about the deep waters of the world that remained unknowable, yet always, always, irresistible.

On the operating table of a Spanish hospital, Griffin gave a deep sigh in response. The surgeon said in Spanish, "Holy Mother, I can't believe it, but I think he's going to survive."

High in the mountains of Riley, Georgia, Alice woke in the icy lake where she'd taken refuge during the night, and her misery became a slow keen of confused wonder. She'd never heard anything so mysterious and so beautiful.

Lilith ran up the path to the seaswept mansion, calling for her sisters. She and they had lost their souls, their passions, their family's future, years before. Now, Griffin Randolph and the long lost Alice Riley would bring it all back.

Lilith sang.

The Nagas of India were matriarchal tribes named for the mythological serpent children of the Goddess Kadru. They were said to host fantastic undersea mansions and keep mystic books of wisdom, and in return, the goddess granted them long lives. What a beautiful story. All true.
—*Lilith*

Three
~

I rescued the governor's granddaughter. *The governor of the entire state of Georgia,* I write in my journal, as if there were any other state. He commands that world from the mountains to the sea, all the small towns with their Confederate memorials and barbecue festivals, the pragmatic little cities ringing themselves with identical shopping malls and stucco townhouses on tiny lots, and the stewing megatropolis that is Atlanta. In my intemperate and worried mind, he is suddenly elevated to royalty, the king of a kingdom, also ruling our major league sports teams, our Olympic legacy, our mythical Tara, and me.

His son, the prince, is a well-to-do young lawyer, and the son's wife is a lawyer, as well, with a long corporate pedigree attached to her name. Not the type to welcome strange

27

mountain women into their circles or to admit any carelessness. They had lost track of their little girl while setting up camp for a hike up Riley's high ridges and granite over looks, that border the national forest. She had wandered to a picnic area near Lake Riley's massive concrete dam and mistaken the frail ice around a dock for a skating rink.

"You hid in the bushes and watched her until she fell in, didn't you?" an investigator asked me. "You knew whose granddaughter she was. It's been in the local paper—that the governor's family was up here, hiking. You knew if she fell in you could get publicity for finding her. And a reward."

"I didn't mean any harm," I kept repeating, which probably did not sound innocent, now that I think about it. "I was only out for a swim, and I heard her scream."

How did you hear her scream from your end of the lake, Ms. Riley? That's a mile away. How did you get there in just a few minutes? Nobody swims that fast. Your relatives say you're frail. You have allergies. You're sickly. You can't swim like that. No one can swim like that, Ms. Riley. An Olympic gold medallist couldn't swim that fast. How did you know where to look for the little girl at the bottom of the dam? How did you find her down there? Why were you swimming naked in weather cold enough to make ice on the water? Why didn't you feel the cold? When you got to the dam, how did you dive under for so long the fire department had time to drive way out to the lake and put on their scuba gear before you surfaced with the little girl? That was over fifteen minutes, Ms. Riley. That's not humanly possible. Not possible. Not damned possible.

Tell us, Ms. Riley. How did you do something no one can do?

Tell us, Ms. Riley. How did you pull off this hoax. And why?

"It's not a hoax," I told them. "It's just what I can do." They only stared at me in disgust. After some discussions outside my earshot, they decided to let me go about my business for now, but I'm still terrified. I know what can happen when people want to convince themselves there's nothing to fear from me.

~~~

Freak. Weirdo. Let's see if crazy Alice really has tits. A half-dozen of Riley High School's most popular boys held me down one September day when I was fourteen years old while several girls watched, laughing. I was a pale pencil of a teenager with huge green eyes, auburn hair that grew so fast I had to trim it daily, and a mouth so pink in contrast to my complexion that I sometimes smeared white corrector fluid on my lips to dull the effect. I hid behind oversized clothes and speechless passivity, though that rarely prevented trouble. People were afraid of me. I saw it in their eyes, and I began to realize that only by acts of bullying cruelty could they prove I couldn't harm them. That year, I had returned from summer vacation with some semblance of a bosom growing on my stick-thin body. My classmates dragged me into the woods behind Riley High and pried my plaid blouse open to see if I had developed breasts like a normal girl. Then they tore my loafers off and looked at my webbed feet for proof I hadn't really changed. Finally, they poured a tepid bottle of cola down my throat and watched in curious disgust while I vomited and broke out in large, seeping hives. My allergies were as peculiar as the rest of me.

After they left me that autumn day, I hid in a grove of laurel shrubs and sobbed while vomit dried on my disheveled clothes. When my legs stopped shaking, I raced through the deep firs and hardwoods of the forest outside town to my beloved, isolated lake. I stripped, dived in, and tried to drown myself—intending to, meaning to, spiraling down nearly one-hundred feet to the bottom of the lake's dam, where I curled up in the pitch-black darkness inside the rusted cab of a junked car.

A long time later, when I realized I simply wouldn't die, I floated wearily to the surface. My skin had turned the lovely color of a pale blue Easter egg. I had a ravenous craving for pure, creamy butter, and my cheap wristwatch had stopped from water damage.

I stared at it. I had been under for nearly an hour.

That was the first time I realized just how fully different I was. Every human physiology book I'd read said my abilities simply were not possible. And none of the great religions explained the meaning of my unnatural existence, although some hinted darkly that I might be the spawn of dark forces. My Great Aunt Judith, who never married and was treated as a servant by the other Rileys, raised me like a wild yard cat she was forced to feed. I crept unnoticed through her stern brick split-level in town, peeking out her polyester drapes at a dull lawn she paid a neighbor boy to mow like a bad crewcut.

Marooned on that loveless island, I escaped by reading every novel in the Riley Municipal Library, losing myself in the melodrama of operas and symphonies, and scribbling disjointed poetry.

Water. Smooth. Life. Flow.
How do I find it?
How will I know?

Whenever possible, I ate only oily canned tuna, sticks of butter, and soda crackers dipped in bacon grease. Otherwise, I became dreadfully ill. Great Aunt Judith seemed to think I was infecting myself, a natural wick, soaking up germs. She cited that bizarre rationale when she sprayed disinfectant throughout the house and helped me cut my auburn hair, so that it remained only about an inch long. My nickname throughout elementary and high school was bleakly funny but excruciating. *Eraser Head*.

When my great aunt died, she left me her house as if in apology. I sold it and bought my little cabin in the woods beside the lake. In the years since then, I've filled the tiny place with good books and art posters I buy at a flea-market frame shop over in Hightower, the county seat. My furniture consists of odd pieces I've purchased at yard sales and refinished in soft white shades, the colors of sand and sun-bleached shells. I've painted the cabin's walls blue-black and the ceilings pearl gray, the way the sunlit surface of the lake looks from underneath. I pretend I live inside a vast, beautiful sea.

A few years ago, I saved enough money from my job at the Riley Pet Shoppe (where I specialize in fish) to purchase a computer, which I adore. I correspond with oceanographers, marine biologists, retired naval officers, and other folk who love the world's great bodies of water. So I have been content enough. I swim in my lake, I communicate with the world, I stock my refrigerator with butter and canned seafood, I clip my hair daily with a thick electric razor, and I keep my thoughts to myself.

Until now. I am so frightened and lonely.

Reporters have already begun asking about the fact that my pretty, teenaged mother, Joan Riley, drowned herself in Lake Riley. I was only two days old when my mother walked into the water, thirty-four years ago. The Rileys say my father was an evil stranger who never looked back once he ruined her good-girl life. Mother obviously agreed since she killed herself rather than raise me. There's no rational reason why I swim in the lake that took her, except I can't resist a body of water.

And it can't resist me.

I sing to the water, and the water sings back. These songs—if that's what they are—come to me as naturally as my other unnatural talents. I've read about echolocation in dolphins and radar in bats, and what I do must be similar. I sense objects in the water by vibration, shaping them in invisible waves of sound, feeling them echo in my brain before I can see them with my eyes.

Perhaps that explains everything. I'm a human dolphin-bat. Simple.

I keep thinking of the imaginary man with the black hair and hard-jawed face, floating in his own blood. Somehow I knew he could hear me, was like me somehow, had resources buried in the molecules of his body that sustained him but condemned him to a loner's life. I keep trying to see him again when I shut my eyes, but I can't.

Reality, such as it is, has trapped me in a very public torment. I am hiding in my house with the lights off. People drive up my gravel road and yell. Sometime late tonight, when it feels safe to go outside, I'll swim in the deep sanctuary of the lake. Such a trite thing to say, but true: In the water, tears are simply a gift to a greater tide. Nothing else in my life makes much sense. I come from something I don't understand, I am something I don't know, I cannot explain myself.

Except for that one moment, when I touched the man, and the child.

Then I was real.

<div align="center">~~~</div>

Alice, who are you? Where are you? What are you? What am I?

Griffin had very few lucid moments, and most were devoted to the mystery woman, Alice. *Hell of a way to end a career as a treasure hunter,* he thought. *By losing my mind.* He lay in a room in a private Spanish clinic available only to the rich and well connected. His right leg was encased in a cast from knee to ankle, and his left arm from elbow to wrist. He was covered in bandages over sutured wounds. His veins were fitted with IV's, his chest with electrodes, his nose with an oxygen tube. He drifted on a slow tide of medication, and when he thought about what had happened in detail, he sweated.

All his life he'd fought a secret fear of the ocean. Now he lay in bed, dreaming in fluid fantasies that became nightmares. This was not the first time he'd imagined women rescuing him from deep water. He was four years old, broken, bleeding, sobbing, with the ocean pouring down his throat. He floated more than seventy feet below the surface of the cold, stormy Atlantic off the Georgia coast.

Mother. Father. He struggled to point his broken arms toward the bottom. *Go get them, too.*

Hush, child, the water has fallen in love with them. They can't come back.

The voices of the Bonavendier sisters vibrated inside him, their music fearless in the vast, deadly deep, their souls at home in an ocean world where he would never feel safe again.

You hate my parents; you killed them, he cried.

Shhh. Remember only the love.

But he couldn't. Not then, not now.

"Whatever you're dreaming about, stop moving, or I'll get the nurse to pop you with some more painkillers," demanded a voice hoarse from decades of whisky, cigars, and the wrong women. Griffin woke in a groggy daze, tied down by tubes and wires. He looked up at a rugged older man in rumpled khakis and an old flannel shirt. A tiny gold crucifix gleamed in one of his ears. His silver hair was disheveled as always, framing a cynical face tanned brown by the ocean sun.

Charles Anthony Randolph, known as C.A., first cousin to Griffin's father, Porter, gently wiped Griffin's sweating face. "Whatever the hell you're dreaming about, stop it."

"Trying, but I can't," Griffin mumbled, floating in a dream world where the

Bonavendier sisters and a phantom named Alice sometimes gazed at him with amazing green eyes. Alice in Wonderland. "Tired of looking though the looking glass to find nothing. Nothing. Have to find. . . *Alice.*"

"If I take you back to Savannah babbling like this, the family will think you're as crazy as me." C.A. laughed ruefully. As a young man, everyone had expected him to become Porter Randolph's right hand at Randolph Shipping. But then Porter had drowned off Sainte's Point and C.A. had gone off some deep end of his own. "I'm not going to tell any of them the details of this little event of yours," C.A. continued. "Because you know it's a miracle you survived."

"No...miracles in the water. Except Alice."

"Look, I don't know who this *Alice* is—some lady-friend you left behind or not—but God bless her if the memory kept you fighting. You were under water for over ten minutes before your crew was able to find you. The doctors don't understand why you don't have brain damage. They don't understand why you're not crippled. Hell, there're nuns in the hospital chapel who cross themselves every time your name is mentioned. A religious man would say you've gotten a second chance. Time to change your life, hmmm? Toe the straight and narrow? Come in from the sea and settle down? You don't want to end up like your ol' cousin C.A, do you? A salty drunk with strange ideas." C.A. dabbed a cool washcloth on Griffin's head, his touch gentler than his voice. "I don't recommend it. "

"I think. . ." Griffin murmured, "I can breathe underwater."

"Okay, we settled one question," C.A. said with great patience. "You're definitely crazy. I won't tell anybody, I promise. But that's no reason for you not to thank God and haul your ass back into the family fold. Just use me as a bad example. You can change."

Change into what? Griffin thought and tried to remember what he might have been when the water loved him like blue sky.

In our version of Noah's Ark, the world was destroyed by a great drought.
—*Lilith*

Four
∽

After a week of public humiliation and private interrogations, the governor and his minions still can't decide what to do about me, so they've decided to give me an award for saving the little girl. I tried to decline it.

"You will go, Alice, and you will accept," my mother's eldest sister ordered. "Or the people in this town will drive you out like a sick bird in their house. And I'll be at the head of the crowd."

She's told me all my life that I'm a burden, that servitude and gratitude are my only hope of paying back the misery I represent. She has pointed out time and again that my mother won the Miss Riley County Pageant the year before I was born. That she had a scholarship to a state university and had planned to become a teacher. That the son of our Baptist minister was in love with her and they had planned to announce their engagement when she turned eighteen. That she had gone to the coast that summer to work as a counselor at a church camp. And that there, under the sultry sun of the beaches and coves and magnolia-scented ocean, she had allowed some perverted stranger to ruin her and all she would have been.

"Go to the damned ceremony, Alice," her eldest sister says now. "Or else."

So, tomorrow I will accept my *award*.

That's what they call it, anyway.

~~~

"We've forgotten to take chances, to love new people, to attempt dangerous things," Lilith said. "We've created a safe little world on our island. We've become accomplished cowards. But no more."

"The world comes to us," Mara said, scowling. "We haven't been lonely. We have our kind. That's all we need."

"Liar," Pearl said gently.

"We're going to get Alice," Lilith said firmly. "And then we're going to sing Griffin home, too."

"Please slow the car down, Barret. These unnatural heights make me dizzy," Pearl begged.

Barret filled the car's driver seat next to her like an aging, Teutonic wrestler, though dressed in the finest of dark suits. "Yes, my darling," he answered, embroidering the affection with a thick German accent. She gently patted his shoulder in thanks.

The Bonavendiers' old silver Mercedes lumbered toward a bridge high over a mountain creek bed strewn with boulders and lush green rhododendron. Ice glinted on the boulders in the cold winter sunshine.

Lilith tilted her head near a backseat window and stared down into the creek gorge grimly. *What an unfriendly part of the world this is, where water is reduced to sneaking between huge hummocks of land like a tiny, living vein in a dull stone.* She spread a hand over the opalescent gray weave of her dress suit. She, too, felt breathless.

"Oh, I'm dizzy, yes, I am. I'm going to be ill from these heights," Pearl moaned again.

"You can't possibly feel air sick," Mara snapped. Seated beside Lilith in the Mercedes' backseat, Mara faced straightforward, nonetheless, as she twirled one long end of a sheer, emerald-green shawl over her soft white suit. "These are not the Alps or the Rockies. People can't even ski here; there isn't enough snow. It's just all ordinary and rude and *low*." Her blush-pink mouth flattened. She, too, avoided glancing at the deep mountain ravine beneath their car. "You see?" she went on. "I'm not air sick. Lilith's not airsick. And our new mystery 'sister' doesn't get air sick, obviously, since she's lived all these years up here in these godforsaken termite mounds. I say Alice Riley is nothing but a typical, senseless *Lander*."

Pearl coughed. "Breathing is not about altitude, Mara. It's about *attitude*." Pearl steepled a fragrant, manicured hand to the throat of her silk jacket, the nails deep peach against the material's brilliant sapphire blue. Colorful. The Bonavendier sisters were as colorful as tropical fish. "I can only assume poor little Alice has adjusted as best she can to her circumstances, surviving by inherent strength of character. It's a great testament to her Bonavendier lineage if she's managed to survive on such thin air."

"You're assuming poor little Alice *has* a Bonavendier lineage," Mara retorted. "I say 'poor little Alice' is going to be a huge, ordinary disappointment. She's not father's daughter; not really. It just can't be."

"Oh, you're such a cynic! You have the heart of a shark. Yes, a shark." Pearl fluttered her hands. "Keep away! I'm as heartless as a Killer White! I'm Menacing Mara, Queen of the Unimpressed."

"Oh, go swim up a sewer pipe. And take 'poor little Alice' with you."

"I'll hear no more of such nonsense," Lilith said quietly. "Pearl, restrain your whimsies. Mara, hold your sarcasm. I'm tired of you both. This is about our family honor. Our family's past, our family's future. We're going to meet Alice Riley and determine precisely where she belongs. And if what I suspect is true, we're going to beg her forgiveness. Now, *be quiet*."

Pearl and Mara traded accusing glares as if they were teenagers scolded by a teacher. *Don't encourage Lilith's noble guilt,* Mara hissed silently to Pearl.

I like noble guilt, Pearl glared back.

Barret guided the car with mysterious German precision up a twisting mountain road that crested a forested ridge. He devotedly managed the sisters' cars, their boats, their home. He had loved Pearl nearly all his life. *Life*, Barret Anzhausen mused, *ebbs and flows with the gift of extraordinary unknowns and the deepest of faith.* He moved his crippled right leg gingerly as he braked the car. "There is the town of Riley."

In the small valley ahead of them, the plain, pragmatic town of Riley peeped from among skeletal trees and brown pastures, a sterile mountain burg anchored to bone-dry land surrounded by hulking, dry mountains wreathed in winter clouds.

Lilith shut her eyes, filled with pity, regret, and memories from thirty-four years before.

~~~

Young, then, dark-haired and somber, Lilith stood at Joan Riley's grave in the cemetery of a Riley church. Autumn leaves danced across the raw rectangle of red mountain clay. A plain granite marker read simply, *Joan, 1950-1968.* The Rileys had not bothered to list Joan's stillborn baby, though Lilith had understood the baby girl's body lay with its mother's. Lilith shut her eyes. *My half-sister.*

Gold and red mountains looked down like silent guards, making Lilith draw up straighter in response, even as despair weighed her into silence. She touched Joan Riley's engraved name. *My dear, I'm so sorry for my father's indiscretion*, she began, then stopped. There were no words for this tragedy, no song for it.

There was no answer but the unforgiving wind.

Lilith bowed her head in thought as she walked back to the cemetery's gravel drive. *I should have come here sooner. I could have taken care of her and her child. I should have known there was a child.*

The churchyard lay on a knoll overlooking the town of Riley. Pulling a soft cashmere wrap around her pale suit, Lilith looked down at the pragmatic mountain town, sunken into forest. In the distance, the woodland parted to outline a pretty lake, where poor Joan had gone after giving birth to a Bonavendier. It was the only place that would have made sense to an ordinary girl thrust into extraordinary circumstances. Joan had tried to find the water's magic again.

Lilith heard a calling, the tiniest cry, and listened with her head up. But, no, it was just a hawk, screeching in the unfriendly mountain sky. Yet she stood there a long time, searching, not knowing why. Her effort faded. Her shoulders slumped.

We have to move forward, she thought wearily, and *listen no more to the past.*

～～～

Now, years later, Lilith regretted the tiny

song she'd ignored so long ago.

Oh, Alice. I'm so sorry I didn't listen harder. But I promise you, I won't shut my heart again.

∼∼∼

An amplified voice boomed over me. *"And we ask that You look down upon Alice Riley with a true and knowing heart, and show us all her grandness of spirit and weakness of flesh."*

The minister of Riley First Baptist—who, as a young man, had been engaged to my mother—spoke those ambivalent words. He was now an aging small-town preacher with a kindly, dutiful expression. He'd volunteered, when no other minister would, to lead the town in prayer at my award ceremony. His public prayer implied I was neither evil nor saintly but simply a soul in limbo whom no one but God could understand.

I cringed and sank lower in my metal chair. My stomach roiled. The minister droned on. Then, suddenly, *someone touched me without using any hands.*

I felt an odd tingle begin at the back of my skull, like fingers massaging my scalp, but then I realized it was a vibration, humming against my skin, seeping into my brain, calling to me. My heart pounded. I kept my head bent and eyes shut. The humming in my head became so insistent I put my hands to my temples as if in pain. What was happening to me? I imagined my brain actually shimmying between my ears.

A hundred determined Riley citizens

hunkered around me in hard chairs on the cold brown lawn of the town square. A freezing wind whipped the limbs of several stalwart sour-woods, and the last of the season's huge acorns banged like gavels on the roof of the bandstand that served as the ceremony's stage. Every bang made me jump.

The silent song grew louder inside me.

Sweat gathered between my shoulder blades and breasts, melting me front and back, pooling in the creases where my thighs joined my body, wetting me between the legs and under the armpits. I wore a long wool dress, a quilted blue coat, insulated gloves, and a thick polyester scarf wrapped around my throat—all for discreet public effect only. My cold-natured body was roasting alive.

And then, as the vibrations inside my brain rose to a crescendo, a voice whispered to me. *Meet us at the nearest water, my dear.*

A voice. Inside the song inside my head. Feminine, gentle, firm, elegant. Not spoken so much as insinuated. I swayed in my chair. What insanity was this? What delusion was I suffering *now?*

Stand up, Alice. Strip off your ugly, miserable wrappings and bask in the winter sun. Fling a smile at these ordinary fools as you glide away without a shiver. Leave them sitting here bundled up like gray rabbits in their ignorance. Stand up, Alice. Stand up for yourself.

I opened my eyes and scrubbed perspiration from my face. *Leave me alone. Who*

*are you? You don't understand. This life is all I have.
I can't ruin it.*

*You're wrong, Alice. We've found you. We're
here, Alice.*

Who? Where?

Behind you. Turn around and look.

I began to swivel in my chair. A dozen
Rileys, including my mother's eldest sister,
stared at me. I faced forward again. My skin
burned. I was not only hearing voices, I was
replying to them and looking for the owners.
Horrified, I riveted my attention to the
preacher. He raised his head, shut his Bible, and
stepped aside for the mayor. The mayor, a
woman with stark brown hair and the
methodical manner of a woodchuck gnawing a
hard tree branch, began giving a short speech
about me. "No matter how Alice saved that
beautiful little child," she said in a toothy voice,
"it's her secret. We know she'll tell us the real
story about her heroic act someday. We know
she's just too shy to tell us yet. We know the
truth is as heroic as Alice's storybook
explanation."

*How dare she, Alice? Stand up and tell that
pompous little woman your veracity is beyond
question.*

Please, I begged. *Stop.*

"Alice, come up here," the mayor ordered.
Sitting behind me like a watchdog, my mother's
eldest sister clamped a hand on my shoulder and
shoved me slightly. I wavered to a stand, locked

my trembling knees, then slowly made my way across a mere yard or two of winter lawn, every step requiring total concentration. Beads of moisture slid down my face. On the bandstand's stage, a stern man in a gray suit and overcoat rose from a chair beside the podium. I made my way up the bandstand's whitewashed wooden steps as if blind, never raising my eyes to either the people on the stage or the crowd on the lawn.

"Alice," the mayor chewed into the podium's microphone, "please welcome the governor's dear friend." She named the man's name, but it didn't matter. He was a substitute for the little girl's family, an insincere stranger sent to shield them from my strange self. He rose firmly and began to speak, holding up a plaque bearing my name and the insignia of some obscure foundation I'd never heard of, possibly one that had been made up for the occasion. "The governor and his family are sure of one thing—sure they're grateful their precious little girl is alive, safe and well. You did the right thing, Ms. Alice Riley. You know in your heart you did the right thing by saving a child's life, and that's all that matters."

How dare he imply your motives remain in question, the voice whispered.

I gripped my hands together. The presenter held out the plaque almost like a challenge. Several reporters posed themselves to snap pictures, and the white-hot light of an Atlanta TV crew suddenly scalded the scene. I blinked hard. This was my life—eccentric and ugly—this was how people saw me, and suddenly I realized this was how I would always see myself, too, shrinking inch by inch until one day I would simply evaporate.

Sweating, shaking, I turned my head toward the crowd with excruciating care, squinting directly into the TV light, bracing my feet wide apart as my breath shortened to a dizzying pant. A hundred pinched and disapproving faces stared back at me, just like the award presenter, shortening me, melting me, and me letting them. My heart sank. No one was out there but mirrors of those faces.

But then.

But then.

She stepped into a grassy aisle that divided the rows of chairs. She stepped out of the light, it seemed to me, and walked right up that center aisle with a stride more graceful than a dancer's, and she stood, tall and beautiful, silver hair piled in some soft, intricate fashion on her head, her body cased in a beautiful light suit not at all right for the place or the weather. Her eyes were the deepest green, lined at the corners with wisdom, utterly hypnotic. I could not breathe. She didn't lift a hand, say a word, even nod. She sang to me with the silent vibration, the voiceless whisper.

Alice, my dear.

Behind her stood two others, just as amazing, one luxuriously dark-haired, one a flamboyant redhead, their hair upswept, their manner regal, their green-eyed regard so stunning that everyone, *everyone* turned to stare. They wore the finest rich silks, pearl bracelets, diamonds, delicate and elaborate gold pins with handsome gemstones in them. They stood out like angelfish among plain brown trout. Every man in the crowd wanted to touch them. Every woman wanted to be them. I had never seen females so beautiful in my life.

"Alice," the silver-haired doyenne said aloud, in a voice as lyrical as a southern trade wind. She put more devotion in my name than I'd ever heard before. *"Alice, my dear. We're your sisters. Your father's elder daughters."*

Everyone gasped. I took a step back, shaking my head. No one knew who my father was. How could they know *me*? How had they found me?

My Riley aunt leapt to her feet. "Alice," she called out loudly. "I don't care what this is about, just take that award and say thank you, *right now. Alice.* Get off the stage. If you know what's good for you, take the award and quit standing there like a fool."

My gaze sank, defeated, away from the silver-haired woman's troubled scrutiny. Shame clouded my vision. I slid my shaking hand out to take the proffered plaque.

Alice, don't accept so little when you deserve so much. Look at our feet, Alice. Recognize your own kind.

I peeked furtively through the bandstand's

railing. All three women slipped off their exquisite shoes on ground so cold particles of ice crunched in the dead grass. *To show me their feet.* Delicate, arching feet. Perfect, strong feet. Sensual feet, outrageous feet. Adorned with jeweled ankle bracelets, the nails gleaming with glossy polishes. The silver-haired one shifted one naked foot just so, arching it like a swan's head, spreading her toes. The others did the same. I uttered a low, keening sound.

Webbed feet. Like mine.

"Take the damned plaque, Alice," my mother's eldest sister warned again.

My head snapped up. I looked at her, then at the presenter, then at the plaque. I jerked my hand away. I staggered down the bandstand's steps, threw off my coat, and fled, gasping for breath.

In the chaos that ensued, Pearl Bonavendier sighed in dismay. Mara Bonavendier rolled her eyes. "Pathetic," she couldn't help saying.

Lilith frowned and signaled for them to follow.

*Land People fight and struggle and yearn to
find magic in their lives. Water People hide behind
that magic, but realize the loneliness of it.*
—*Lilith*

Five

〜

I hovered like a ghost, shadowed in the
ultraviolet glow of the fish tanks at the Riley Pet
Shoppe. It was a Sunday, and the shop—or
shoppe, as the owner insisted on calling it—was
closed, the lights off, the blinds drawn. The
gloaming of the winter afternoon dropped deep
shadows over the shelves and cages. Watching
me was a menagerie of hamsters, mice,
parakeets, snakes, iguana lizards, and hundreds
of small fish. Every creature, whether fin, fowl,
fur, or reptile, moved to the fronts of their cages
and tanks. The parakeets twittered at me; the
hamsters made soft, squeaking sounds. The fish
merged in neat schools, all facing toward me. I
was a magnet for small creatures, beloved by
them, trusted. I sang to them every day. They
listened.

So did I. I waited for the three web-footed
women to find me. I smelled the fragrance of
their fine perfumes and fabrics as they made

their way down the alley behind the shop; I heard the whisper of their fabulous feet on the concrete lane, there; I imagined just the slightest, alluring tang of sea salt in the air around them. My chest heaved. I clutched a countertop for support.

I jerked my gloves off and dropped them on the floor, tore my scarf away and lost it somewhere on a shelf. The sound of my breathing made a low roar in my ears. *Click.* The shop's back door opened, followed by the softest padding of footsteps beyond the doorway to a storeroom. "Alice," the silver-haired one called quietly from the storeroom. "Shall we enter?"

It was a little late for niceties, now that she'd been inside my head. I backed into an alcove fitted with floor-to-ceiling fish tanks—a dark, safe cave, I'd always thought, surrounded by bubbling water and friendly, swimming creatures. "I'm here," I said in a voice that shook. "With the fish."

The three women entered the shop's main room with the gossamer grace of leaves floating on a stream. I straightened, clenched my hands by my side, and stared at them from my dim corner. They gazed back, the dark-haired one looking impatient, the redhead very kind and earnest, Silver Hair frowning at me with wistful eyes.

"Yes, I'm pathetic," I confirmed quietly, and Dark Hair grimaced.

Silver Hair stepped in front of the other

two like the queen of a small delegation. "No, you are simply—" she paused, searching for the right words—"simply unaware of your true nature."

"Who are you, please?"

"My name," she said, "is Lilith Bonavendier." She nodded toward the dark-haired woman. "This is my younger sister, Mara." And in the other direction, toward the redhead. "And this is my second younger sister, Pearl." She paused. I suddenly noticed that the fish, the mice, the hamsters, the snakes, the lizards, and the birds now faced *her* way. None of them moved or made so much as a peep. "And you," Lilith Bonavendier went on, looking straight at me, "are, indeed, our *youngest* sister."

"Only our half-sister," Mara corrected, then blanched when Lilith gave her a hard look.

I took another step back, pressing myself against a wall of aquariums. Like all the other small creatures, I gazed at the three women in hypnotized wonder. "What kind of game is this?"

"Oh, Alice. Sisterhood is never a game." Pulling something from a tiny silk purse bound to the waist of her exquisite suit, Lilith moved toward me slowly, as if I might bolt, which I might. She laid the offering on the top of short display shelf. "A photograph," she said, "of your mother with our father."

I picked up the old snapshot. My hand shook. I gazed at my teenage mother, smiling on a sun-drenched Georgia beach beside a handsome, white-haired man. Both were dressed in swimsuits, her looking like a wholesome girl next door on the cover of a Beach Boys album, him looking fit and suave and incredibly desirable. And, quite possibly, fifty years her senior.

"This man," I said, "could be my grandfather."

"I assure you, he is not. Father was not an ordinary man. He was, after all, a Bonavendier."

Mara added tightly, "We Bonavendiers don't look our age. Father was eighty-five when he died that summer."

"But still quite a charmer," Pearl amended.

I laid the photograph down. "And if I may ask, how old are you-all?"

"How rude," Mara said instantly.

Lilith nodded to indicate her own lithe form. "I am seventy and quite pleased to be so." She lifted a hand toward Mara, who yipped in dismay. "Sixty-five." And Pearl, who laughed. "Sixty-two."

I stared at them. Mara and Pearl couldn't possibly be much older than I, and Lilith had the skin of a beautiful forty-year-old, despite the silver hair. Southern socialites are notorious for lying about their ages—gilding the magnolia— so to speak. But none ever claim they are thirty years *older* than common sense says is possible.

Remain polite about their delusions, I told

myself, staring at the floor to hide my alarm. "I see."

Lilith watched me closely. "No, you don't. We don't live by the rules of ordinary people. You know that in your heart. You know anything I tell you may be possible. Look at me, Alice. Please."

I raised my eyes to hers. Her expression softened. "Study our eyes. Vibrantly green, like the sea. Just like yours. An extraordinary color. Unique to our kind. To our family. Mara. Pearl. Look at her eyes. Let us all look straight into Alice's eyes. And Alice, you look at *us*." She paused. "All four of us standing here today are linked by the most amazing destiny. We have our father's eyes."

In the deepening silence between words, the pauses of reflection and emotion, the acidic wash of stark scrutiny and shock, in those spaces where the truth lives, I knew, I felt, I saw. A long sigh escaped me. A sound of awe.

Lilith Bonavendier immediately swept toward me. "*Alice.* Your father's name was Orion. Orion Bonavendier. Our mother, the love of his life, had died not many years before he met *your* mother. He was still grieving, distraught—dying of a broken heart. Nothing could stop that."

Lilith touched my face. "He met your mother when she came to work as a counselor at the children's camp called Sweetwater Haven, on a brackish river along the mainland, not many miles from our island. This young counselor—your mother—was bright and beautiful, and we all appreciated how she drew our father out of his misery. I can't say I'm proud he seduced her, but I'm sure he never meant to destroy her, Alice. And I am certain—in the depths of my dreams, in my soul, my instincts, my sisterhood with you—that your mother adored him, and she was only driven to disaster by her family once she returned here."

She had cast a spell over me, but those last words broke it. I stepped back. "She drowned herself in the town lake," I said grimly. "After she saw the web-toed mutant she'd birthed."

All three women stared at me in horror. "Web-toed mutant?" Pearl cried out.

Lilith touched a hand to her heart. "Is *that* what you've grown up believing about yourself?"

"It's the truth."

"*No.* I have notes your mother wrote to Father. She was in love with him. She wanted to stay with him. She wouldn't have rejected any child she had with him."

"No mother can turn her back on a Bonavendier baby," Pearl said. "We're quite alluring, even in the crib."

"You were taken away from her, Alice. That's the only explanation that makes sense. That would have driven her to despair. I expect the Rileys intended to place you for adoption."

My thoughts whirled. I felt as if I was

struggling just under the surface of shallow water, caught in a vortex. "You're offering me a convenient rationale, I'm afraid."

"I'm offering you the *truth*. Come with us, Alice. Look at the proof we can show you of your heritage. See where you belong." She paused, her expression becoming supplicating and sad. "Accept our apologetic and sincere love."

Love? I had *never* known love in my life, and the use of it as a lure from strangers enraged me. "Let me understand this," I said between gritted teeth. "You're saying my mother, a very young woman—not even out of her teens quite then—a small-town girl raised in a time and place where morals were very strict and the rules undeniably severe—you're saying she was willing to give up everything for a summer seduction orchestrated by an eighty-five-year-old grieving widower? And I am supposed to believe she adored him—and wanted to bear his child? *Me.* And you actually *care*?"

"Yes. Absolutely. Listen to your instincts, Alice. Trust your faith."

"Faith is a blind word, used to excuse every mistake."

"No. Alice, say what you will, but you do *want* to believe me."

"This is all an elaborate defense for a tragedy that shamed you."

"Yes, I'm ashamed we hurt your mother—and you. And yes, this is an elaborate effort to redeem that terrible crime. But, then, we

Bonavendiers are an *elaborate* kind of being."

"Oh, more than elaborate," Pearl inter-jected brightly. Mara scowled at her.

Lilith put a graceful, opalescent-trimmed hand on my shoulder. "Our father—and yours—went out into the ocean one day and never returned. We found him later—his body. The dolphins brought him home. We were all heartbroken, including your mother. She left the coast immediately—returning here, to this town, to her family. I wrote to her kindly. She never answered. I learned later that she'd died. I also learned she'd borne a child. I was certain, of course, the child was Father's. I was informed that the child had died, too, at birth."

I exhaled a long, rattling breath. "The Riley family told you I died?"

"Your aunt told me."

My mother's eldest sister. Anger became a widening torrent. "My aunt."

"I should have known better, Alice. I should have felt your presence in the world. I should have heard you calling. I've dreamed about you for years. Why didn't I hear you singing before now? That's a question I have to answer for myself."

"If I am going to believe any of this," I managed, "then please tell me why we're so different from everyone else."

"You aren't ready to hear that yet. You're consumed with anger and pain and distrust. Come with us to our home, Alice, and learn about us, and learn about *yourself*. And then you'll understand. And you'll believe."

"I prefer clear answers instead of vague promises. *Simple* answers."

"That's not possible. The truth, my dear, is far more complex than you've ever imagined—and far more wonderful." She went on in her lovely voice, telling me that she and her sisters—*my* half-sisters, if I believed her—come from one of the barrier islands off Georgia's coast, a small isle named Sainte's Point. She said it has been owned by Bonavendiers since the late 1700s. "Our ancestor was a French privateer," Lilith said.

"A pirate," redheaded Pearl interjected eagerly.

Lilith silenced her with a stern glance. "A *privateer* in service to the American revolutionary government. He fought off a British warship that threatened an American village on the mainland. After the war—in return for his service—President Washington deeded him the small island across the cove from that grateful village. Our ancestor named the island Sainte's Point. He settled there quite happily, bringing with him a quite *remarkable* wife."

"And *she* is responsible for the very special circumstances that have existed in all her Bonavendier descendents ever since," Pearl put in, shaking an elegant, webbed foot for mysterious emphasis. "Because she was a . . ."

"*Shhh.*" Dark-haired Mara hissed at her.

Pearl's eyes widened. She huffed.

Lilith gave both women a rebuking stare. They lowered their eyes. Lilith looked at me again. "Our family has so much lovely history to tell—so many traditions, so many proud memories. But, you, of course, simply need to know your own history at the moment."

I took a deep breath. "If I do believe you, then tell me this much. *What kind of monsters are we?*"

Pearl sputtered. "Monsters? *Monsters?*"

"How dare you," Mara hissed. "You weakling. You . . . you *pretender.*"

Lilith inhaled sharply. "Say no more, either of you."

"But we're *not* monsters," Pearl cried, her expression wounded.

"Pearl, say no—"

"We're *mermaids*!"

Silence. Pearl pressed her fingertips to her indiscreet lips. Mara gave me a slit-eyed glower, while Lilith watched me with quiet concern. Neither attempted to explain, correct, or dismiss Pearl's claim.

"Oh," I said. "Mermaids."

And, moving as casually as I could, I left them there with the fish.

～～～

I am not one to accuse others of frail whimsies and lunatic notions, considering my own strange afflictions and tastes, but the Bonavendier sisters were crazy. Not crazy in an evil way, I decided, or even a clinical one, but deluded, gently fantastical, dancing with moonlight. I never doubted that they and I shared the same freakish talents; I never seriously doubted we were blood kin. The difference, I concluded, was in defensive rationalizations and adjustments. I tried to be clear-eyed about my bizarre qualities. I mourned my oddity and went about my life as if it were a daily *mea culpa* for my unnatural ways. But the Bonavendier sisters were smug, vain, and wealthy, all of which grants lunacy the soft succor of respectability. They had designed a world for themselves in which lovely notions of mythological mermaidhood explained the unexplainable. They had clearly survived by designing their own fairy tale and inhabiting it.

I would not be taken in. Though I wanted to be.

That night, I sat in a small blue rocking chair in the deep-sea-themed living room of my cabin, my head in my hands, not a single light turned on, the darkness of early evening as tight as shut eyelids around me. I had no idea where the magnificent, insane Bonavendier sisters had gone after I left them in the pet shop. As I rocked, head in hands, mourning the day's events, I pushed my bare, webbed toes into a pile of seashells one of my e-mail correspondents had sent me. I'd arranged them prettily at the base of a water garden in a ceramic pot. I caressed my conch shells and sand dollars for an unwitting moment, then jerked my feet away.

Mermaid. Then where were my iridescent scales, my transforming flippers and coquettish charm and subverted genitalia? In the water I was still two-legged Alice. And how was it that I came by my mermaid-dom through a father, not a mermaid mother? I shuddered at the Bonavendiers' nonsense, hugging myself inside a thin white robe over plain white underwear. I was rooted in cotton reality, not silken dreams. The Bonavendier sisters could console themselves with ludicrous whimsies, but the world operated by harsher rules: We were genetic freaks, not mythological marvels.

"My father was not a merman," I said aloud, just to assure my own intelligence.

The sound of several cars turning into my long driveway made me jerk to attention. I hurried about my dark cabin, changing my robe for an ankle-length denim skirt and oversized denim jacket.

So tell me, would you save that child again, knowing the consequences?

I stopped stock still in the middle of my own floor. The humming filled my head again. Lilith Bonavendier was speaking to me *again*. I groaned in defeat.

Yes, I would.

Then you've got nothing to be sorry for, Alice. And nothing to keep you here anymore.

You are my family in name only. I don't believe in you. Where are you now?

Nearby.
Stay away, please.

I began frantically lacing up high black boots on my feet. Since high school, I'd made it hard for anyone to jerk my shoes off. Trembling in denim and Victorian leather, I walked out onto the cabin's dark porch and pressed a switch. A tin light fixture cast its glow on the yard and the winter woods beyond. Below the sloping backyard of my house, the lake waited with dark, quiet appeal. I fought an urge to run down the bank, pull off my baggy clothes and strict shoes, dive in, and escape.

Car lights pierced the cold dusk.

The vehicles contained my aunt, plus about a dozen other Rileys—older ones, younger ones, men and women—stern upholders of the family's hard, respectable philosophy. My aunt commandeered my yard, a strong, stocky woman with my mother's russet hair but nothing resembling any maternal charm. She was about sixty, and my mother, I realized in passing, would have been a little more than seven years younger, if she'd lived. Suddenly I could see my mother—*Mother*, I thought of her, for the first time—in a way I'd never imagined before. Smiling and kind, loving and doomed. I'd heard glimmers about my aunt's hard feelings toward her over the years. Duller and stauncher, my aunt had always been the family's girdle, while my mother had been its crown.

"You've humiliated us in public. This is

the last straw. We want you out of here," my aunt said.

"Did you hate my mother?" I asked. My aunt scowled and buttoned a long gray coat tighter around herself. The other grim Rileys traded grim looks.

Good for you, my dear. Lilith, again.

"Were you glad she fell from grace?" I persisted. I was vibrating, picking up Lilith's goading song and singing it myself.

My aunt's face contorted. "She threw away her life. She had everything a girl could want. What happened to her was her own fault."

"Did Grandmother and Grandfather Riley take me away from her against her will?"

That froze my aunt. The others shifted unhappily. I studied their faces, watching anger mix with embarrassment, and I saw the answer. My heart squeezed in on itself, then began to weep for ruined joy. "I see. She *did* want me, but they took me away from her. And she couldn't bear it." I stepped forward, my voice rising with the movement. "Wasn't that enough punishment? *You-all killed her.* Did you have to make my life miserable, as well?"

"You weren't meant to be born," my aunt spat out. "You're a mistake of nature, you're just a sickly thing, you're nothing like a normal person, and you're a peculiar troublemaker, to boot. Whatever happened in the lake between you and that little girl will cause gossip forever around here. And those females . . . those flashy women who waltzed into our business today—they can say whatever they want about being your kin. I don't know, and I don't really care. They only feel *sorry* for you, Alice. Or they want something from you. They figure you're a celebrity. Yes. That's it. That's why they came, Alice. To see what they could get out of you."

All of that was a possibility, of course. I couldn't really defend three strangers who secretly claimed to not only swim with the fishes but to *be* fishes. I said nothing and began to sink inside my own skin.

"We're going to buy this cabin from you," my aunt went on. "You've got some savings already, and with the money from this house you can start over somewhere new. Somewhere where people won't know about you. It'll be better for you and us, too, Alice."

I held out my hands, trembling. "I've done nothing to deserve this. Isn't it possible to forgive me for being different and let me stay here? The talk will blow over. I won't encourage people to notice me. I never laid claims to any miracles when I rescued the little girl. And I never asked for any awards."

"Miracles? I don't know *what* to think about you and your strange ways, Alice, but I'll tell you this much: I *do* believe in miracles. But I believe in evil, too. And I believe *you are evil*."

I put a hand over my stomach as I fought nausea.

Lilith's elegant voice rang out, filled with

disgust. "You're motivated by nothing except petty revenge. And thus, your beliefs regarding Alice are absolutely meaningless." Everyone looked around wildly, me included. Lilith stood in the light at the edge of my porch, facing my aunt and the rest of my tormentors.

She was naked and wet.

Her soaked silver hair was plastered over her, front and back, offering just enough modesty to reveal only glimpses of youthful breasts and the long, slim belly of an accomplished swimmer. Her soft, flawless skin, ivory and peach, glowed with diamond ankle bracelets and a thick pearl choker around her throat. Her body steamed in the cold air, lifting a silver mist around her. Lake water trickled down her body and limbs in caressing streams. She was absolutely calm, regal, totally in charge.

All the Rileys took several steps back. Real fear clotted their eyes. My aunt raised ruddy hands to her throat as her gaze hung on Lilith, and Lilith gazed at her. There was a long pause, tension gathering in the air like the carbon scent of ozone just before lightning strikes.

"Be gone," Lilith ordered very softly and very clearly. *"Before I lure you into the lake."*

Her innuendo filtered into the crowd like icy tentacles. I saw the horror of it snare people, raise the whites of their eyes, hold them very still. This was no dimestore threat, built on cheap theatrics. All of us standing there at that moment would have done whatever Lilith

Bonavendier asked, including sink into the lake with her lithe hands around our throats.

My Riley kin flung themselves toward their cars as if released from a slingshot. My aunt fumbled as she climbed inside her vehicle, slammed the door, and locked the locks. So did the others. I watched in amazement as my aunt and the rest drove away quickly. My mother's family disappeared from my life as if swallowed by the night.

Lilith looked at me and I at her, searching each other's hearts and souls. I felt a surge of joy, but a lifetime of bitter pride made a hard shell for it. "You want to turn me into someone who doesn't exist," I accused hoarsely. " I'm not a mermaid. There's no such thing."

"My dear, whatever you want to call us is fine. But we do exist."

"So my father was a *merman*?"

"Your father was the great-great-grandson of Simon and Melasine Sainte Bonavendier, she of the Water People, as the Old Ones called themselves. And like all of us who are descended from her, your father was of her kind."

"He lived in the water and sported a fine, finned tail?"

"No fins, I'm afraid, and no stereotypes. We are people, not fish, my dear."

"Then I assume that we two-legged descendents of Melasine are, biologically and genetically speaking, *watered down*?"

She smiled beneath her cool eyes. "How

droll you are. Such flowing wit. You realize, of course, that just meeting us has begun to change you? Your voice, your manner. You sense who you are, now, and you're more confident."

"You're wrong. You have provoked my worst nature. I apologize. I'm not a sarcastic person."

"My dear, no need to apologize. You think I'm absolutely delusional, and you're trying to reason with me via humor. And I am humoring *you* because deep inside I recognize every bit of your urgent need to believe in us— and yourself."

"I can't live up to your fantasy."

Lilith touched my face with the back of one hand. Even in the steaming cold, her fingers were provocatively maternal and warm. "You already have. Come to us whenever you're ready. Just follow the water to the sea."

Something or someone splashed in the dark lake. I jumped. A glimmer of porch light caught the emerging heads of Mara and Pearl. Their bare shoulders gleamed like wet porcelain. Their hair floated around them in graceful swirls. They were amazing, sensual, ethereal. Mara looked me up and down with disdain, but Pearl issued a reassuring smile. "Let's go home, Alice. The water there is much finer."

Mara raised a hand and tasted the lake on her fingertips. She grimaced. "Needs salt," she said.

I stared at them, then Lilith. "I need to

think."

"You need to *dream*. You'll float to us on your dreams," Lilith replied. "We'll be waiting."

~~~

Sometime during the night, I went out to my small backyard dock and stood there naked, grieving with deep loneliness and fear of the future, preparing to swim in my lake one last time, before the mob of Rileys returned. I spied a small gift box, which someone had set quite obviously on the edge of the dock's weathered floor. I knelt warily and opened it. On a liner of dark silk lay the most beautiful emerald ankle bracelet. I opened a small, folded note tucked beneath it. Lilith's handwriting was beautiful. Her message was clear.

Adorn your special feet and celebrate every step you take toward your true kind.

The term "mermaid" is literally translated as "virgin of the sea." And thus I have never considered that popular term a particularly apt or complimentary name for our kind. To celebrate the water is to celebrate the consummation between water and earth, female and male. To have never experienced that unity is to be half-lived.

—Lilith

Six

~

"So handsome. Look, *Senor*," a nurse said, holding up the newest issue of *National Geographic* for Griffin to see. "You will look like this again when you are well."

The woman propped the magazine on her hands with the pages folded to a story titled "Secrets Of The Mirabelle." Griffin and his crew posed atop the deck of the *Sea She* with a deep-blue Caribbean sky behind them and the coral-encrusted cannons of a sixteenth-century French warship at their feet. The nurse looked from the picture to him with a sigh, as if assessing the sad contrast between the adventurer and the bedridden invalid. Griffin squinted at the magazine through swollen, bloodshot eyes, his face covered with black beard stubble, a sutured wound making a raw pink slash across the right side of his jaw.

"Handsome bastard," he managed in a hoarse voice.

"Oh, *Senor*, yes. Yes, you will look that handsome again. And all the ladies who have tried to come here and visit you will be waiting."

The woman didn't understand. He didn't give a damn how he looked, or whether his women came back to him. "Take it away, please." Sighing, the nurse folded the magazine and left the room.

His head diver came to see him the next day. "You know," Enrique said in a thick Brazilian accent, "the men will wait however long for you to work again and go wherever you say. You know that."

"Pay them and tell them not to wait. I'm done. I'm going home."

He had no idea how he could salvage something valuable from his own life. He was very good at finding what the oceans had stolen from human kind, but not what they'd stolen from him as a child. He only knew he had to return where the fear took him, where the singing of the Bonavendier women in his painful dreams called him to go. He believed they might be deadly, the Bonavendier sisters. But he didn't know about the other woman, the one who had saved him.

Alice. He only knew he had to go where he might find her with the equally mysterious Bonavendiers.

Sainte's Point.

∿∿∿

Potential treachery. Enemies and allies. The sinister unknowns that surround the Bonavendier legacy. The absurd claims. Lilith sensed Alice's thoughts as cold February turned to windy March and yet still, Lilith knew Alice couldn't resist. Somehow she'd make her way to Sainte's Point. It had only been three weeks. No time at all in a Bonavendier's long life.

"Oh, Lilith, let us go back to the mountains and get the poor child," Pearl urged. "She'll curl up and die from fear of us. We should just kidnap her and tame her by force."

"I doubt we'd have much luck," Mara retorted. "Oh, don't worry; she'll show up on our island one day, needy and embarrassing, covered in baggy denim with her feet bound in those sadistic granny boots of hers." Mara sniffed. "A fashion disaster."

Lilith scowled at them. "We'll leave her alone to make her own choices."

Alice was coaxing herself along roads that followed the rocky streams flowing south out of Riley down the mountainsides. She had hesitated when she reached the foothills, easing worriedly past the huge electric dams and man-made conduits of Atlanta, then floating with the slow, lazy waters that stretched their fingers across the state's coastal plain. Alice was sliding down the state of Georgia, drifting over the bony edge of the North American continent, flowing naturally to the Atlantic.

One day very soon, the knowing waters would deposit her at Sainte's Point.

~~~

Mermaids giggled at me in my dreams. *You couldn't possibly be one of us, Alice Riley—not one of the world's mystical undines, hailed in song and literature throughout history and in every culture of the planet. Mysterious, confident, alluring, a queen of the vast deep. Not you, you scrawny, fearful, two-footed thing, hiding in a cheap motel on dry land. And we do mean hiding.*

I am sitting in a small motel in the middle of the Georgia, near the small, dry city of Macon. I have gone to ground in the state's flat navel, burrowing like a crab. For the past two weeks, as February has given way to March, I've huddled in my room, surrounded by my jeering, mythological phantoms, fighting motion sickness even when I'm not moving. I trim my impossibly determined hair every morning, and I take long soaks in the bathtub, pining for water. My life is in tatters. I am *bereft*, in every melodramatic sense of that fine old word. I'm an arcane woman floating in a sea of strangers with normal toes. I got this far on my journey to the sea, but now I'm hiding, yes.

You're a fish out of water, the mermaids laugh.

I prefer to think of it as being stranded on high ground.

You see, I don't own a car. Before the

upheaval in Riley, I had never spent a night outside the town. Never rented a hotel room. Never ridden in a cab, a commuter train, or any other public conveyance. I'm a swimmer first, a walker second, a traveler, never.

I have decided to go no farther than Macon.

So I'm reading the local newspaper, trying to work up my courage to apply for a job at a pet store, and making lists of apartments located near ponds, lakes, or even small creeks. I eat the motel's vending machine crackers and cans of vegetable shortening I buy at a convenience store next door, run by a kind family of Mexican origin. I speak to them in fluent Spanish—languages come to me as easily as breathing—and they are quite friendly to me.

"A person can lose her voice so easily when no knows how to listen," the mother of the family confessed to me in her singsong words. "Sometimes I become so quiet I can't even tell myself what I am thinking."

I couldn't agree more.

Pull to and fro, Row men, row! Keep your eyes upright and your ears shut tight! The devil's in the sea but he won't get thee! Pull to and fro, Row men, row! The devil looks up from the depths below!
Ballad of the Merfolk
British sailors' song, eighteenth century

Seven
~

The nurse's aide wasn't more than twenty-five—not quite young enough to be his daughter, Griffin decided, but close. Apparently her main duty was to touch him as often as possible. She was pretty, with bright blond hair, and looked as if she belonged not in the ponderous Victorian confines of Randolph Cottage but in a smoky urban club, some dark, loud place where goateed college boys sucked pacifiers and traded small packets of pills beneath retro 1950s diner tables. Her typical work outfit consisted of snug little sweaters cut low enough to show cleavage and tight black pants with a little flair at the ankles. The pants stretched just enough to emphasize every flexing inch of her, front and back. She smelled of good perfume. Her name was Kelly. She spelled it Kellee. C.A. had hired her.

An efficient male nurse named Ben

helped him with his baths, his medications, and trips to the john. But Kellee fetched and toted, brought him books to read, kept his water pitcher full, artistically arranged meal trays he barely touched, and tried to give him erections.

That didn't work either and worse, he didn't care that it didn't work.

"No, thanks," he told her gently and cupped a scarred, pale hand around her face. She cried and left the room.

Griffin, who had never had a problem with either the obvious reaction or the obvious follow-through to female attention, laid a pillow over his groin. From then on he spent the time gazing, hollow-eyed, out a large window that faced Bellemeade Bay. Randolph Cottage sat on a spit of sand dunes two miles south of the bay's namesake—Bellemeade—the village Simon Sainte Bonavendier had rescued from an English warship during the Revolution.

The cannon battle between Bonavendier's ship and the English had taken place right off the cottage's shores, just inside the bay's narrow mouth, bracketed by the island on the oceanside and this jutting peninsula of sand dunes and sea oats on the bayside. Bonavendier had cornered the English warship there, pounded it with cannon fire, and let the villagers of Bellemeade finish it off.

Behind Randolph Cottage, buried under dunes, lay the coquina foundation of Fort Bellemeade. Two cannonballs—one from

Bonavendier's ship and one from the fort's artillery—graced massive newel posts at the foot of the cottage's staircase. One of Simon Sainte Bonavendier's own swords—a gift to Randolph ancestors who had commandeered that fort—hung in the cottage's living room.

Randolphs and Bonavendiers. Land and water. They had been allies then, but the friendship had faded over the generations. Randolphs were merchants at heart, Bonavendiers, pirates.

On the clearest March days, Griffin could see across the bay to Sainte's Point. The island made an ethereal blue-green strip on the horizon. He knew that a mile beyond it, beneath the jagged waters of the open Atlantic, pieces of his parents' sailboat still lay on the ocean floor. Pieces of his childhood. Only the island stood between him and that place.

He waited to grow strong enough to cross the bay.

~~~

Our kind will go the way of unicorns and dragons. Reduced to fantastic illusions, dismissed by science, forced into hiding. It is so much easier for people to believe nothing extraordinary exists in their own nature.

On the cusp of a new millennium, with magical technology folding the world in on itself, Lilith diligently wrote in a large journal atop a slender, gilded desk in her private office. Her great-grandparents had salvaged the delicate writing desk from a wrecked French cargo steamer in the mid-1800s. The steamer's journey had begun somewhere off the coast of Europe, and it had been heading for one of the Randolph estates near Savannah. The desk was rumored to have belonged to Napoleon.

The Randolphs suspected but had never proved anything. The Bonavendiers considered the desk a small commission for rescuing the rest of the steamer's cargo, not to mention the passengers and crew.

Lilith knew precisely where remnants of the steamer's hull lay off the island's shoals, alongside the shells of other vessels once employed by Randolph Shipping. One of her many projects involved cataloging all the romantic and tragic ships that had sunk in the island's arms—some modern, some ancient, some fact, some merely lore.

She had dutifully researched her family's diaries and letters and had explored the underwater wreck sites herself, of course, like many Bonavendiers before her. She meticulously recorded locations, circumstances, how many passengers were rescued by Bonavendiers, and how much property. She wasn't compiling the journal to brag about the family's reputation for wit and bravery in the old times, before ships circumvented the island's deadly shallows via satellite tracking systems and computer-aided navigation charts. Nor was she gossiping about the goods they'd plucked from hapless brigands and schooners and steam-powered paddlewheelers and diesel tankers during two hundred years of Bonavendier history on Sainte's Point. She was writing it all down as a gift for Alice and Griffin. Whether they knew it or not yet, they understood the desire to bring back what the sea would give and forgive.

One page of the thick leather journal remained blank except for a few small notations at the top. *The Calm Meridian*, she wrote quietly, followed by the date of the small sailing yacht's demise: November, 1967. Thirty-five years ago. She had listed three passenger names: Undiline Randolph, Porter Randolph—the parents. Griffin Randolph–their young son, and only survivor. She included the latitude and longitude of the wreckage, and a brief description of the scattered woods and metals that had once comprised the handsomest and fastest luxury sailing yacht on the Georgia coast. Beneath it all she wrote this small epitaph.

God rest your sweet soul and forgive Porter for his cruelty, dear Undiline.

She stood resolutely and closed her journal. Beyond her parlor's louvered Spanish shutters and hand-blown English windowpanes, the first balmy hint of spring put a tinge of green on the massive maritime oaks on the front lawn leading to the cove. Seagulls and pelicans shared squatting privileges on the cove's docks. Dolphins surfaced like gray-blue cats arching their backs. Barret kept a ferryboat named the

Lorelei ready to leave at a second's notice. Thirty minutes of peaceful passageway would take Lilith and her sisters across the bay to the mainland whenever they wished.

Alice would arrive at the coast any day now, and they would go immediately to welcome her in style.

But it was time to welcome Griffin home, first.

∾∾∾

"Thank you, Barret."

"You're most welcome."

Barret offered a brawny hand as Lilith stepped from the *Lorelei's* broad, mahogany deck onto the dock at Randolph Cottage. Barret took a small, finely engraved wooden box into his arms, then limped onto the dock. "I should carry this for you, Lilith."

"No, I can manage." After wrapping herself in a light shawl over an ice-blue suit, she took the box from him. He turned toward Pearl and Mara, who stood on the *Lorelei's* deck, looking anxious. "We'll go to the village and have a vodka while we wait, yes?"

The younger sisters trained their gaze on Lilith and could not be distracted.

"Griffin will reject you," Mara said. "Why should anything have changed?"

"I think a great deal has changed inside him."

"He hates us," Pearl added mournfully.

"Then it's time we offered him a chance to understand us instead."

Mara scowled. "You know we can't risk that."

"He's Undiline's son. She'd want us to try."

The mention of their dear Scottish cousin silenced Mara and Pearl. They looked at the box in Lilith's arms. Lilith nodded.

Barret guided the ferry away from the cottage's ornate wood-and-coquina docks. Mara and Pearl waved goodbye. Lilith carried the elegant box up a weathered boardwalk between huge dunes. Ahead of her, Randolph Cottage loomed with the quaint majesty of shingled turrets and fading gingerbread trim. Undiline had lovingly restored the old place after her marriage to Porter Randolph. Some earlier Randolph had built it as a country retreat, but it was far too old-fashioned and far too isolated for the rest of the family's sophisticated tastes. Lilith sighed as she noted the generally unkempt condition to which the house had fallen once again. Even Griffin, who had inherited it on his twenty-first birthday, had tried to let it succumb to the winds and the tides, though he'd loved it as a little boy.

She stepped gingerly onto the creaking boards of an empty veranda Undiline had once filled with fine wicker and ferns. When she pulled the ringer on a brass chime, a blond young woman in jeans and a fat blue hiking jacket opened the ornately carved door. Her luggage—a pair of canvas duffels painted with bright streaks of color—lay on the old Turkish rug in the foyer behind her. "Oh, I thought you were my ride," she said.

"I'm here to see Mr. Randolph."

"Okay. Whatever."

Lilith stepped into the shadowy foyer, long empty of furniture. Tall transomed archways led off to other parts of the house. Drafts crept across the floor, and dust motes floated in the light of an old crystal chandelier. *How sad, Undiline. I remember your parties, your music, your lovely furnishings.*

The girl watched Lilith, transfixed. "You glow in this light," she whispered.

"Oh, it's a trick of the shadows. Now, you go about your business. I know my way through this house, my dear. Go wait for your ride. I'll find my way upstairs without your escort."

The girl said nothing else, looking dazed and suddenly miserable.

Lilith reached out and stroked her hair. *Talk to me,* Lilith urged silently, the slightest song.

The girl immediately complied. "Would you tell Mr. Randolph something for me, ma'am?"

"Yes, dear."

"Tell him . . . tell him I'm not a *whore.* I just needed the money from this job for tuition at art school. I really appreciate the way he treated me. That he didn't encourage me."

Lilith hid her surprise and pleasure at Griffin's honor. Randolphs, by nature, were users. "I suspect he knows you were forced into an unseemly position."

"But I would have done anything he asked. He looks awful and acts like nothing matters. He paid me a lot of money to leave, but I wish he wouldn't send me away. He fired his nurse, too, and told his cousin to beat it. He doesn't want people around. I don't understand why, but I . . . fell in love with him, anyway." Tears slid down her face. "He was a gentleman, even though I decided to sleep with him if he asked. But he didn't ask, and I love him. Go figure."

Lilith sighed at the girl's confusion. The water wrapped itself around the land, or the land around the water. Dominance was a matter of perspective, and pleasure did not always equal power. "He's a charismatic man."

"Yeah. Yeah. He's got some kind of . . . of talent."

He's a special kind. You poor, dear Lander.

"Go back to college in Savannah. Use your feelings for him as inspiration, paint great art, and demand his brand of nobility from every man you love." Lilith touched her face, released her, and the girl, nodding and crying, grabbed her luggage and disappeared out onto the veranda. Lilith shut the door, then gathered her thoughts for a moment before she began to climb the staircase.

Oh, Undiline, how did your dreams for him come to this?

As for Bonavendiers, add to our psyche the spoiled attitudes of a silver-spoon upbringing in the deep, coastal South, and you have that most dangerous of all combinations (and here I stoop to use two common stereotypes.) Southern Belles who are also mermaids. Gilding the magnolia, to say the least.

—*Lilith*

Eight

~

1959. Dressed in slender Chanel cocktail dresses, their webbed feet hidden in exquisitely jeweled pumps with stiletto heels, Lilith, Mara, and Undiline drew eye-popping attention from the enthralled partygoers each time they stepped from the shadows of the moss-draped forest. The Randolph fete was being held at an aging church camp along the sleepy Sweetwater River, which flowed through the deep coastal forest to the saltwater marshes of Bellemeade Bay. Dozens of kerosene torches and colorful Japanese lanterns lit the ethereal recesses of the lawns beneath gnarled live oaks and enormous magnolias. A small orchestra played *Mack The Knife*. Long linened tables were laden with chowders and fresh seafood, barbecue, and martini pitchers. Black men in waiters' uniforms ferried trays of liquor and finger sandwiches among rich whites whose ancestors had, in many cases, owned the waiters' ancestors on coastal cotton and rice plantations before the Civil War.

"Stay on the edges, out of the light. We're here to represent our family, not cause a scene," Lilith said. "There'll be no showing off, Mara, and no seductions."

"No fun at all," Mara sighed.

"Oh, you're wrong, cousin; it's all wonderful and glamorous just to watch," Undiline proclaimed in her lyrical Scottish voice. "Lilith, do no' be slow about pointing out Porter Randolph to me the very second you spy him. I want to see the notorious ladies' man for my own self."

Lilith said nothing. Her only mission was to pay polite homage as society celebrated Porter Randolph's ascension to the throne of Randolph Shipping. Lilith, then twenty-seven and already wiser than her years, sipped an iced vodka with the weary air of an emissary sent to do diplomatic duty. She and Father had decided modern times called for modern relations between Bonavendiers and Randolphs. When Porter Randolph himself had sent an invitation for his river soiree, Father had said, "He made the offer. We'll accept." But Father, nearly eighty and still grieving for Mother, who had died the year before, remained at Sainte's Point to help Barret care for Pearl. Pearl, only nineteen and still so girlish she chewed bubble gum, was pregnant and ailing. The baby was the first of three children she and Barret would lose to miscarriages.

Rebellious Mara, twenty-two and already a threat to all mankind, draped herself against a ramshackle bench of the river landing's church camp, near a wooden sign that proclaimed the landing, with its charming collection of cabins and pavilions, Sweetwater Haven. Randolphs owned the property but donated its use to their church.

Mara snorted. "Church folk, indeed. Randolphs. *Murderers.*" She despised all Randolphs and blamed their huge, diesel-belching cargo ships for killing Mother. "They poisoned her," Mara always insisted. Mother had fallen ill with inflamed lungs after leading the local dolphins away from an oil slick caused by a Randolph ship. Mother had been only 70, still young and beautiful before the infection withered her. Undiline had come from Scotland to help nurse Mother and had stayed on after Mother's death. It had been a very hard year.

"I could happily drown them all," Mara went on. "You know Porter thinks he's going to be the one to eradicate Bonavendiers from the coast once and for all. You *know* it, Lilith. Inviting us to his little fete is just a ruse of friendship. He thinks of Father as old and widowed—and vulnerable. He expects to slide into our good graces and buy the island from us.

I've heard all the details. I have my sources."

"Pillow talk," Lilith said bluntly.

"Men tell me anything I want to know once I get them into bed."

"Oh, how brazen you are!" Undiline said with a jolly roll of her green eyes. "Mara, you make Porter Randolph sound like a monster! I just don't believe it. You hate all land-lovers--"

"*Landers,*" Mara corrected. "Don't sweeten the sound of them. Ordinary, dry-footed, barbaric Landers. That's what they are." Among Water People, *Landers* was the derogatory term of choice for the world's non-mermaid population.

"Landers, land-lovers. Whatever," Undiline sighed. "Either way, you won't give a Randolph a fair chance." Tall, exuberant, and stunningly beautiful, she patted an errant swath of her copper hair back into its upswept style and then prodded Mara's shoulder. "I think this Porter Randolph must be the only man you haven't bedded. Aren't you a wee bit put out about that?"

"If I ever touch a Randolph, it will be to ruin him."

Undiline sighed. "A pity. They're handsome men. Tall and black-haired, straight of limb and strong of shoulder, with their dark, earthy eyes. Ah! The land will always lure the water, Mara. And the water lures the land. It's so. We're as much drawn to them as they are to us."

Deborah Smith

Mara turned to her spitefully. "Oh? You think a Randolph can respect our kind? Understand our kind? *Believe in our kind*? Then kick off your fine shoes, Undiline, and watch how Porter reacts to your webbed feet. Show him how long you can stay under water. Let him hear you singing to the dolphins—and the dolphins singing back. Admit all that and more about our kind—tell him we come from ancestors spoken of only in fables and fairy tales—then watch him proclaim you a freak or a crazy woman. To a Randolph we're a sinister mystery. Best to keep it that way."

Undiline laughed but looked at Lilith with somber eyes. "Do you agree?"

Lilith touched her shoulder kindly. "I prefer your perspective to Mara's. Mara, pull in your claws. That's enough."

Mara slid an arm through their cousin's. "You know I adore you. I just feel it's my duty to educate you about Landers in general and Randolphs in particular."

"Ah, you kind devil," Undiline said quietly, gave her a subdued smile, and turned back to the festivities. Lilith watched worriedly. Though Undiline's family in Scotland was quite wealthy and sophisticated, they'd been very isolated on their windswept Scottish island. Before coming to America, Undiline had met very few people other than her own kind. She was too vulnerable to the charms of ordinary folk—Landers, as the Water People derisively

88

called them. And she'd never seen such a thoroughly American event as this river party of Porter Randolph's, with its Old South atmosphere and modern savoir-faire.

"There's the subject of our debate and your intrigue, Undiline," Lilith said, as the crowd suddenly divided and broke into applause. On the opposite side of the glen, a tall man stepped out of the shadows, nodding to his assembled guests and family. Dressed in a tuxedo and imbued with the quiet command of coastal aristocracy, Porter Randolph was enough to make any woman's heart race.

Lilith tried to recall all she knew about him. "He's thirty-five," she told Undiline. "He was bred and raised to take over Randolph Shipping. His father retired last year. Porter has been managing the family's South American operations, but now he's returning to Savannah. I believe he has quite a reputation for racing yachts. He's considered very brilliant and athletic." She paused. "And as you've heard, he's considered quite notorious in his ability to break women's hearts."

All this was wasted on Undiline, who had gone very still, very quiet. She pressed her fingertips to her heart as she watched Porter Randolph shake hands among the crowd. Lilith and Mara traded worried looks.

"I am very sorry, my cousins, to upset you," Undiline whispered. "But I'll no' be telling you lies." She began to tremble. "I believe in love at very first sight. And there he is."

Before Lilith could stop her, Undiline strode forward into the light, halting only when she stood directly in Porter Randolph's path. Her arrival drew instant gasps from the crowd. Undiline was One Of Them, kin to the mysterious family whose whispered peculiarities had entered the realm of lurid coastal legend. Porter Randolph turned toward the commotion—or heard her singing to him and could not resist.

It was a moment no one who witnessed it would ever forget.

He seemed to lose all track of the people around him, the event, his status. He looked at Undiline and simply stopped. Stopped his life, stopped his fortunes, stopped his heart, slid that heart from his body, and handed it to her. People gasped again as he held out a hand to her, a stranger. Lilith groaned when Undiline walked straight to him. The orchestra began to play an achingly romantic ballad. He drew her into his arms and they danced slowly, while everyone else stared in wonder and disbelief.

A Randolph, publicly smitten with *One of Them*.

Late that night, in her bedroom in the mansion at Sainte's Point, Undiline could not suppress a song of pain and determination.

Lilith reached her first. Undiline was seated on the room's Turkish rug, a razor in her hand, her crimson blood soaking the rug's elaborate patterns. Shreds of her skin lay about her like small offerings. She had spread her toes and sliced out the webbing between them. Lilith sank down beside her and clasped her tear-stained, joyful face.

Undiline smiled. "Do no' be angry with me, cousin. I will do whatever it takes to be his kind of woman."

Lilith put her arms around Undiline and rocked her like a ruined child. "Oh, my dear," she whispered. "You'll have to cut out your soul."

"Then I will," Undiline whispered in return.

Often we read the hoary old tale of dangerous sirens luring ships to their doom and men to damnation: The Cyrenes of Homer's Odysseus, beckoning ordinary men and their possessions. The truth, dear readers, is far more sentimental; our kind tends to rescue hapless travelers and take only a small commission in return. It is the travelers who steal from us.

—Lilith

Nine

⁓

"Here to finish off what you and your sisters started when I was a kid?" Griffin asked.

Lilith acknowledged the insult with an arched brow as she entered his bedroom at Randolph Cottage. She carried the box to a small table in one corner, set it there, then returned and seated herself near his bed, settling gracefully on an aged armchair of cracked leather. "No matter what you still believe about the past, I mean you no harm, and neither do my sisters."

"I'm not in any shape to uphold the Randolph tradition of avoiding Bonavendiers right now." He glanced at the box with a frown but clearly wouldn't ask.

Lilith studied him sadly. He lay against a mountain of pillows on a big four-poster bed of wood and iron, a bed Undiline had shipped here from Scotland during her honeymoon with Porter. Griffin was well over six feet tall, a commanding presence, even deposed in the antique bed. He had a sailor's rope-working hands, big-knuckled and coarse. His skin was weathered, and squint lines fanned from the corners of his hooded, long-lashed eyes.

And his hair, his hair. Like anyone of their kind, he must keep it trimmed almost daily or risk having others notice its extraordinary rate of growth. Undiline had taught him as a child to clip his hair every morning. But he'd let himself go now, and the sight was astonishing. He had hair just one shade lighter than true black—Randolph hair, in color. In only a few weeks' time it had grown into thick, shaggy waves that curled below his shoulders. Even more startling, his facial hair had grown at an equal rate. He had a luxurious black beard halfway down his stomach.

His eyes burned like dark jewels, the burnt-brown color of fertile garden loam, the essence of earth. Lander eyes. Lilith frowned. *He has never known what his mother really was, or what he is. Now is not the time to tell him. But I have to make a connection, somehow.* Lilith leaned forward and touched a long fingertip to the foot of his bed. "You were conceived in this bed nearly forty years ago. Souls are drawn back where they began. You belong here. Take comfort."

Griffin clenched a fist around a mug he perched on his belly. "You're looking at me as if

I'm a monster," he said with a mercurial smile.

"Another day or two without shaving and you'll sport a grand black beard like Blackbeard the pirate. When the English cornered him, they swore he lit small candles in his beard to make himself a terrifying sight. Will you set yourself on fire to frighten me away, as you've chased off all others who care for you?"

"Now, I've been called a lot of things, but being called a pirate by a Bonavendier is ironic. Half the ships at the bottom of the Atlantic out there—" he jerked his head toward the island— "went down because your ancestors conveniently manipulated the lighthouse during storms." He took a drink. "Sinking my parents' sailboat must have been easy."

Lilith shut her eyes for a moment. *Ah, Undiline, I know he's half yours, and his heart is good, but he has been taught such prejudice against our kind, and he has no idea of the truth.* She stood. "Your father was a proud fool and drove your mother to torment. He and he alone decided to take the *Calm Meridian* out that day. He alone is responsible for what happened. Why have you come back here? To confront the truth? Or to hide from that truth while blaming others?"

"Your family didn't admit a thing then, and you won't now."

"Listen to your heart. It will tell you the truth."

"You didn't come here to give me advice. What do you want from me?"

"I have come to ask you for a favor. You

are kin to me after all. Distant kin, but those bonds are important to me. And should be to you."

He held out one large, long-fingered arm, his hand palm up, as graceful as a courtier. The movement revealed the sensuously entwined woman and dolphin tattooed on the underside of his forearm. "Madam Bonavendier comes here thirty-odd years too late, not to confess how she and her sisters killed my parents--" he smiled grimly--"But to remind me we're related and ask me for a favor."

Lilith walked to the box. She laid a hand on it. "This keepsake box belonged to your mother." Her gaze bored into him, conjuring the spirit of his mother around him, riveting his attention. She laid a key atop the box. His sardonic smile faded to a shadow. Lilith nodded. "You'll know when to unlock it."

He wet his lips, struggled for a moment, then repeated in a low voice, "I said, *What do you want from me?*"

"I want you to watch out your windows for a fellow lost soul. Take care of her when you see her waiting at the docks we share, speak to her kindly if she asks for your help, and don't frighten her away. Because she fears the land as much as you fear the water."

"Then I feel sorry for her. And I can't help her."

"She is my half-sister. She is a treasure you must reclaim for us all." Lilith paused. "Her name is Alice Riley."

What was left of his color drained from his face. After a long, quiet moment, he exhaled. "Alice," he said.

Lilith's heart made a thready leap. *He's heard her singing; he's felt her touch somehow. There is hope. He can hear the songs of his mother's kind.*

"I'm sure you'll take care of her as if she holds your heart," Lilith whispered.

He said nothing, but she knew.

Alice already held it.

~~~

I froze in a front aisle of the convenience store with a container of whipped butter in my hands, while a sad young man with dirty blond spitcurls waved a pistol at both me and the Mexican cashier who had befriended me. Her name was Maria.

"Give me your damned money," he screamed at Maria and me.

Maria shrank back. I could not make myself move an inch. I felt doom swirl around us like a pulling current.

Make him look at you, Alice. Make him put down the gun or he'll shoot.

The deep male voice rose inside my mind out of nowhere, filling me with the vibrations of a low-pitched hum. My spine arched; I gasped as if electrified. *Him. The face in the water. The injured man.* Fingers of sensation webbed my skin and delved inside me. I felt my womb loosen, welcome, and then retract. Moisture spread between my legs, and my knees went weak.

Pleasure, at a moment like this. Life. *That voice.*

"Please, don't hurt us," Maria begged and began fumbling with the cash register. She knocked over a jar of pennies, and the robber jumped at the crash.

"I'll kill ya!"

"No, you won't," I said. Just like that, in a low tone. The robber swung toward me furiously.

Make him look at you, Alice, the voice urged again. *The way you looked at me. Sing to him.*

My head came up. I squared my shoulders, tilted my chin just so, feigned grace and patient command. I stared into the robber's eyes, past the bloodshot whites and wide-open irises, inside the dark, fluid pools of his brain. So much of what we are is water. We change with the tides, we struggle in our own endless seas to transform ourselves into something or someone splendid. I dived beneath his fear and confusion, his paranoia, the currents of drugs and abuse and hopelessness that pushed him away from every shore. I made a mewling sound of sympathy.

Float, I sang in my mind. *Breathe. Become who you truly are.* I began to hum to him, a silent, erotic, spiritual song.

He wavered. His hand, bearing the pistol, slowly eased to his side. His expression stilled. Without a word he turned unsteadily and walked out the front door. A tiny set of metal wind chimes sang in his wake. The sound filled the stunned silence.

"How did you do that?" Maria cried. "You charmed that crazy snake!" She pressed a button behind the counter. The door lock slid into place, alarms began to ring, and the police were summoned by some faceless computer somewhere. Out under the awnings of the gas pumps, the robber wobbled to a halt, sat down on the ledge of a pump, and gazed back toward the store, watching me. He began to cry and dropped his head into his hands. I began to cry *for* him, and my knees went weak.

You did it, Beautiful.

His voice again, the stranger. All my life men and boys had stared at me oddly, taunted me, ignored me, avoided me. My fantasies of loving and being loved by a man were just phantoms, my sexuality confined to stroking my own body in the lonely nights of my bed. I didn't trust men this easily and did not want any man inside me, body, mind, or soul, without my explicit permission.

Where are you? I demanded. *Who are you? How do you know me? What do you want from me?*

No answer. Silence.

Sobbing, Maria ran to me and threw her arms around my shoulders. "You are a hero!"

Not again. Oh, my god. My knees collapsed. I sank down on a stack of canned soft drinks while she continued to hug me and cry.

          ~~~

Griffin stumbled to a window overlooking

the cottage's front yard, crashing the cast of his injured leg into a table, slamming the cast of his broken forearm against a wall. He gripped the edge of a captain's desk and looked out over the bay as if it held answers.

All his life he'd had quirky moments of prescient knowledge, and people often commented on his uncanny ability to find rare objects underwater. But he had told them it was because he read, he studied, he was an accomplished if uncredentialed archaeologist and historian. He regarded his abilities as just trained instincts, like following the stars across the ocean. Nothing like what had just happened.

Randolphs did not have psychic experiences or melodramatic spiritual epiphanies. They were staunch Protestants, raising each new generation to a stiff-upper-lip standard of worshipful decorum. Religious experiences ought to be practical, socially responsible, and good for business. Telepathic hallucinations were looked down upon.

Griffin scrubbed a shaking hand over his black hair. He dragged an armchair to the window and, gasping for breath, folded his body into the seat. He feverishly set his gaze out the window, watching the sand dunes and docks, the bay, the long, white lane of the driveway. Proof of reality had better, by God, arrive soon.

Come on, Alice. Prove there aren't any mysteries of the deep inside either one of us.

"I have heard the mermaids singing, each to each, I do not think that they will sing to me."
—T.S. Eliot

Ten

∼

I wouldn't risk a crowd of strangers coming to examine me like a specimen in a zoo. I wouldn't wait to see them remember my name in the media. Never again.

Maria and her entire family saw me attempting to drag my belongings down one of Macon's back street and rushed after me. I halted and began backing away. But Maria smiled. "Where are you going, dear friend?" she begged in Spanish.

"To the bus station. I've decided to travel on to my relatives' home." If I could just get within walking distance of the coast, I would find my way to Bellemeade and then to Sainte's Point, and I would never set foot on the continent again, never risk being seen as a monster *or* a hero again.

"Oh, no," Maria protested. "You saved my life. We will drive you wherever you want to go."

I stared at her. Before I could say another word, her brothers—men from high deserts—

100

began loading my boxes into a car. These people knew how to seek water. I would be in Bellemeade within a few hours, and then, Sainte's Point. Maybe I'd be better off out on a barrier island with three half-sisters who made me feel ordinary by comparison. Relief weakened my restraint. I pushed the strange events of the day from my mind.

Please, leave me alone, I said to the unknown man.

Once more he didn't answer. Or didn't exist. Or was lurking in some recess of my life, down the road somewhere. Afraid of his silences and my own, I left one stranger and hurried into the car of another stranger's family.

I had taken a step forward. I was on my way to the sea and the Bonavendiers.

And to him?

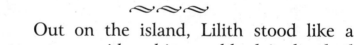

Out on the island, Lilith stood like a statue atop a wide, white-marble dais that had been carried to the New World in the hold of an Italian frigate. The frigate now lay in the waters off Sainte's Pointe, and the dais, a stunning work with gentle tendrils of vining roses carved around its circumference, lay grandly on the wooded banks on the island's bayside. A massive maritime oak dipped its limbs around it and wept in mossy tendrils on its surface. The shadow of the nearby lighthouse fell across the oak and the fantastic marble dais at certain hours of day, marking the passage of forgiving time.

Lilith shielded her eyes and gazed across the bay to the southwest, just making out the sand dunes and turreted roofline of Randolph Cottage, sitting like a separate world from Bellemeade. The cool wind melted a flowing white top to her body in the breeze, and a long skirt of sheer silks swayed around her bare legs and feet. She moved with the wind and she listened.

Something had stirred inside Griffin, some part of Undiline's heritage that vibrated like the lightest touch on a symphonic chord. And something had happened inside Alice because of him. Lilith pressed a hand to her chest and bowed her head. They were both safe, for now. She held out her arms to the water with grateful joy, knelt down for a moment and pressed a kissed fingertip to the dais, then went to call her sisters and prepare for Alice's arrival.

Alice Bonavendier—not Alice Riley—was finally coming home.

<center>~~~</center>

I left Maria and her family in Bellemeade, lying to them, saying I had arranged for relatives to meet me and that I would wait alone.

"It will be dark in only two hours," Maria protested.

"I'm not afraid of the dark." She sighed. Her brothers carried my boxes to the veranda of a charming bay front inn called WaterLilies. I thanked Maria and she hugged me.

"You have a special power," she said.

102

"May you find happiness and bring it to others."

"I'll be looking," I answered, my eyes already shifting helplessly to the bay across the street. Not more than twenty yards from me the water of the world lapped one tendril of its vast tongue at Bellemeade's coquina seawalls and weathered docks, beckoning me. As Maria turned to go, a quiet sense of knowing came over me. "Maria," I called. She looked back, and I spoke to her in soft Spanish. "You will have the child you want, within two years. A boy. Healthy."

She put a hand to her heart and stared at me. She and her husband had been told she would never conceive. "Mia Madre," she whispered, "you are truly gifted, I pray." Then she turned and hurried to her car.

My knees wobbled. Now I had become a fortuneteller, divining people's lives. Another talent of mermaids? I shook my head to clear it. As soon as Maria and her family drove away, I deserted my boxes and stepped off the inn's elegant porch, moving like a nightwalker across a sleepy street lined with beautiful shops, passing, hypnotized, beneath the winter shade of small pines twisted like bonsai by the wind. At the docks, pleasure craft and shrimp boats nuzzled one another like tethered ducks, bobbing on the quiet surface of Bellemeade Bay. I went to the edge of the seawall and stroked the coarse surface embedded with sand and broken shells. As I looked out at the little marina and the bay and the island, I began to tremble.

The wind was cold, a bright blue sky domed the world, and my heart was pounding in my chest; my eyes were on Bellemeade Bay because something I've always feared happened instantly. I fell in love with the ocean at first sight. I might never admit it to anyone, but I was home. *Where are you?* I called out to the stranger. No answer.

I turned, trailing one hand along the seawall, and walked the tiny main road out of town, passing beautiful little cottages with tree-shaded yards. I caught a wisp of wind-blown moss from the trees on my hand, let it go like a butterfly, every texture imprinting on my skin.

"Find your way east out of town to Randolph Cottage," Lilith had instructed weeks earlier, when she left me in Riley. She had said something about the Bonavendiers sharing a mainland dock and boathouses with the Randolphs, an old coastal family on the mainland.

I walked beside the waters of the Atlantic, the edge of the waters of the world, scented with brisk brine and fish, adorned by hardy white seagulls and gliding brown pelicans. I walked on the unnatural heels of my laced black boots, the salty breeze curling around my stiff denim skirt and jacket like annoyed fingers. I carried nothing but my awe along a flat, narrow two-lane road where even the concrete was mixed with crushed shell. Sand seeped in pretty patterns onto the pavement from the roadsides, and palmetto grass rattled its hard fronds. Pine woods shouldered me on my right and the long, placid, gray-green bay on my left. On the horizon, fringing the line between water and sky, lay the mysterious silhouette of Sainte's Point.

I couldn't take my eyes off the island, the bay, the womb where my teenage mother was seduced by a man old enough to be her grandfather. I was worried but hypnotized by my own conception in this magic, and now I took the first small step to understanding how euphorically she must have danced, my young mother, to Orion Bonavendier's enchanted song.

I began to hum to myself, my gaze always turned to my left, out there, off the edge of the continent. The water. The bay. The ocean. I had tried to imagine the ocean all my life, but my fantasies had been a dull substitute. I moaned silently with the sweet surf out beyond the horizon; I arched in the perfumed air and smiled at the squawking of the gulls. I reveled in the perfection of it all, what I'd lived thirty-four years without. Tears slid down my face.

People passed by in pickup trucks and salt-rusted cars. Suddenly, they began to turn around, to follow me, and then a dozen or more pulled off the road. Just simply pulled over on the landside. Hardworking fishermen, house-wives, and tanned children got out of their vehicles, then stood silently, smiling.

I halted anxiously. "Hello. I'm just walking to the docks at Randolph Cottage.

Going to wait for Lilith Bonavendier from Sainte's Point Island to meet me , thank you."

Men nodded. Women pressed their hands to their lips or their hearts. Children studied me with wide eyes. What had I done? Yet, there was nothing fearful about their scrutiny of me.

A little girl darted forward, her puzzled eyes riveted to my spiky auburn hair. "Ma'am, if you're a mermaid like the other ladies, where's the rest of your hair?"

A mermaid.

Ludicrous.

Her mother hurried up, smiling, and took her by a hand. "Miss Bonavendier, you're mighty fine lookin', just like we expected."

"I . . . my name is not . . . I'm not a . . ." my voice trailed off. "Thank you," I managed. Clearly these people, these townsfolk of Bellemeade, indulged the Bonavendier claim of mermaidhood, no doubt because the Bonavendier family was rich and powerful. Money and influence put a respectable polish on even the most bizarre traditions. Poorer people conceded. I had conceded all my life.

I bent to the child and smiled. "I'm certainly glad to be here, with or without much hair."

The girl giggled. I nodded to everyone, then forced myself to turn and walk on. The people stayed in the road, like a royal procession, and newcomers pulled over as well.

Soon, fully two dozen cars and at least fifty people lined my way.

My face burned. Lilith and her sisters had brainwashed these kind souls, and I was determined not to fall completely under a spell myself. I kept walking, a mile or two or ten—I was no good at calculating land distances. The crowd let me go on alone, but waved and called out good wishes. I locked my fragile attention on the cool, magnificent bay and Sainte's Point Island. Tears slid down the back of my heart, unseen.

I had never been welcomed anywhere before.

~~~

Griffin looked away from the sand dunes and gray docks, the gothic, cedar-and-coquina boathouses, and the dark, shimmering bay below his bedroom window. The sun was sinking in a blue-gray mist along the horizon. His head throbbed with bourbon and fatigue. His legs had stiffened like raw logs, his broken bones seemed to grate inside their casts, and a muscle low in his wrenched back flexed with a pain like a sharp filet knife splitting his spine. He lowered his head, cursed under his breath at the state of his body and mind, then dragged his head upright and forced his gaze back out the window.

And there she was.

Alice.

The world is a very narrow stream for most people. They never realize how many other streams flow to the same ocean.

—*Lilith*

Eleven

~

Alice Riley stood with her back to him, gazing out on the bay with her hands by her side and her head up. She made a long shadow haloed by sunlight glinting off the water. The diamond-fettered light began to silhouette her, flashing between her splayed fingers and feet, illuminating and hiding her at the same time. Griffin flattened a palm on the windowpanes, framing her between his thumb and forefinger, trying to capture her and the magic

Her long skirt and bulky denim jacket gave her the shapeless form of a cloistered nun, and her hair, what he could tell of it from the backlit sun, was cropped as close as a boy's. But still she made an ethereally seductive sight amidst brilliant illuminations, not reflecting, but instead defining. She slowly knelt by the water's edge. White dunes framed her on a miniature beach packed hard and smooth.

Turn around and look at me, he urged. *Let me see you and hear you, too.* But she didn't hear him, or was silent. The water held all her attention.

She leaned forward, scooped the surf into her hands, and nuzzled her face into that small pool encased in her palms. She tilted her face up, raised her hands, and let the ocean water trickle over her eyes and mouth, shimmering in the sunlight. Her empty hands flew to her bulky bluejean jacket; she wrenched it, still buttoned, over her head and threw it on the sand behind her, revealing a plain white T-shirt that clung to the supple outline of her torso. She sat back on her haunches, pulled up her long, coarse blue skirt, and jerked at the laces on her ankle-high black shoes. Moments later she sent them flying behind her on the sand, too. She got to her feet, swaying as she pulled on the waistband of her skirt. It dropped to her feet. She bounded out of the material as if sprung from a trap and ran toward the nearest dock.

Break the sound barrier, he caught himself thinking. *Sing to me.*

He caught only glimpses of her face, the large eyes, the solemn mouth, an expression of reverent passion. Beneath her white T-shirt she wore smooth blue panties that clung to her taut hips, cresting high on long thighs molded like an athlete's. Her skin was flawless, a sheath of fluid silk with the opalescent quality of a blush pearl. She skimmed the sand in graceful strides, piercing the ocean wind, the sunlight silhouetting her classic profile and lanky body, lithe and long, her shoulders and hips moving in perfect sync, her breasts high and round, every muscle curving and flexing in waves of pure, feminine power.

Set free, she was the most beautiful, breathtaking sight he'd ever seen.

She bounded onto a dock and headed straight for the end. Griffin staggered to his feet, clutching his window ledge and watching her with disbelief and fascination. Had she lost her mind? The waters off the coast of Georgia were frigid in March; he spread his hand on a windowpane so cold that the sensation pierced his skin. She raced along the dock's length, bounded high off the last gray board, and arced like a bending arrow toward the deep, gray-green water of the bay. She disappeared into that water with barely a splash, the bay closing over her pointed feet as if inhaling her.

The water, the sunlight, the air, all went still and quiet, devoid of her energy. Griffin exhaled hoarsely, dragged a hand over his eyes to clear them, and waited to see her surface. A mantel clock above the room's cold fireplace ticked ten, twenty, thirty seconds. Then a minute. No sign of her. *Oh, my God. Come up, Alice. What the hell have you done?*

Another ten seconds. Another fifteen. He strained his eyes, searching everywhere beyond the docks and around the boathouses. Maybe she'd surfaced on the other side of them, where he couldn't see her. That had to be it. His gut twisted. *The water's too cold for swimming. She's disoriented, passed out, drowning.*

Drowning. Griffin swung about and lurched for an antique cane standing beside the room's door. A brass sextant clattered from a table. Leaning heavily on the cane, he struggled out of his room, yelling, filling the house like a bellows with the terrible frustration he felt. He made his way as quickly as he could down the long staircase, cursing the ocean.

Give her back.

≈≈≈

I swam the way a bird flies in a perfect sky. Curving and turning with joy, letting the currents lift me and carry me weightlessly. There was nothing between me and the very ends of the earth except water, and water held out an infinite, open invitation; I could travel as far as that vast current would take me, flowing from one great underwater world to the next. I might surface beside the white cliffs of Dover, along the sultry cape of Africa, in the port of Shanghai, or before a blue-white glacier at the top of the planet. I might discover the lost continent of Atlantis. I might even find my place in the scheme of things.

Or I might simply stay close by small, beautiful Bellemeade Bay, with the moonlight-and-magnolia southern mainland behind me and mysterious Sainte's Point Island shadowing my intentions.

Hello, my dear ladies, I would call to the Bonavendiers with great dignity as I rose like

Venus from the surf. Hello to the exquisite Lilith and sarcastic Mara and sweet Pearl on the island's shore. *I made my own way here without help, you see.* Confidence obscured all memories of my time spent in cowardly hesitation. I was drunk with elemental discoveries and became a braggart.

Behind me on dry land Randolph Cottage sat empty, deserted—or so I thought. It looked romantically gothic, and if I hadn't been transfixed by the water, I would have studied it more before I lost myself in the lure of the bay. Musings about the local landmarks would have to come later.

I sang out in water so dark I couldn't see my own hands in front of me. Waves of sound illuminated my way, giving back echoes that outlined fish, great and small, crabs on the sandy bottom, diaphanous shrimp skittering along, and even, across the bay, the huge, submerged landmass of Sainte's Point Island itself.

I circled back toward the docks, filling my senses, simply wandering. Suddenly, my reverie erupted. The water surged with shock waves and bubbles. I flattened myself on the bottom. Someone or something had plunged off the end of the dock no more than a few yards from me, clumsy but powerful, churning water and sand as if dredging for gold. The invader headed straight toward me. I whirled around to escape, but he touched me.

Fingers. Hard, thick, human fingers

grazed my right ankle. *Alice*, he yelled inside me. *I've got you.*

Him. The voice. I gulped down water, gagged, then slipped through his raking grasp and surged into deeper territory, not stopping until I'd put a good distance between the stranger and myself. I felt him flailing along the bottom, searching for me, refusing to give up. I could feel his determination. I sank my hands into the sand and held on. Had he led me here? Or had he *followed* me? Was he a noble protector or a scheming magician? I was so unnerved I sank down like a flat gray stingray, wishing the sand would hide me. My heart nearly exploded. Men or boys only chased me to humiliate me. Panic, pure and simple, overrode all sense. This was primal. This was survival.

Don't touch me. Stay back. He did not answer. I waited for a minute, then ventured the slightest reaching-out, a careful hum, searching for him.

The horrifying truth roared back at me. Pain, confusion, fury, terror. He was too weak, the water was too cold, he was struggling, sinking, weighted somehow. This man was dying in the water I loved. This man had *known* he might die if he went after me. He would rather die than let me die.

I propelled myself like a shot through the dark water, sang out strongly, and found him. He floated just above the bottom of the bay, facedown, bubbles frothing from his lips. I squatted on the ocean floor, burrowed my feet into the sand, latched a hand around his wrist, and launched myself toward the surface. He lifted from the bay floor with heavy and cumbersome retreat.

The echo of his pulse beneath my fingers said his life was still potent. I tugged him quickly to the shore, swimming on one side and scissor-kicking. Then I stood up in the shallow water a few yards from the gray beach before Randolph Cottage and wrapped both hands around his waist. The bay itself gave a slight, tidal heave to help me. We laid him on the sand with his upper body safely anchored to dry earth.

Crouching beside him, I studied him with terrible fascination. I laid a hand on his chest and felt his heartbeat. I sang out to him, a silent vibration. And then I said loudly, "You forgot to breathe again."

He arched his back, coughed violently, then rolled over on his side and retched water. He smelled of liquor and illness, of fear and despair, yet his writhing was powerful. Thin blue pajamas clung to him like cellophane. His body was tall, muscled and lean, his skin ashen but textured like canvas aged in the sun. He kept his eyes shut as if even a single ray of light would burn the back of his brain. Thick black lashes swept sleep-deprived blue smudges on his skin. His pajama top hung half unbuttoned, and when his beard draped aside, I saw lurid pink scars and healing gouges among the dark hair of his broad chest and stomach.

I winced. One arm was encased in a cast from elbow to hand. A scar protruded from his thick beard atop one cheek. His lower right leg was also covered in a cast. How he had thought to swim with that anchor on him, I could not imagine. I shamelessly noted the impressive outlines of his sex and the explicit tattoo of a naked woman embracing a dolphin on his inner left forearm. I drew back with alarm but also a trill of intrigue. I had never seen anyone like him except in my imagination.

He seduces the feminine in every way. What a magnificent, dangerous beast he is.

When the shaggy-haired stranger rolled over on his stomach and dragged himself a little further out of the water, I looked quickly at his exposed feet. No webbing. My heart sank. So he was not like me, though he obviously shared my strange new talent for telepathic hallucinations. His eyes still shut, his chest rising and falling swiftly, he shivered in the cold air and continued to cough up the cold bay water. I flinched with every gasp of his lungs. Desperate, I blew out a long, coaxing sigh and watched in wonder as the rhythm of his chest slowed.

So I did have a *little* control over him.

Suddenly I recalled some object falling away as he floated in the water. "You lost a crutch or cane in the water, didn't you? I'll retrieve it for you, and then see about getting you into your house." I leapt to my feet, glad for the escape. I turned to wade into the bay.

He clamped a hand around my ankle.

I jerked wildly, fell, then tried to crawl away from him, but he held on. I managed only to splash my outflung hands into the water's edge, searching for handles that didn't exist. His strong fingers tightened around my tender anklebones. I flipped over on my back, drawing up my frcc leg to kick him. His eyes were bloodshot but dark and intense, like the shadows inside deep water. Urgent. Compelling. But not angry. Just holding on.

I stopped struggling. "Let me go, please," I demanded in a low tone.

"You've saved my life. Twice."

"Only paying a debt of honor. You've saved mine as well. So let's be friends and you let me go."

"How did you do it? How did you stay under so long?" His voice was just as it had seemed in my mind, deep and worldly, hinged with melodic Southern vowels but trimmed with a hard edge. The hoarse quality of it vibrated through my bones.

I shook my head. "I'm a strong swimmer."

His fingers pressed harder. I felt the pulse in my ankle throbbing under the pad of his thumb. "I have to know that I wasn't imagining you before," he said, "and not imagining what you were able to do in the water out here."

"I have questions about *your* abilities, as well. Your motives. You're a very reckless stranger."

"Not a stranger, Alice. Your name's Alice. I know you, *Alice*. Alice."

He spoke my name like a caress of lace on my skin, and I stared at him. My name always sounded plain, ugly, basic. The Riley family had labeled me as an afterthought; no favorite grandmother had borne my name, no beloved friend. It was a name they assigned me as casually as clerks marking a sales tag on damaged merchandise.

I stiffened and replied quite formally, "You were told to expect someone named Alice Riley?"

He leaned forward, dripping, still breathing hard, coughing between almost every word. "I dreamed about you. I spoke to you in my dream. Alice . . . I'm on the edge, here. Are you with me?"

I shivered, almost undone by his plea, but too afraid. *Trust no one.* "I am *here* as a guest of Lilith Bonavendier of Sainte's Point Island." Lifting my chin, I recited this information as doggedly as any prisoner of war, giving only the essentials. "I was told to come to Randolph Cottage, where the Bonavendier family shares boat docks—"

"Did you make the man put down the gun?"

I froze. The stranger and I stared at one another. He searched my eyes, taking deep breaths. His voice grew stronger. "You did hear me this morning, wherever you were then? *Was there a man with a gun?*"

"Whatever you think me capable of doing," I said, "is your fantasy, not mine."

A tremor went through him, and he clenched his free hand atop the other, still holding my ankle like a jailer. "You *did* hear me. You *did* make him put the gun down. I can hear it in your voice. I see it in your eyes." He groaned. "So I'm not crazy—or at least we're crazy together. Tell me what's happening to us."

I moaned silently and looked away. *I didn't know.* "If you suspect me of strange intuitions, then why haven't I divined something as simple as your name?"

"Maybe you don't want to listen; you're afraid of what you'll hear. I understand. I'll make it easy for you." He watched me urgently, as if his mission in life was to tell me all about himself and learn all about me. "I'm Griffin. Griffin Randolph."

I drew back, contemplating the unexpected lyricism of his given name, thinking of mythological beasts of many parts, wondering why his parents had named him so. Now he had a visceral voice, a form, a face, a paternal and maternal claim to recognition. A lion's head and claws with the wings of a bird of prey. A hunter on land or in air but hating the water. A strange pirate. Yet his hand still made a vise around my ankle. He might eat me alive.

"If you continue to hold onto me and

make bizarre claims, Mr. Randolph," I whispered, "I'll pull you back in the water and finish what the water began."

The air stilled between us. His stark expression said he believed me but could not quite admit it. Neither could I after a moment of stunned thought. Never in my life had I uttered a death threat. I recalled Lilith's sinister words to my aunt and the others in Riley and their fear. My blood chilled. I was learning very bad habits. "Mr. Randolph, I only want you to release me—"

"You're a Bonavendier, that's for sure. Deadly."

"Me? Please, I. . ."

He continued to hold my ankle but pushed himself up to a sitting position. His shirt flayed open, streaming water. Droplets trailed down his chest, pooled in the awful puckers of his scars, tracked the flexing of extended muscle, the tendrils of coarse, masculine hair. He planted my foot on his knee, then placed a trembling, big-knuckled hand atop my toes. Slowly, he parted two of my toes, spreading them with his fingers. The webbing, iridescent and softly folded, fanned out for his inspection. He touched it with just his blunt fingertips, studied the butterfly shades of it with a look of fierce wonder, then raised his eyes to mine. "Lilith and her sisters have webbed feet. A family trait. Interesting deformity. My mother didn't have it, but she was just a distant cousin.

There are people around here who say the Bonavendiers aren't quite human." He nodded at my toes.

"Don't make fun of me." My voice was low, pained.

"I'm sorry. I never meant—" He spread his hand and released me.

I got to my feet, shaking. "I only want to be left alone, Mr. Randolph. That's all I ask for. *Privacy and respect.* A *very* human desire."

"Wait," he began. I could see the apology in his eyes, but I pivoted toward the bay, flattened myself in a long, shallow dive, and arched into the dark sanctuary of the water. Within a few seconds I found his cane. The feel of it told me it was old and important, possibly an heirloom. I pierced the surface with it clutched in both hands, and then I stared at the ornate silver handle. A mermaid of typical lore—finned tail and all—curved in sensuous splendor atop a cluster of silver shells. Etched distinctly on one of those shells was a small, perfect family crest of classic style and a Scottish surname, McEvers.

I frowned from the odd, beautiful cane to Griffin Randolph. He pushed himself to his knees, then with wretched, painful effort, employing extraordinary discipline, he got to his feet, balancing uneasily on his one good leg. I could tell how he suffered—cold, wet, an invalid who had strained aching bones and muscles. He took a step toward the water, then halted, staring at it fearfully. Yet he stood in the edge, determined. His valor made me plunge toward him, standing, wading, thrusting the cane at him, mermaid-end first.

"Don't be afraid of the water," I said with a certain smugness. "We web-footed fish freaks won't harm you." He took the cane from me, then sank the tip in the sand and leaned heavily on it, one big hand covering the silver mermaid entirely. He held out his free hand to me. "Don't be afraid of the land," he countered. "I won't hurt you, either. I promise. And I'm sorry I frightened you." He paused. "I know how awful I look."

My breasts tightened against the sodden material of my bra and T-shirt, and my womb opened. But I stayed in the safe water. "Not awful. Just wounded."

"You're kind."

Some large creature swirled past me. I looked around with new fear. A tall, blue-gray fin crested and submerged. And then, nearby, another. And another. One by one, nearly a dozen dolphins joined in circling me. I looked up at Griffin Randolph for explanation. "They used to come here," he said, staring at me. "For my mother."

A bottle-nosed head emerged from the water, and I found myself looking down at a dolphin. It uttered a soft series of clicks and whistles. A wave of warm friendship slid through me, a translated communication. "Hello, ma'am," I said in wonder. She whistled at my greeting. All the others then raised their heads from the water to chatter at me, too, and I, quite naturally, began to sing silently to them. This sent them diving and swirling around me, grazing my legs like cats, and the next thing I knew, I sank my hands in the water and stroked them as they flew past. I began to cry with joy and confusion, then beseeched Griffin Randolph with one more look and discovered we both wore tears. At that moment I would have come out if he had asked me, and he would have come in if I had called.

I had to get away from this seductive border between the water and the shore. "You stay there," I yelled hoarsely. "And I have to stay *here. Please.*"

Upset, operating on foolish pride and not a shred of common sense, I plunged deep into the bay. The coterie of dolphins formed an escort around me. I surfaced a long time later—two miles away, at least—in the very real shadow of Sainte's Point, within yards of the island's wooded banks. I squinted back across the bay, trembling. I could see Griffin Randolph, still standing on his own shore.

Watching after me but remaining in his own world.

For now.

A notable percentage of the world's popular singers and operatic stars are Water People. Good manners and common sense prevent me, of course, from naming celebrity names.
—*Lilith*

Twelve
~

The villagers of Bellemeade sent word to Lilith excitedly. Alice Riley, identified by her name on boxes she'd left at WaterLilies, had arrived. A group had gathered to watch her walk to Randolph Cottage. Though Alice's precise whereabouts eluded Lilith, she assumed Alice was now waiting at that cottage under Griffin's care, and she had a deep feeling that whatever had happened between the two of them was meant to be.

"In due time she'll be one of us, at home and at heart," Lilith promised aloud as she hurried into a very private sunroom in the mansion at Sainte's Point. Anatole, the cockatiel, preened his white feathers from a brass perch hung below Tiffany windows a dozen feet tall. Remnants of the day's sunlight poured through their stained glass, shading the aviary's palms and orchids in pale gold and green hues. Lilith brushed a wisp of Anatole's pinfeathers off a small marble pediment, then went along the other tables and shelves, touching a fingertip to the blooms of the rare orchids. She re-arranged crystal and silver servings on a tall English cabinet of brass and teak, once bound for Windsor Castle. At the center of the room, a pair of miniature pagodas held up a thick glass tabletop in exotic wood and gold, gifts from some passing trade ship a hundred years before Lilith's birth. Lilith fluffed a blooming bromeliad in a marble planter on the table's center.

This was her favorite room in the mansion, filled with tropical plants, private family albums, discreet portraits, Anatole's feathers, and the pale-green aura of transmuted daylight, the color of the ocean. She stood for a moment, gazing at a closed set of white velvet drapes that covered a portrait on one wall. "You wanted us to find her, I know," Lilith whispered.

She swept out of the room in a filmy swath of pale silks, her bare feet adorned in anklets and delicate twines of sapphires and pearls, inventively fastened. Alice would be greeted in warm Bonavendier style at the docks on the mainland and not be overwhelmed again.

"Come, my dear sisters, " Lilith called as she went down the broad main hall, straightening perfect vases of flowers, smoothing invisible dust motes from side tables and lamp sconces, nodding to a shrine-like procession of Bonavendier ancestors in elaborate portraiture. She halted in an alcove before a portrait of her own parents and gazed up at them quietly.

Her father, Orion, looked not outward but inward at her mother, Helice, an English beauty who had been lured from her own waters by him in the dark-haired charm of his prime. They had been acknowledged like royalty among a very exclusive private society that encompassed the waters of the world. Lilith remembered fabulous yachts filling the harbor and fabulous, often barefooted peoples filling the mansion. It had seemed in her childhood that the island was home to a special kind of magic.

"Mother, I am welcoming Father's fourth daughter to this house today," Lilith said to the portrait. "This is no shame to your memory. It was his grief for you that made him love again, and even if he chose an ordinary young Lander to love, she was very special in her own way." She paused. "Father, the halfling you created out of loneliness will never live in loneliness again. I promise you."

Mara spoke sadly behind her. "Can you promise us that Father's bastard isn't meant to doom us all with her useless, ordinary, Lander problems?"

"Oh, Mara," Pearl rebuked but sounded worried.

Lilith turned to find her younger sisters staring at her. They were adorned like solemn dancers in some antique Grecian tableaux—robed in whispers of sheer aquamarines and mauves and golds, their *je ne sais quoi* attitude saying it was no surprise that others of their kind were some of the world's leading fashion designers. Their bare feet gleamed with exquisite gemstones. Pearl's flame hair and Mara's mahogany cascaded in waves down their backs, decorated with tiny, interwoven diamonds here and there. Pearl wore a little gold angel on a gold chain around her throat, having decreed that an angel would be the emblem of Alice's mother from now on. Lilith's younger sisters had decorated themselves ceremoniously, if not spiritually, to greet Alice. Lilith sniffed at their melodramatic concern. "I have never felt more *right* about a decision."

"Oh?" Mara bobbed her head, sending waves of dark locks past her eyes and a tiny diamond bouncing in its nest above one eye. She shoved her hair back impatiently. "You've lost track of Alice. Please, admit it. You don't know where she *is* right now. That's significant, Sister. Has there ever been a time when you couldn't say where one of *us* was?"

Lilith stiffened. "Why, she's at Randolph Cottage. Waiting for us to fetch her. Perhaps because her mother was not our kind, my connection to her is not quite strong enough to be more specific."

"Or, *perhaps,* deep in your heart, you know she doesn't belong here. Sister, please reconsider. What say we take her in, give her money, find her a home elsewhere, then send her away? She'll be happier with her own people—Landers."

"She's not a pet to be placed with a good family of strangers, Mara. She's our sister."

"*Half-sister*. Oh, Lilith, I have intuitions, too. I feel you're not telling us all your motives, and there's going to be trouble. There's always trouble when we're careless about the outsiders we trust. Plus, you're cultivating Griffin, and you know that's not right either. I don't care if he's one of us . . . he doesn't know it, wouldn't accept it, and you know what could happen—"

"I never recall you suggesting that his mother should be avoided, even after she married a Randolph and pretended to be ordinary for him."

"Sweet Undiline," Pearl moaned. "Poor, dear Undiline."

Mara paled. "Yes, and look how badly Undiline's life turned out because she tried to belong to both our world and the ordinary one. Because she loved a Randolph. Look at what we've been forced to hide from her son. And don't forget our own forays into the world of dry land-lovers. Isn't all that testimony enough? We have to keep to ourselves. Our own kind."

The distant sound of the dock's bell broke through the tense moment. "We *are* going across to the mainland now," Lilith ordered softly. "And we *will* welcome Alice. And we *will* come to understand all her mysteries, as she will understand ours. And I *will* believe that Griffin's homecoming is a sign that he is meant to be among us, too. Do not speak to me of degrees of rightness. I know our *kind*. Our kind consists of those whose love carries beyond any tide. What point is there in our existence, otherwise? Are we to be the remnants of worlds long forgotten and nothing else?"

She left the mansion angrily with her subdued sisters following her. They went out into the bright blue late-winter day, down the pathway that led from the great house, past the statuary and tables and winter gardens and draping, massive oaks. Barret waited on the main dock, beside the *Lorelei* with its handsome cabin containing fine and sumptuous accommodations.

Standing with him, dwarfed by the aged German's height and heft, two cherubic, silky blond men and a woman waved their hands in concern. The middle-aged Tanglewoods— brothers and sister—were plump and asexual, all dressed in pale, baggy trousers and cashmere sweaters dyed various shades of delicate gold and white. Like overgrown Renaissance angels, the employees hurried up the path, invisibly winged and gentle and alarmed. Loyal Tanglewoods had fluttered around Bonavendiers for two centuries.

Kasen, the eldest and leader, drawled breathlessly, "Oh, here now, we've filled the boat with vodka and flowers and gifts, yeah, Lady Lilith, but look, look, something's happenin'; look out in the cove."

Even the unflappable Barret was frowning at the cove, his hands shoved in his trousers, his thick fur coat pushed back behind them. He turned to watch Pearl with adoring concern as she, Lilith, and Mara walked out onto the dock. "The dolphins are singing to you, my ladies."

The dolphins crisscrossed the small cove in exuberant flashes of blue-gray choreography, churning the water. When Lilith reached the edge of the dock, their matriarch thrust her head from the water. She and Lilith regarded each other in singing silence. Lilith gasped lightly, raised a hand to her throat, and gazed out at the edge of the cove, where the surf broke on the cove's narrow mouth. "*Alice,*" she said.

There, indeed, was Alice, looking back at all of them from the water. Steam misted around her boyish hair and large-eyed face. She seemed uncertain, nervous, a little lost. Yet she'd just managed two miles of unfamiliar water littered with small sharks, jellyfish, and treacherous currents. And Lilith had never heard her coming.

Remarkable. Troublesome.

"*Alice!*" Pearl echoed. And then to her eldest sister, with bewildered alarm, "Lilith, how did she swim the bay without any of us suspecting it?"

"She's a show-off," Mara said loudly.

"And a sneak."

"I would have fetched her in style," Barret complained. "She doesn't even trust us for transportation?"

"The Alice!" all three Tanglewoods chorused, using one of several peculiar titles their family had assigned to Bonavendiers over many generations of spellbound service. "She is a most forward person, isn't she, Lady Lilith?" one drawled worriedly. "To appear out there, just appear, without tellin' you."

Lilith held out her arms and called loudly. "Welcome home, Alice. What an extraordinary entrance you're making. One for the Bonavendier history books."

Pearl began to cry and applaud. Mara sulked. The Tanglewoods cheered. Alice swam toward them slowly, clearly none too eager to believe it was all right to show up this way. The dolphins swept around her like joyous heralds, with pristine gulls dipping and screeching above and the slanted sunlight raising diamonds like unreal promises on the harboring cove of Sainte's Point.

Lilith stripped off the silks she wore and dived in naked to greet her father's lost daughter. Pearl followed enthusiastically, and Mara, reluctantly. Alice gasped, then plunged out of sight. Lilith feared she had deserted them out of modesty, then felt her movement in the water. As Lilith and her sisters frowned and treaded in place, Alice circled their bare lower bodies. Her hands darted out, examining their naked thighs, their knees, their feet, even prodding their buttocks. Pearl yipped. Mara kicked at her. Lilith was compliant. This strange affront continued for several minutes.

When Alice surfaced, Mara gave her a furious look. "How rude."

Alice said nothing but heaved a sound that might be relief, disappointment, or both.

Lilith heard the explanation in that breath and said gently, "Don't confuse fantasy with the glorious mysteries of the truth, my dear. And don't assume we're lunatics because you didn't discover the type of proof you *expected*. Realize that subtle facts are far more precious than fairy-tale theatrics." She gently touched Alice's bristly auburn hair. "Become your own proud self. That is the transformation you should expect now that you're here, where you belong."

Alice bowed her head, blushing, acknowledging the ludicrous idea she'd needed to set aside right away.

In the water, no one had grown a mermaid's tail.

～～～

During the darkness of that eventful March night, Griffin poured his liquor into the drains of the cottage sinks and flushed pain pills down aged toilets gurgling below porcelain water tanks high on the cottage's ornate plaster walls. At the last moment, he looked hard at a row of soda bottles, opened them, and poured them out, too.

Sweating with exertion, he stripped and sank himself in the tepid water of a claw-footed tub, propping his sodden cast on the rim. The wind sang melancholy warnings he ignored. He soaped and washed the stink of defeat from his skin. Armed with scissors and a package of disposable razors, he shaved off his ragged beard and cut his hair.

It was after midnight when he finished drying and dressing himself in faded gray sweats. He limped to a small temporary kitchen C.A. had installed in a corner of his upstairs bedroom, where he drank a pint of thick cream and ate several cans of tuna.

Finally, he went to bed, straightening the careless covers, aligning himself with staunch, painful discipline instead of drugged chaos, lying in the dark with his gaze trained on the vista of black ocean, cold white stars, and thoughts of Alice Riley. She was out there, on Sainte's Point, her solemn, stunning face turned up to this same sky. If he could unravel Alice's mysteries, he might unlock the secrets he was now convinced that Lilith Bonavendier and her sisters had kept from him. He might understand their relationship with his mother and what they knew about her and his father's deaths, about his own survival, then and now. There was something, *something* he had to find out—he couldn't name it but could now identify the longing at least. Alice might piece it out, help him, be persuaded to tell what she learned from her new kin.

The hard course of desire rose in him at that thought, and he realized he wanted answers but he also wanted Alice Riley, or even Alice Bonavendier, whoever and whatever she was, whether he deserved her or not. He laid a cool, strong hand on himself.

He lived tonight because of Alice Riley.

Ali, he decided to call her, changing her just as she'd changed him, owning her gently, by a new given name.

The Celts called him The Waterman and said he was once a sea-god named Dewi. In Christian times, he became Saint David. By any name, he was reported to be irresistible when playing the harp and singing. No doubt, since he was one of us.
—*Lilith*

Thirteen

~

If the sisters suspected I had met their Randolph neighbor, they said nothing and neither did I. I tried to put him out of my mind and intended to keep him out, if possible. Everything was too confusing.

I have come to Paradise, I wrote in my journal. My first few days on Sainte's Point have been spent in dazed silence. I'm drunk with the beauty. The ancient island lies along Georgia's sultry coastline among a slender chain of its sister isles, many of which have names as rich as a lover's sigh—Ossabaw, Wassaw, Sapelo, and grand, majestic Cumberland, home of the Carnegies. Tiny Sainte's Point is the least known to the curious public, the most private, the most ethereal. An island of misty forests, long beaches, moss-draped oaks, ancient shell middens, and the peculiar, elegant old estate of the notorious, elusive, mysterious, and very rich Bonavendiers, descended from a French pirate and his wife, Melasine, a woman of origins and rumors too wild to be true.

I swim; I walk the shady island trails, exploring brackish, enchanted pools, the lighthouse at the island's southern tip, and even the coquina remnants of a sixteenth-century Spanish monastery. I study fanciful books written about long-dead Bonavendiers *by* long-dead Bonavendiers, and I gaze at pictures of my father. Sometimes I stand for an hour before the foyer portrait of him and his wife.

What kind of man were you, and what did you do to my mother? I whisper.

But neither he nor the sisters can adequately answer that question for me. Their own lives and loves appear just as enigmatic. Apparently, none of the sisters have children, and I don't understand why only Pearl—via Barret, the mysterious German—enjoys a lusty, permanent paramour. I passed by the half-open doors to Pearl and Barret's suite one afternoon and heard undeniable murmurs and sighs of passion, with tender words called out by both. I hurried away for fear they would catch me listening, though to say the sisters aren't prudish is an understatement.

The old mansion is conducive to trysts and secrets without a doubt. It is huge and gothic and luxurious and stunning—a jigsaw puzzle of stone, wood, fine metals, porcelains, and sweeping vistas hooded by hoary maritime oaks balanced like spiders on limbs that dip nearly to the ground. One limb curves like a natural seat beneath my own main-floor bedroom window. My bedroom is a seduction in vibrant aquamarines, silvers, and antique white, a nest of silks and fine cottons and cashmere, with an enormous four-poster bedstead that Lilith says came from an early nineteenth century English ship. She makes no apologies regarding the family's talent for found goods. Maritime law allowed a bounty to those who rescued human lives.

"Were you pirates?" I asked. I'm careful to refer to Bonavendiers as separate from my own lineage. I simply do not feel I am, at heart, one of them.

"We were *privateers* in service to the government, my dear," Lilith answered without a shred of irony over such a small distinction.

At any rate, the bedstead must have belonged to some princess or high courtesan, at least. I have equally stunning armoires, lamp tables, and bookcases, which are filled with first-person accounts of sea-going adventure and texts on oceanography. Lilith surmised my favorite topics, of course. I have a writing desk stacked with stationary bearing the Bonavendier crest, and a cache of old-fashioned gold and silver fountain pens that produce script with the fluid grace of a sloop skimming the ocean. I have a sitting room, where an antique Italian cabinet offers a disarmingly high-tech music system, including a collection of my favorite operatic and instrumental music on CDs. In a pearl-hued bathroom, I dry myself with thick white towels from a cabinet smelling of fine soaps; I indulge in canisters of fragrant bath salts and slide a hand around the carved edge of a white marble tub so smooth it is like my own skin. Above me, of all things, a chandelier scatters dewdrop rainbows on my face, just as stained-glass transoms fill all the rooms with lyrical light.

My suite leads into the main house through double doors with scrolling gold Bonavendier crests inlaid in some fine wood. The crest, I note, is a traditional coat of arms but is bordered by two controversial figures in honor of Simon Sainte Bonavendier and his supposedly fin-endowed wife, Melasine—a naked man with his genitals discreetly covered by a twining sash and a classic mermaid. The two curve toward each other around opposite sides of the crest, clasping hands at the top. At the bottom, the mermaid's elaborate, swirling tailfin curves possessively around the man's feet. A phrase in Latin, scrolling beneath the pair, says the rest.

Hidden Between Water And Earth Await Miracles.

～～～

"What are you doing?" Pearl asked me when she found me reading on the beach. "Reading again? Thinking some more? Oh, now stop that. *Feel* your way along, Alice. *Sing* your way. That's what we mermaids do. We sing out, and we sing inside ourselves. Don't let all the nasty tales of evil *sirens* color your idea of our kind. We are the keepers of the waters. And all the other creatures and forms and beings and even the ordinary people cannot resist our joy."

I told Pearl patiently that I'd learned Sainte's Point was approximately twenty-five thousand years old in geologic age, that the warm waters of the Gulf Stream flowed south to north about one hundred miles east of these shores, that the island was perched on a broad continental shelf that sloped out to that Gulf Stream current, then plunged toward the Atlantic's abyss. I told her that the windward side of the island was dangerously endowed with fast currents and shoals, including a limestone reef, and that ten miles out, the Point Trench formed a large, undersea valley that had once been an ancient riverbed. I told her the climate was sub-tropical, the fishing excellent, that all manner of small mammals roamed the forests, that terns and skimmers nested behind the dunes, that loggerhead turtles hatched their eggs on the beaches.

She sat down next to me as sweetly as any sixty-two-year-old child, if I believed the claims she and her sisters made about their ages, which I didn't.

"In short, this is an incredibly complex habitat," I explained to Pearl with great kindness.

"Habitat?" she chirped as dolphins rose

just beyond the surf to watch us. Pearl fluffed a silk sarong she wore over a flowing white shift. Her flame-red hair tumbled down her back and onto the sand. Her bare, webbed feet twinkled with jewelry. Her breasts, unfettered by any underwear, bounced in perky unison as she laughed. I stared at them and frowned over the thought of my own breasts bound under my denim jacket.

"Habitat?" she called again to the dolphins, and they whistled and clicked as if laughing, too. "Why, this is your *home*, Alice. Not a habitat. We're not a science experiment. And neither are you." I smiled but accepted nothing. "So," Pearl said. "Tell me what your books say about mermaids. I *know* you've been studying the fairy tales. You're very interested in proving one thing or another."

"I've researched a good deal of the mythological and sociological lore. The idea of a union between humans and the sea dates back to the dawn of human history. The Babylonians, the Assyrians, the Egyptians, the Greeks and Romans, not to mention all the ancient Asian dictates, and those of the Hindus, the Polynesians, the Africans, the American Indians, et cetera—all the ancient cultures focused on the worship of the water as a womb, the female river deities, the oceanic goddesses, fish goddesses, the fertile sea kings, et cetera. For example, many of the Greek and Roman deities were water-based. Aphrodite, Neptune,

Poseidon, et cetera."

"Et cetera," Pearl said solemnly.

"Since most of the world's great early civilizations developed in coastal areas, it was natural for people to personalize the vast, mysterious oceans. The idea of half-human, half-fish creatures seemed quite plausible and helped explain both the danger and the allure of water. The notion of mermaids—and to a lesser extent, mermen—came to embody a certain sinister charm—no doubt largely a fear of the ocean and a fear of women's sexuality, at least in terms of European patriarchal attitudes, as the centuries progressed."

"Et cetera," Pearl intoned.

"By medieval times, the pagan gods and goddesses were declared demonic and reduced to caricatures of sexual provocation and evil. Yet the image of mermaids and mermen has been resilient enough to survive as rather charming, though seductive beings who inhabit all forms of water. Hans Christian Anderson's *The Little Mermaid* gave birth to the modern notion of lovesick mermaids transforming into two-legged human beings at will. Well into the nineteenth century, the belief in real, flesh-and-blood mer-people was taken quite seriously, with numerous reports of sightings and captures. Britain even had a law on the books claiming sovereign rights to any mermaid or merman found in British waters."

Pearl yipped. "They should have looked

right in their own royal house. Just why do you think you never saw Henry VIII without shoes? Hmmm?"

I ducked my head and studied her carefully. "All right, tell me the truth about Water People, as I've heard Lilith call them. Are there many around?"

She gazed at the ocean in deep thought. "Well, let's see. I personally know at least a thousand. We Bonavendiers have a great many relatives and friends among the other Water People of the world."

"All . . . web-footed and imbued with certain remarkable abilities?"

"For the most part. But of course there are, hmmm, *degrees* of our kind, just as in any kind of . . . kind." She glanced at me with a wistful smile. "Those of us with the glorious feet and singing ability are regarded as the most blessed."

"Does that opinion extend even to someone such as myself, who has webbed feet but comes from . . . mixed parentage?"

"Why, yes. The traits of our kind are strong in you. No one will ever call you a false-footed *poseur*."

"But you're saying there are others who are *not* endowed with webbed feet but are considered merfolk?"

"Oh, yes. You can hear them humming a little. They listen to us calling, and understand what it means, perhaps on a subconscious level.

They have certain abilities. Just lesser."

"Then they don't *know* that they're merfolk?"

"Some do. Most don't. They only know they're drawn to water, and to the singing." She rattled off a long list of admirals, explorers, and celebrities, including some of the world's finest singers and most charismatic actors. "All of them are our kind," she announced blithely. "The beautiful people. Especially the divas."

I sat for a while, not daring to say a word, pondering her claim. When I finally got myself under control, I said solemnly, "I've always suspected Diana Ross, I admit."

"Oh, indeed."

"Are there any mermaids or mermen who fit the classical description?"

She looked at me askance. "You mean preening before seashell-encrusted mirrors and flapping about in gilded cities beneath the waves? How Hollywood! Certainly not!"

I blushed. "I'm sorry. Forgive me for asking."

"But . . . I thought you knew. Don't you understand?" She bent toward me, peering at me as if I must be playing. "About Melasine? The one from whom all Bonavendiers are descended for the past two centuries?"

I bent toward *her*. "Lilith promised to tell me more, but hasn't . . . yet."

She frowned and bit her lower lip, squinting, clearly debating what to say. "I suppose I might as well be the one to spring the truth on you, then."

Prickles ran down my spine. "What truth, Pearl?"

Pearl looked at me with somber, guileless import. "She had the loveliest tail."

I went very, very still. "Pearl, please don't—"

"But it's true. We call her kind The Old Ones. We believe there are only three of the Old Ones left in the whole world—and they are not given to socializing. In fact, it's believed they're loners to the extreme, living in the greatest depths, in the most isolated realms of the vast waters." She nodded sagely. "This probably explains why merfolk haven't taken over the whole planet. We're not mixers."

"You're saying that our . . . great-great-great grandmother was a true, fin-bearing, half-human, half-fish mermaid."

"Well, now, if you're going to get technical—" she flashed an exasperated look at me—"I don't know if 'half-fish' is biologically correct. Perhaps 'half-aquatic mammalian' is more accurate. At any rate, she is a good deal more exotic-looking than the standard portrayals show a mermaid being."

My ears rang. "And she sprouted legs and walked on land when she pleased?"

"Now, *listen*. I'm telling you, forget what you *think* you know about the Old Ones. Melasine lives entirely in the water. None of this melodramatic transforming—that would be physically impossible, not to mention quite preposterous, you know!"

"True." I wondered why we were talking about Melasine in the present tense.

"Simon was no doubt devoted to her, body and soul. They wed in the sea after settling here, and she *remained* in the sea while he built the Bonavendier estate. But he also built a beautiful stone chalet right on the cove's edge, with sections submerged in the water, and certain submerged doors open to let the water flow inside. Simon shared that chalet with her— half on land, half in the water. She bore their children in the watery chambers of that lovely place. She and Simon were quite happy together for many decades. It was a remarkable bonding, considering that the Old Ones rarely stay in one place or love an ordinary person for long. Simon was no doubt a quite alluring man." Pearl sighed. "But, of course, he eventually grew old and died, and Melasine was left bereft and alone. She was so distraught she ordered the chalet torn down."

I'd perused the ornate Bonavendier cemetery, an ethereal place of fine marble crypts and monuments in a shady grove overlooking the bay. I'd visited my father's grave more than once, and spoken to his spirit, in that place. And while there I'd studied Simon Sainte Bonavendier's elaborate monument, with his name and dates melting into the marble. There was *no* monument for a wife at all, and certainly none marked with the name Melasine. "I suppose Melasine's body was committed to the water when she died?"

"Oh! I should have explained. *She's not dead.*"

I got up from the sand very slowly. "So you're claiming Melasine is still alive, somewhere?"

"Absolutely. Why do you think we call her kind the Old Ones?"

"Ah! Because they live to be very old."

"Oh, thousands of years."

"Thousands of years."

"Of course, as her two-legged descendants, we tend toward more ordinary lifespans. Perhaps a century, occasionally more." She grinned. "So at thirty-four, you're just a teenager."

I nodded toward the Atlantic. "I assume she didn't linger around here?"

"Who knows? Despite her love for Landers, she is a lone creature at heart."

"Landers?"

"Land people. Ordinary people."

"I see."

"Once Simon died she disappeared."

"And has never been seen again, then?"

"Well, no, there have been sightings, but there's no *proof* of her."

I breathed easier, realizing Pearl had told me the perfect fairy tale, a sweet homage to every mythological being who conveniently never reappeared. That was all. "What a lovely story," I said.

"A story?" Pearl sighed, got up, and came to me patiently, prying my arms loose from the hug I was giving myself. "Dear Alice, there are many kinds of transformations. Believe what you can, but always leave your heart open to Melasine." She laughed. "No need to look so solemn about her. When I was a child, I called her 'The Great And Powerful Flipper.' "

I didn't even know what to say to *that*, and she didn't seem to expect an answer. She tweaked my nose affectionately. "A mermaid's mind is best suited for cultivating beauties and nurturing interesting philosophies—you know, tidying the great depths of the heart. One has to be careful not to burden us with too much sorrow. We have to remain buoyant or we'll sink."

"I see."

"No, you don't. Not yet. But keep looking for 'Et cetera,' and you will." She laughed, threw off her clothes, and dived, naked, into the surf.

And I stood there on the beach, bound in denim and logic.

I had to find Lilith.

∾∾∾

Lilith loved the mansion's plant-filled sunroom. I could see that, see the contentment in her face anytime I met her there. Her cockatiel, Anatole, shrieked with interest when I walked in. Lilith looked up from the fabulous glass table at the room's center. She was writing in a journal—a passion we shared, to her delight. She closed the book when she saw the expression on my face. Without a word, she gestured to someone behind me, and I realized one of the sweet Tanglewoods had appeared magically in my wake. He closed the room's glass doors, giving us privacy.

"Ask me," Lilith said quietly.

"Do you really believe Pearl's fairy tale about Melasine?"

She sighed and stood in a sleek rustle of raw peach silk. She walked to a lovely marble wall across from us. It was one of the few areas of the sunroom not crowded with exotic trees or potted plants. On it hung a set of white velvet drapes, always closed. Lilith stood to one side, pulled a delicately tasseled drawstring, and the drapes parted. They revealed a rectangular portrait hanging longways, filling most of the wall, dwarfing both her and me.

I put a hand to my mouth. The colors were rich and old, the style was classic eighteenth century portraiture—dramatic, romantic, vibrantly realistic, yet very soft. The setting was a chamber of stone and rich fabrics, fringed pillows, gilded vases—what any fine lady of the time would want in the ambiance of her portrait. Through an open window, the ocean crashed on a sandy shore. The lady clearly wanted water behind her.

Because the lady, lounging decorously on an ornate chaise, was a mermaid.

"Melasine," Lilith said.

Her skin was ivory, her lips deep red. Her eyes, large and ocean-green, were tilted on the ends, with no lashes or brows, giving her face an ageless patina, a face like an oval moon, like a fine porcelain doll's. Yards of dark gold hair streamed over her bare breasts and jeweled arms, draping in luxurious waves across her pale stomach.

Her hands were larger than normal and webbed in opalescent skin. Her smooth, bone-white torso was perfectly human and perfectly beautiful, tapering at the waist, rising at white hips, merging below a perfectly ordinary navel, adorned with a gold waist chain and an emerald pendant. But at the vee of her thighs the milky skin merged, and there *were* no thighs.

There was a very different kind of being.

She glistened with pale blues and pinks, just a shimmer to her skin, a different texture, not scales, but a body meant to glide through water, like the lower half of some iridescent white dolphin. Sleek and smooth, that part of her bore ornamentation, too. A swath of gold cloth wound around her where the thighs might have been on one of us. It was tied in a large, ornate rosette over the middle of her, and I wondered, dazed, if it discreetly hid some sort of genital opening.

I couldn't begin to form that question into

words.

Her body tapered with aquiline power to a long, slender tail. Its twin white flukes streamed over the chaise's upholstered end with gossamer beauty, like the divided train of a wedding dress. As I pulled my gaze back along the length of her, she looked at me with her surreal face, the magic of the portrait placing her gaze directly on mine, and I was caught up in her gray-green eyes.

"See the resemblance to us?" Lilith said quietly.

I did. I couldn't speak. I couldn't move.

"I've never seen her myself," Lilith went on, "but I can tell you I've felt her presence at times, out in the water—and in that way I do believe she exists. In some form, Alice, either like this physically or not, her spirit is this grand. And when you need her, you'll know she's there."

I finally nodded.

I couldn't leave the parlor until Lilith closed the drapes, so I no longer saw Melasine. And Melasine no longer seemed to see *me*. Then I walked slowly out, went to my rooms, and laid flat on my back in the bed. When the spell began to fade, I started rearranging everything I believed, everything I assumed, everything I thought I knew. I wasn't sure what to think, instead, or what had just changed in me, but I couldn't *not* believe, anymore.

The education of Alice had begun.

Some Water People use the word halfling as a slur when someone exhibits Lander-like traits. That usage, however, is generally considered both inaccurate and ill mannered.

—*Lilith*

Fourteen
∼

"Someone has taken all my clothes," I announced, standing in a parlor of the mansion where the sisters and Barret gathered for tall glasses of vodka every evening.

"Those were not clothes," Mara retorted, "they were body bags."

"We took your hair clippers, too," Pearl confessed, looking gently distraught. "I couldn't bear the thought of you mutilating your lovely hair anymore."

I stared at the two of them.

Lilith watched quietly. "You'll find new clothing in your armoires," she said. "But if you wish, I'll have the old things returned."

"I don't want to be a charity case."

"*Charity case?*" Lilith straightened regally in a damask lounge, where she lay like a silver lioness, swathed in white silk and holding the finest crystal tumbler of pure, uncut vodka. "You are a Bonavendier. You have an

150

inheritance here. You have rights. You have an image to uphold. And you're a beautiful woman, as all true women are beautiful."

"In other words," Mara snorted, "we're tired of you looking like a skinny turtle in a denim shell."

"Oh, Sister," Pearl rebuked.

My face flamed. I didn't know what else to say, so I finally muttered at Mara, "Better a turtle than an ill-tempered crab."

Mara's mouth drew up in an angry bow.

Pearl burst out laughing. "An ill-tempered crab," she agreed, nodding at her aggravated sister.

Even Lilith repressed a smile with the back of one long hand. Her gaze went to me proudly. I was talking back. She approved.

In my rooms I indeed found fine cottons and silks, dresses, robes, flowing tango pants, delicate shoes, lovely blouses, even svelte, classic swimsuits, though no one around there seemed to swim clothed. I now owned the latest, sleekest, yet most classic fashions, owing to Lilith's impeccable and expensive taste. I knew the first moment I slipped into a clingy dress with a draping neckline and tiny straps that showed off my shoulders that I was being seduced. After thirty-four years of being ignored, chastised, or taunted like a sexless freak, I was now adorned in silk by the most beautiful crazy women in the world.

The thought drugged me with hope.

I walked out, head up, cheeks red, and returned to the drinking parlor. I stood in the doorway, staring over everyone's heads, waiting for execution via laughter, polite smiles, and Mara's taunts.

Silence.

Then—

Pearl ran to me, crying and applauding. "So beautiful!"

Lilith stood, the glow on her face beaming with pride. Mara gaped at me in silence.

"All right, put her in silk, and she'll more than do," Mara said finally.

High praise from the priestess of insult.

I thought my heart would burst with gratitude. *Wish it, believe it, and it will be so.* A saying I made up when I was a child.

Wish it, believe it, and it will be so.

They *are* seducing me.

∽∽∽

In the evenings the island fills with azure mists. Traces of red-gold sunsets finger through the oak's greening boughs, setting ruby fire to the first tiny fronds of ferns unfurling from the leafy ground below. Spring is nearly here. I think of everything that's happened in the past few weeks and of Griffin Randolph's provocation, of Lilith's expectations, of the adoring townsfolk lining the road out of Bellemeade, of Melasine's portrait. I see the sisters swim with the wild dolphins every day, and when I swim the dolphins accompany me, too.

Across from my bed are French doors, and through them I gaze into my own tiny garden. The mansion juts out on one side here, forming a privacy wall to my left. The ocean lies in front, and the island's forest begins on the right. I go outside often and climb into the oak limb's coarse, moss-covered cusp, gazing, enthralled, at the white surf of the Atlantic. I am happy facing the ends of the earth, defined only by water. When I'm satiated, I lounge on the oak's cradling arm and gaze into the lyrical shadows of the deep forest. A white, sandy lane arbored by oaks beckons me into that palmetto-and-vine wilderness. Every morning, several large deer gather there, watching me placidly. I watch them back.

Is it really so safe here?

They flick their tails and go back to grazing on spring greenery, as if a peaceful appetite is all that matters. Judith Beth, the female of the Tanglewoods, slips into my suite every afternoon and leaves a silver service on a small dining table in the sitting room. Liquored tea steams from an exquisite silver pot there, and a crystal decanter glistens with fine vodka. To my amazement, I can drink most liquors unscathed, in quantities that would kill any normal person. Beneath silver hoods on small china plates Judith Beth has placed mounds of pure butter filled with fresh herbs, saucers of heavy cream to be eaten like a dessert, and salty biscuits. Here my cravings are known before I admit them. Known, and encouraged. Lilith says my appetites are perfectly appropriate for *our kind*. Merfolk, if I believe the fantasy, are metabolically fueled by a diet of liquors and fats.

Not a bad fantasy.

All right, so the sisters don't sprout fantastic tails in the water. They transform themselves with fantastic *tales* instead, and I am becoming their willing accomplice. In my bath I study my naked self in each of several large, gold-framed mirrors hung on stone walls colored the soft white hue inside an oyster shell. I admit the sisters are perfectly formed, and I am a thin edition of them, but for the first time in my life I think I have potential. Sometimes I don a soft silk robe Lilith placed in my armoire. I stand in the middle of my bedroom, excited, sexual, confused, forlorn, listening to some ethereal hum that must be the island singing to me, or might be the future, warning me to beware.

The golden sunsets fall on my bare feet as I sit in the oak. I spread my toes, remembering the erotic invasion of Griffin Randolph's fingers. Griffin. Man-Beast. I drop his last name and admit we are acquainted, have been intimate, have saved each other from harm but might harm each other in the future. Yet my webbing looks invigorated, translucent and gilded, and my skin glows. My hair grows approximately two inches a day. Am I being transformed?

Maybe.

But I cannot possibly live up to the color of this light.

~~~

A typical breakfast at Sainte's Point consisted of creamy shrimp pudding laced with sherry. Puddles of butter adorned the top. This delicious dish seemed to strike no one as an inappropriate morning meal, and I had consumed perhaps a half-gallon of it every day in helpless adoration. We ate at a linen-covered table in a nook overlooking a rose garden and a tall stone fountain. Through an open window we listened to the music of saltwater splashing from a stone shell onto a pair of naked lovers, who held the shell aloft. Water trickled down their bodies into a base surrounding their webbed feet. Most mornings I could barely take my eyes off their fluid congress.

Lilith waited until I was sufficiently hypnotized one day.

"What happened between you and Griffin Randolph the day you arrived?" she asked without warning.

I sat back from the table, a silver soup spoon idle in my hand, and kept my gaze focused on my fingers. *She knew.* I had never mentioned meeting Griffin, never indicated I even knew his name. Of course she'd divined it all along. I shivered and looked at her apologetically. I told her everything. And then, "He saw what I can do in the water. He said he wants to know all about me and you-all, too. It's my fault. I apologize."

Lilith inclined her head. "Nothing is your

fault. This was meant to be. And there's a history to it you don't know. There are serious issues between his family and ours. There have been feuds for two centuries. We live *in* the sea, and the Randolphs live *on* it. A subtle but significant contrast. To them we're troublemaking oddities, pilfering from the waves, shirking real commerce. To us, they're—" she lifted her fine hands and gazed out the window at the naked lovers beneath the fountain waters—"they're *dry* goods. They have an insatiable need to dominate the ocean, and that, my dear, is an insult to every living drop of water, inside our bodies and out." She sighed. "Yet we can't do without their kind. The ocean is defined by the shore. The shore is defined by the ocean."

She told me about Griffin's work and the accident that had nearly killed him in February. She told me, in vague terms, that his parents had died when their yacht sank in a storm off Sainte's Point when Griffin was a boy, and that he'd nearly died, too. "You see, he's come full circle," she said. "Confronting life and death as a child in the ocean, and now again, as a grown man."

"His fear of the water began in childhood?"

"Yes. He's fought it ever since, but after the recent accident it's taken over completely."

"I don't understand why he and I connected suddenly. Just as I don't understand why you and I . . . Why, Lilith? I spent thirty-four years of my life alone in my own strange silence, then suddenly—" I spread my hands "—I'm hearing beautiful things."

"When you chose to save that small girl in the lake—when you chose to risk your life—you opened yourself to everything you fear and everything you want to love. Just as Griffin did when he risked his life to save a man in his crew. Those events were the catalysts of your souls and mine. You're not hearing voices that don't exist. You're hearing voices that finally have meaning for you. We all are."

"What does he want with me? How does he think I can help him?"

"You're an answer he's seeking. You're a way out of the confusion that has always marred his life. The endless questions he asks himself about himself." She paused, looking at me with her beautiful head tilted. "And, Alice, whether you believe it or not, you're a desirable young woman."

"This situation isn't—" I shook my head "—this isn't about that sort of thing."

She smiled knowingly, sipped her tea, and gazed out the window. "Every aspect of life is about desire, Alice. Every passion, every dream, every danger. Griffin keeps taunting the ocean to kill him, and if he doesn't stop, it will soon grant his desire. You, my dear, must change him. It's one of your desires in life, I am certain, to be taken seriously, to make a difference in the world. No doubt he has a purpose in your life, as well."

I went very quiet inside. "You believe in destiny, then?"

"No doubt. Every drop of water is destined to find another, my dear. From the clouds to the seas to our bodies and back again, an endless cycle since the beginning of time. An ancient stream. Nothing is lost, and there is meaning in every current." She paused again, looking at me kindly but steadily. "He has vague childhood memories—dreams—in which my sisters and I rescue him from the ocean floor with our own hands. A feat which is impossible." One more pause. She had impeccable timing. "Of course, we *did* rescue him."

I exhaled a long, shaken breath. "Do you think you can ever tell him?"

"Yes, but *how* to tell him is the problem—how to help him understand."

"Perhaps all of this—" I indicated the house, the finery, the indulgent food, the whole, lovely world in which she and her sisters had cocooned themselves "—is a false dream, and Griffin can prove it doesn't deserve to exist."

My honest rebuttal didn't seem to bother Lilith. She looked at me sadly. "I am willing to risk having you and Griffin destroy all that we Bonavendiers have created, in order that you may learn to believe in it."

I laid my hands flat along the table's lacquered edge. "I was speaking rhetorically about his justifications. I can *assure* you I'd never hurt you in any way. I am eternally grateful for your kindnesses. I'm just not sure I can share your faith in the explanations for what we are or how we fit in."

"That is precisely why you must try to *listen* and to *trust*. And so must Griffin."

I considered everything in silence while she sipped herbal tea and our breakfast pudding cooled. "His mother," I said slowly, "was she like us?"

"Yes, my dear. The traits, the talents, the exquisite taste." Lilith smiled wistfully.

"And so . . . he is, too?"

"Yes. Of course, with his father being a Randolph, and not at all of our kind, Griffin's not as blessed as you or I. But he is a remarkable young man, Alice, and I certainly consider him more Us than Them."

I stared at her. My heart constricted and expanded; joy raced through me. "So he's odd, like me," I whispered happily.

"He's special, like you," Lilith corrected.

"Special."

"Believe it."

"Should I be afraid of his powers?" I had a distinct feeling there was quite a bit she hadn't told me. And wouldn't tell me . . . yet.

"Only if you forget to lead as well as follow."

"Should he be afraid of *mine*?"

"That," she said with a sad smile,

"depends on where you lead him."

~~~

I floated on the edge of forever. Below me, I could sense but not see forms that must have been pieces of the *Calm Meridian*, and just beyond the wreckage site a depth as big as the sky. The Point Trench. A vast underwater valley beyond the shallows of Sainte's Point, curling out into the deep of the Atlantic. A dozen yards above me, the pale green water of the ocean surface had begun to fade to the dark hue of the deep sea. I could just see the hazy glow of the sun, lighting schools of small, dark fish that swirled and turned, agitated by the dolphins who had followed me. The dolphins' songs were curious, bewildered. They were not afraid for me but were not certain why I'd come out so far and down so deep.

To help Griffin, I told them.

I turned my attention to the graveyard below me and went down, singing.

Soon, I entered pitch-black water and was cocooned in the indescribable silence of the ocean. I sang out and shivered at the huge shape that came back to me. Slowly, I settled beside it. I pressed my palms to it and froze. I was touching the barnacle-encrusted bow of the *Calm Meridian*. The nose of the old yacht jutted upright on the ocean floor like a pointed hat some giant hand had set down neatly. I felt my way around it, tracing the outline of a porthole, finding no other openings. The sand fell out from under my feet, and I floated free, startled for a moment, before I regained my footing. I sang out into the Point Trench.

The remnants of the *Calm Meridian's* bow perched precariously on the slope of that ancient space, and a small shiver went up my spine. This site was dangerous. Like a tuning fork, my shiver became a song. Shapes bounced back to me. I slid away and explored the safer territory nearby. There lay the other scattered remnants of the classic yacht.

The years and the currents had collapsed the amidships and stern of the wooden vessel into a jumble of timber, all thick with barnacles. I skirted the perimeter of the wreckage, feeling my way around the bottom, scooping my hands into the sand. I began to find small, buried items—a brass cleat, a shard of some heavy, ceramic dishware, a door hinge as might have been on a cabinet in the yacht's galley. I pulled a small nylon bag from inside the sleek black maillot I wore, carefully tucked my findings into it, then tied the bag around my waist and eagerly returned to digging in the sand. *Treasure hunting is exciting,* I thought, then caught myself. I sat back on my heels. *This is a graveyard.*

I started again but felt subdued. The lure of a wreck site surprised me. Or was it just my nature to pluck curiosities and fineries from the ocean? Was I indeed the natural inheritor of a mermaid's talents and a pirate's tendencies? Nonsense. I busily scolded myself until my hand sank into soft sand and clasped something new. It was heavy and odd-shaped but smooth. I pulled it to the surface and ran my hands over it, sang to it, outlined it in my mind.

It was a marble figurine of a child riding a dolphin's back.

Oh, Griffin, I thought sadly. Traces of him as a little boy clung to the figurine. He had loved it. His mother had given it to him. He had carried it with him everywhere, even on the last trip he took with his parents. My hands shook. I carefully set the precious piece inside my sack. Singing out to the dolphins to follow me, I headed for Bellemeade Bay and Randolph Cottage.

To Griffin.

Land People fight and struggle and yearn to find magic in their lives. Water People hide behind that magic, but realize the loneliness of it.
—*Lilith*

Fifteen
~

Traveling on dry land is overrated, Griffin admitted as he managed the last few exhausted paces into the cottage's sandy yard. Every bone in his body ached, and his scars felt raw. Doctors had removed the casts from his leg and forearm, and he stepped steadily, though with a slight limp. He had just forced himself on his daily fitness hike, a grinding four-mile tour along piney backroads where no one was likely to notice him. A sweaty flannel shirt hung open down his chest, and his old khaki pants had settled low on his hips. The tie-strings on his heavy-soled walking boots had come undone, but his still-healing back was too stiff for him to bend and tie them. He gave in now, in the sanctity of his own yard, and leaned on the mermaid cane as he walked.

"Ready to take on the world," he intoned, "as long as my pants don't fall off my ass, or I don't trip over my own shoelaces."

You're doing fine. I left you a gift on the dock. Alice's voice, elegant and somber, sang inside him.

He halted instantly and scanned the bay. There was no sign of her, but she was out there. His heart raced. *I'm glad to hear you again,* he answered. *After that first time—well, I wasn't fit company.*

I left you a gift. She wouldn't openly react one way or the other to what had passed between them before, or whether he was fit company anytime. *Look on the dock.*

He tossed the cane, limped through the heavy sand with as much *machismo* as he could feign, and made his way down the dock's alley of heavy, gray plank. His gaze went to the top of the endmost piling. When he saw the small marble sculpture there, he slowed. When he reached the piling, he braced himself on it with one trembling hand. Reaching up with the other, he gently lifted the figurine down.

You found this out there?

Yes, but so could you if you tried.

Slowly, his legs folded, he sat down with the boy and the dolphin cradled in his lap, and bowed his head over it. He stayed there a long time, sifting a torrent of emotions caught in the twilight of such old memories. Alice was silent, and when he could finally clear his head, he knew she'd slipped away to give him his privacy.

She had no idea what she'd done. He looked toward the island and beyond, where the

Calm Meridian lay. She had been to the bottom, without scuba gear, and she'd explored the wreckage. Impossible, but she'd done it. If she could accomplish a feat such as that, then so could her half-sisters.

It was no dream. They had been out there that day in the storm. They had rescued him. They knew what had happened to his parents, and they had played a part in it.

Alice could help him prove they were murderers.

$$\sim\!\sim\!\sim$$

Lilith gathered Mara and Pearl long after Alice slept contentedly in bed that night. "Alice confessed something she did today. She was so pleased with herself. And I am pleased for her, honestly. She is growing in confidence every day. She truly wants to do good deeds."

"Oh, God, what's our little angel of mercy done now?" Mara asked, as Pearl looked on worriedly.

Lilith told them about the *Calm Meridian*, the figurine, the visit to Griffin.

Pearl moaned.

Mara grew quietly furious, the combustion ending with a fiery "You knew this would happen!"

"Yes, I did."

"You know what he'll think!"

"Yes, I know. I know he's already making plans. I can feel it."

"And so we're going to suffer for Alice's

naïve bumbling in matters she doesn't understand. *Tell her*, Lilith. *Tell her everything.*"

"No. She went out there on her own. She learned something. She took a chance. She learned an invaluable lesson. I will not sugarcoat the truth or take the experience away from her, dear sisters." Lilith leaned close to them, her eyes and voice adamant. "We will take our chances and keep our silence. And if we have truly been honorable at heart in our lives, then *honor* will preserve us."

"Oh, yes," Pearl said, and sighed. "We must be patient and trust in *kindness.*"

Mara walked away. "Randolphs only understand *revenge*," she said over her shoulder. It was an old argument.

∽∽∽

1949. Water People from all over the world filled the great house at Sainte's Point. The celebrities among them, those known among the ordinary folk on the mainland, included show business stars, artists, sculptors, fashion designers, as well as discreet branches of various royal families, and of course—an afterthought to Mara, though Lilith found them the most intriguing—scientists, philosophers, and writers. Even a few of the most charming politicians in the world.

During a small afternoon soiree, in which one of the world's greatest operatic tenors sang from Verdi beside a piano on the lawn, Mother called Lilith, Mara, and Pearl from their seats in the limbs of the mansion oaks. "Claim your greatness, my darlings," Helice Bonavendier ordered with a proud smile. "Tell us what fine qualities the music inspires in you."

"Honor," Lilith said immediately. "Because without honor, there is only greed and selfish chaos."

"Here, here," Father said, applauding. He had, after all, decreed as a young man that the Bonavendier family would no longer prey on passing Randolph ships. Until his generation, elegant piracy had been not only a Bonavendier birthright but also a duty. Water People often said they owned the ocean and all that passed through it, including ordinary folks' ships.

"Kindness," Pearl announced next, curtseying prettily and with such a guileless, merry smile that everyone loved her. "Because someone must look after people's hearts." There were smiles and nods and enthusiastic glances between the couples, because Water People were notorious flirts.

"You, my sweet Pearl, are the perfect queen of hearts," Father praised.

"Revenge," Mara proclaimed next, standing at attention and eyeing a dashing British admiral as if he would be her military advisor as well as her first conquest. "Because someone has to fight for honor and kindness." She paused, took a deep breath, then concluded, "Or our kind will surely be left high and dry by our inferiors."

Father and Lilith scowled at the high-handed sentiment, but Mother smiled indulgently, and the sterling collection of guests mingled applause with arched brows. Mara was a separatist, and many Water People agreed with her. Father and Lilith, however, did not.

"Let revenge be tempered with honor and kindness," Lilith countered, "lest Revenge forgets she's descended from both the water and the land."

"Here, here," Father said.

Mara bit her tongue and said no more. But from that time forward she had been Revenge in her heart.

Years later, when Undiline married Porter Randolph and brought misery on the Bonavendiers, Mara contemplated revenge on the arrogant Randolphs and settled on a prime victim: Charles Anthony Randolph—C.A.

C.A. was Porter's favorite cousin, like a beloved younger brother, just twenty years old. Tall, handsome, black-haired, dark-eyed, and rich, he was a typical young Randolph, studying business at a fine southern college, already being groomed for a future in Randolph Shipping. But C.A. was more than a pampered son of pampered sons; he was smart, thoughtful, protective of his younger cousins, respectful to his father—a chief executive for Randolph Shipping—and awed by his mother, a tough, old-south socialite who masterminded the restoration of the magnificent homes in

Savannah's historic district, many of them
owned by Randolphs or Randolph kin.

He was irresistible to the daughters of
Savannah's old-blood families and never tried
hard to be otherwise. Yet, during that summer of
the early 1960s, during a solstice dance at one of
the old Savannah rice plantations, he wandered
away from the buffet, the dance floor, the band,
and at least a dozen young women who badly
wanted to be the next keeper of a Randolph
silver pattern. A little drunk on bourbon and
Coca-Cola, he frowned in aroused confusion as a
low, provocative purr grew inside his head,
calling him. The lure led him out on a shadowed
walkway that curled through tidal marshes
singing with night insects and the hot, damp,
ocean breeze. Under a half moon he found his
way, the erotic hum winding down his spine and
through his belly, his dance-sweated khakis
bulging at the groin. He found himself almost
running along the weathered boardwalk, where
long shadows fell between flickering kerosene
lanterns. He had no idea what was happening to
him, only that he couldn't stop.

There, at the end of the boardwalk, where
it became a small, low pier brushed by the marsh
grass beneath—there, in deep shadows—stood
Mara Bonavendier, naked, a river of mahogany
hair drying in thick waves around her breasts
and down her body to her knees. He'd met her
parents at parties along the coast, and he knew
all of *his* family's stories about the strange,

dangerous Bonavendiers. Porter had caused an uproar by marrying a woman from their circles. Not a Savannah girl. A wild Scottish woman, with an odd first name—Undiline. C.A. had come to know and adore Porter's green-eyed, stunning wife, and had even pledged to be one of several young godfathers to hers and Porter's son, Griffin. But he'd never met one of the Bonavendier daughters. Yet he knew instantly who this one was; somehow, she told him.

I'm Mara, the bad one, she whispered in his brain, his sex, his soul.

C.A. stumbled onto the small pier, halted, and stood looking at her helplessly. "My God," he whispered.

She pulled her long, dark hair back from her pale, perfect body, and his knees went weak from wanting her. Her eyes glowed. "You Randolphs cause us so much grief," she said. "Come here and show me why Undiline believes your kind is worth the trouble."

He lurched at her, took her face between his hands, and kissed her as gently as a troubadour vowing his soul. "I love you," he said.

For one instant, her incredible, sea-cold eyes softened with uncertainty. She had not expected him and his boyish impulses to be easy to adore. "Don't you dare be so foolish," she whispered. "I'm going to break your heart and teach Randolphs to stay away from us."

He laughed. Then he kissed her again, and

if she had considered any mercy, that kiss made her recant it. He gasped as she took him off the end of the pier, into the shallows. The water of the marsh surrounded them with its erotic rhythms.

And there she began the slow, thorough process of breaking his heart, and her own.

A mermaid found a swimming lad, picked him for her own, pressed her body to his body, laughed; and plunging down forgot in cruel happiness that even lovers drown.
—W.B. Yeats

Sixteen

I've heard nothing from Griffin since I took him the figurine, and it worries me. I'm not sure I did the right thing. I think I've upset my half-sisters, as well. Mara is avoiding me with bristly, dark-haired elegance, the hint of a quick cat-slap always present in her attitude. I avoid her in return, though I have had the courage to peer into her sunlit workshop off a back hall in one of the mansion's side wings. She designs the sisters' jewelry and is quite talented at it. Her pieces are also sold in a small shop the sisters own in Bellemeade. They own at least half the shops in the pretty little town, including the inn, WaterLilies. The Tanglewoods, among other duties, manage those enterprises.

"Mara's patrons order her designs from all over the world," Pearl said today. "She's quite well connected and very well liked. You know, our family is quite lovable and honorable and . . . and kindly. We've never hurt anyone.

Not deliberately."

Pearl seems strangely intent on explaining life among the Bonavendiers to me. She and each of her sisters have duties, a vocation, a role to play. Pearl acts as social secretary, and judging by the mounds of correspondence in her exuberant, colorful office (jeweled porcelain butterflies dangle from the ceiling on gold wires, need I say more?) the sisters entertain a vast array of guests and old friends. I suspect they've put their social calendar on hold while I adjust. Or am adjusted.

Lilith is the writer and publisher. She compiles histories of the southern coast, botanical treatises, and stories of the oceans provided by god knows who among her far-flung associates. In an office as feminine as a boudoir straight from some Parisian villa, she has shown me little thank-you notes from her past or current collaborators.

"Jacques Cousteau," I said on a short breath.

"Hmmm," she acknowledged, as if the world-famous scientist was just her assistant. I began to realize that some of my favorite books include Lilith's work, under pseudonyms.

"I have been reading her work for years without knowing it," I said to Pearl.

Pearl smiled sadly. "If you want to learn more about her, you won't find the information in her writings. Or about any of us. Would you like to hear our sorrowful stories, Alice?"

A chill went up my spine. I could only nod.

∼∼∼

Pearl and I walked along the island's curving length until we came to a small gazebo mired in the dunes. We seated ourselves in the gazebo's wind-weathered rocking chairs. I tentatively slid my bare feet across the floor and let the soft sand caress the tender webbing. "Tell me, please," I said.

Pearl sighed. "Do you know what every one of us merfolk understands? That sorrows sink us but love keeps us afloat. Love is our breath beneath the waters." Having delivered that philosophy, she nodded firmly. "Why don't you start by asking me some questions?"

I bowed my head. *Let me believe in love.* "You've been married to Barret a long time?"

"He's not my husband."

"Forgive me, I assumed—"

"We try not to draw attention to his circumstances. He's not a citizen, you see."

"When did you meet?"

"Oh, we've been together for nearly sixty years. I was five when we met. He was no more than sixteen. Of course, he was very brotherly until I grew up and we became lovers."

I did some quick calculations and realized her numbers put their first encounter squarely in the early 1940s, during World War Two. "Did he escape the war in Europe by coming to America?" I thought perhaps he was a Jewish immigrant of German origin.

"Oh, no. He came here with the navy."

I looked at her a long time. "Ours?"

She sighed. "Theirs."

The hair rose on the back of my neck. "Pearl, are you saying—"

"There were German submarines everywhere along the eastern coasts, you know. We Bonavendiers were actively involved in spying on them. Father and Mother and Lilith—who was so young then but, oh, what a patriot she was!—they searched out at least a dozen, which Father reported to the authorities. Very discreetly, of course. We have our family traditions, Alice. We don't show off. We don't brag. We are merfolk and specially endowed. No need to gild the water lily."

"There were German submarines," I prodded. "Yes. Go on."

"I was playing in a little bayside cove near the lighthouse one day, and one of them surfaced. I ducked down and watched as the crew climbed out the top and sunned on the deck. I watched this tall, beautiful young man edge away from the others. I sang to him, and he looked right toward me. He leapt into the water, Alice! Dived right in and began to swim for shore. I thought he was playing, but the yells of the others and the way he swam—he wasn't playing, I realized; he was trying to get away."

I inhaled sharply. "Barret was that crewman on a Nazi submarine?"

"Oh, Alice, *yes*, but he was just a boy who'd been scooped up for the service, along with thousands of others. A homesick boy who loved the sea. He hated the Nazis. He hated the war." She paused and looked at me with trust as light as a butterfly's wing. "His great-grandfather was one of our kind, you see. Barret heard me singing in the surf. He knew what that meant. He knew where he belonged."

I spent some time bending and unbending a dried stalk of the sea oats that grew up between the gazebo's floorboards. Gathering my thoughts. Indulging, expanding, resisting. "Barret's great-grandfather was a merman?"

"Mmmm. A Nordic charmer, Barret says."

"Then Barret is also a—"

"A merman?" she finished solemnly. "I suppose. He doesn't have any obvious traits, but then there are many degrees of merfolk. Practically everyone has a drop or two of the old ones in them. But very watered down, of course."

"Of course."

Her face grew solemn. "He swam faster than anyone could imagine, but the crew of his submarine still managed to shoot him."

"His own crewmates shot him?"

She nodded. "They shot him in the back as he swam. He was hit twice. That's why he limps. Why he can't swim now. He was crippled."

"Oh, Pearl."

Tears filled her eyes. "He sank, drowning and bleeding. I dived down and caught him by the arm. I was just a tiny girl, but I managed to tug him to the banks. It's very wooded there, and there was some brush hanging over the sides. I got his head propped above water and hid him beneath the brush until the others left. Then I swam as fast as I could to the cove, screaming for help. Father and Mother came and got him, and then we kept him."

"The family hid him and nursed him back to health?"

"Yes. And we've been together ever since." Her smile trembled a little. "He would have been deported or imprisoned if the government had known about him in those early years. Now, well, no one remembers, and no one cares enough to ask. But during all those years he was in hiding—had become a man without a country—I made my decision to never leave him. We are soulmates, Alice. We made our peace with the forces that brought us together." She looked out at the ocean and added very quietly, "We wanted to have children, but I miscarried, every time. Barret tried to make me give him up because of that. He said it was his fault somehow. But I refused to listen. The ocean gave us to each other. We have been blessed enough."

I sat in silence, reached over and touched her shoulder, and she took my hand and kissed it before she let it go. I was finally beginning to piece my sisters' youthful lives into the patterns they fit now, and my heart ached for them. "Tell me about Mara, please," I said finally.

Pearl told me about Mara and C.A. Randolph's turbulent love affair, and how cruelly she treated him. "He nearly killed himself over her. He threw away everything— his money, his dignity, his family's respect. She broke his heart, then went to New York to work—and married a new lover within weeks. One of our own kind, very handsome, very rich, and devoted to her," Pearl explained. "But she could never quite love him the way she loved C.A. Of course, she was horrified to discover that fact—that even a merman couldn't win her heart away from C.A. She had taken revenge on a Randolph, indeed, but ultimately her revenge hurt many lives."

Mara's husband had taken to flying a small plane over the waters of their coastal New York home. "Merfolk don't fly well," Pearl explained somberly. "We grow air sick at all but very low altitudes, and we envy the ordinary folk for their ability to take to the sky like birds. Perhaps Mara's husband felt he could best her memory of C.A. Randolph if he mastered something so difficult." She hesitated, then looked at me with misery. "But, Alice, he couldn't win. He crashed the plane one day with their two children aboard."

I looked at Pearl quietly. I feared the

worst. "Does Lilith have an equally tragic story?"

She nodded and her eyes filled with tears. "His name was Riyad. He's a Muslim, and a prince. In his country, the families arrange the marriages. When he was a boy, he was promised in marriage to a princess."

"He and his people were all . . . our kind?"

"Oh, yes. Of the same order, like us. He had the loveliest webbing. The color of dark tea."

I sat there thinking, *royal, Muslim, merman.* "How did he and Lilith meet?"

"They were diplomats together in Paris. When she was young, she worked for the embassy there. They fell desperately in love— and I do mean desperately—because our kind does not love lightly. He couldn't bring himself to tell her about his betrothal, and when she found out, she said she could never forgive him. He was heartbroken—and ashamed of using deceit. He returned to his country." Pearl paused, crying a little. "He did not know that Lilith was with child."

I sat back in my chair. Lilith. A mother. And this exotic Riyad, the unsuspecting father. No wonder she had sympathy for my own mother. I thought of the water fountain outside the breakfast nook. Lovers bound in stone. Lilith's affection for that special place was poignant suddenly. "If our kind is so famously psychic, how could Riyad not have sensed his

Deborah Smith

own child's existence?"

"Surely—as you've come to understand—we merfolk can be *quite* stubborn when we want to shut each other out of our songs. Lilith closed herself away from him—oh, such pride, such pain! So he left her, not knowing. She came home, here, and bore the child." Pearl looked at me tearfully. "A tiny little boy. He died within the hour. She went mad with grief. We were afraid she'd die as well. She began to disappear into the ocean for days at a time. Our kind always turns to the water for comfort, Alice."

"Because we're descended from Melasine, who took her own comfort there?"

"Oh, *yes*. There is such *courage* in the Old Ones, such nobility. Lilith believes they understand the deepest love, the truest hope, and are an inspiration we must follow. After all, Melasine was willing to love a man even while knowing she'd outlive him and their children, and even their grandchildren and great-grandchildren and so forth. Knowing that she could never share his world fully, or he, hers. And that ultimately she would spend much of her life only remembering him and what they'd created together. Such is the curse of all the Old Ones who fall in love. And all the Water People must remember to love wisely, too. We're too powerful for our own good."

"I see."

Pearl sighed. "Riyad has lived with his wife honorably, from all we've heard. She died

180

last year."

"Then he and Lilith are free to see each other."

"Lilith has too much pride to sing to him. And she's made Mara and me promise not to contact him." Pearl paused, squinting at me, then gasped. "But *you've* made her no promise! You could sing to him!"

I stared at her. "What? No. No, really. I wouldn't even know how to—"

"You'll learn! It's instinctive! Please, when you do understand, please try!" She rose in joy, clapping her hands and laughing. "Oh, how wonderful! You'll call for Riyad! I knew you'd bring us good luck! We've found you, and now the pieces of our hearts are falling into place! Somehow, Mara and C.A. will reconcile! And Riyad will reunite with Lilith!" She threw her arms around me as I sat there gaping at her. "Oh, thank you, dear little sister!"

She danced away on the beach, leaving me too stunned to speak, much less sing.

～～～

"What kind of crap is this?" C.A. asked, sweat pouring from beneath his shaggy silver hair, his face furious. He paced the dock at Randolph Cottage, glaring at the hulking vessel Griffin had moored to it.

Griffin ignored him for a moment, letting the tension and the scene align themselves. The April air grew hotter every day, the ocean warmer. Great white clouds mounded in the blue sky over Sainte's Point. Griffin had purchased a thirty-foot barge with a large cabin on the bow end and a heavy crane on the stern. Aboard it, Griffin had assembled diving gear, dredging equipment, and other tools of the salvage trade.

"What the hell are you doing?" C.A. said finally. "What is all this?"

"It's a treasure-hunting rig," Griffin replied.

"Goddammit, I know that."

"Good." Griffin limped around the barge's deck, still unsteady but growing stronger. His scars were finer, now, and the work outdoors was reviving the color of his skin. But the rush of blood from his exertions turned the scars scarlet on his chest and back and gave the scar on his clean-shaven face the look of a purplish zipper. Sometimes he worked shirtless, and the men who delivered the gear he'd ordered tended to turn their eyes from him.

C.A. lost all patience. "Goddammit, Griffin, I thought you were giving up your work as a treasure hunter!"

"I am. This gear is for one job only." Griffin calmly straightened, the hot, spring wind ruffling an old chambray shirt he'd pulled on. In a pocket of his faded khaki trousers, he carried a ring of his father's and a small pearl pendant of his mother's. The dolphin sculpture sat atop a piling nearby. Talismans. "I'm going to bring up the *Calm Meridian*."

C.A. paled, put a hand on a dock post, and leaned heavily. "That is the most morbid, useless, obsessive—"

"I know."

"It's lain out there for over thirty years. What's left of it is in fragments."

"Then I'll bring up the pieces."

"If there'd been any evidence of your parents' bodies, it would have been found right after the accident. You know I searched."

"Not the way I intend to search."

"Just what do you hope to prove?"

"I want to know why my father took us out there in a storm. I want to know why my mother let him."

"Those are impossible questions to answer."

"Maybe not. The Bonavendier sisters know what happened. I'm sure they do."

"No Bonavendier will help a Randolph prove they lured your parents into a storm."

"We've always blamed the Bonavendiers. I want to know if they really provoked the accident. I expect they want to prove it, too. If they're innocent."

"Goddammit. Goddammit." C.A. climbed down onto the barge's deck. "There's nothing to prove! Stay away from the Bonavendiers," he yelled. "They get whatever they want, and by the time they're finished with you, you won't give a damn for yourself."

"They're not magicians. They're not

witches." Griffin watched his expression carefully, managing a slight, probing smile. "Are they, C.A.?"

"I don't know *what* they are, but I know you shouldn't get within a mile of them. They've brought our family nothing but trouble."

Griffin stepped toward him, gauging every nuance of reaction, looking for hidden clues. "How was my mother treated by our family? Was she unhappy? Did my father protect her?"

C.A. groaned. "He tried. He did try. It was hard, Griffin. Your mother had wild ideas. She was . . . different."

"My father loved her. My memories . . . I feel it. They loved each other."

"Hell, yes, he adored her. He *lived* for her. She was impossible for your father to resist. That's why I'm begging you to drop this plan. Stay away from the wreck of the *Calm Meridian*. Stay away from Sainte's Point. Stay away from those women."

Griffin put a hand on the older man's shoulder and squeezed. "When I was a kid, I heard some things, C.A. Overheard the adults talking. About you . . . and Mara Bonavendier."

"Stay out of my past. Worry about yourself. You'll end up alone and bitter, too. Because if this . . . Alice . . .this new one—" he jerked his head toward Sainte's Point"—gets her claws into your soul, trust me, you'll wish you'd died with your parents."

He strode away.

The fantastic abilities of Water People are rooted in the physical laws of nature, not fairytales. I say that quite seriously.

—Lilith

Seventeen

~

"Griffin is coming here today to make an attempt at winning your loyalty and estranging you from us," Lilith said to me at breakfast this morning. "Can't you feel it?"

I stared at her. "Estrange me from you? Because he's a Randolph and Randolphs never approve of Bonavendiers? Is that it?"

"I'll let him tell you."

I got up from the table and paced. "I've kept to myself all my life. I don't know much about men. I'm not ready to see him in person again."

A Tanglewood appeared in the enclave's doorway, wide-eyed and excited. "Griffin Randolph is at the docks, madam. He's here to see The Alice."

I froze. Lilith stood and touched my shoulder. "You're ready. Go and listen to him, my dear. See what he wants. And make him listen to you in return." Her eyes were a little sad. "You'll come back with some questions for me and we'll talk."

I didn't like the sound of that.

～～～

Every pair of eyes on this island is secretly looking at me, Griffin thought. He smiled—a defense reaction, a showing of colors—as he stood warily on the dock in the cove of Sainte's Point. The *Sea Princess*—a small ketch that had belonged to his parents and that Griffin had sailed as a boy—was tethered to a piling behind him. Griffin had taken it out of storage and refurbished it. The marble sculpture of the boy and the dolphin was safe in a display case below deck.

He'd neatened his thick black hair, shaved and scrubbed and cologned himself. The scar on his face had begun to fade a little, and he tried not to think about the others on his body. He wanted to erase Alice's memory of the foundling invalid she'd pulled from the water and seen stumbling along the dock when she left the figurine.

Yet the exertion of sailing across Bellemeade Bay had soaked his good clothes in sweat and seawater, so he smelled musky, a man of the sea, as usual. His body ached, and his muscles were shaky from exhaustion. He swayed, regaining his land legs. A gust of wind pulled at his hair suddenly, ruffling it wildly across his forehead, destroying the carefully brushed style. The skin of his big hands was chapped and leathery from working the ropes, and the trip had scraped his palms. He caught himself licking the blood from them as Alice stepped from the mansion's veranda.

She saw him with blood on his lips and halted abruptly.

Blackbeard. He felt what she thought.

Handsome. He felt that, too, and responded warmly, against all will and common sense.

Alice took a deep breath then walked, her head up and shoulders back, down the terraced path from the mansion, stealing his breath with every step. She had changed a lot in the weeks since they'd met, as had he. Now his timid rescuer looked like a midsummer night's wet dream hued in the romantic sexuality of nineteenth century masterworks—the water sirens, the nymphs, the Nereid's. All the legends about Bonavendiers seemed true at that moment. She flowed inside a softly fitted dress with a long, full skirt, waltzing down the stone path with barefooted aplomb, so that the dress's pale silk swirled, outlining her breasts and hips, the vee of her thighs, the athletic swing of her walk. Her hair danced in sync, hypnotizing him. It had grown from a boyish scruff into luxurious, tousled waves, spilling around her face and brushing the tops of her shoulders.

His arousal was instant and urgent. His knees went weak.

C.A. was right. Get back in the boat. Get the hell out of here. Stay away. Stop looking at her. Stop wanting her. Stop feeling her around you every night, and going to her in your mind. You're in over your head already.

Too late.

She reached the dock and halted a few safe yards away from him. She was a tall woman but still a good six inches shorter than he, and his size seemed to worry her. She frowned up at him. Pink splotches bloomed on the pale, perfect skin of her cheeks. A fine tremor animated her hands, and she raised them to her hair awkwardly, pushing the auburn waves behind her ears as if trying to minimize the glorious effect.

"Beautiful," he said.

She blushed harder. "I have very *healthy* hair. I think the salt air has encouraged it to grow at an unusual rate."

"Mine, too. That's just one of many things I intend to understand about us."

She cleared her throat and clasped her hands in front of her as if she were ten years old, practicing for her first formal dance. "Could we hold a polite conversation and not contemplate our mysteries?"

"I doubt it."

"I'll try, at least. Griffin, you're looking much healthier." Her voice became dulcet, her eyes earnest, her mouth pursing slightly in a smile, the richest soft red. "And I'm glad to see you again."

The quiet sensuality in her, the kindness, the honest caress of his name on her tongue made him drunk. He could do no better than a gruff laugh. "So I'm not Blackbeard?"

Silence. She stared up at him woefully. Decorum was hopeless. If he wanted to understand his own mysteries as well as hers, he would have to lure her to him as bluntly as her family had lured his for two centuries. A kind of revenge. The light grew somber between them. "Come with me," he said gently, "and I'll show you where your mother met your father."

Bittersweet excitement filled her eyes, and he knew he had her.

And that she had him.

Of all wonders, I had never been on a boat before. As Griffin skimmed the fast ketch along the bay's wooded shoreline, I gave in helplessly to a new passion. Sailing. I sat on the bow with my bare legs curled over the side, the skirt of my dress jammed unceremoniously between my thighs, my face turned into the tangy, moist wind. Behind me and slightly below the deck, Griffin stood in the cockpit as grandly as a pirate captain, his hands touching the *Sea Princess's* handsome wooden wheel here and there, coaxing, cajoling, seducing the boat, the wind, the water, me. I wouldn't look back at him, though I wanted to. I could barely breathe when I gazed into his eyes. I don't doubt Griffin always invokes a certain raw thrill in people, always enjoining them to challenge the rhythm of the ocean with him, to admit that yes, by

God, a man can make waves and women dance for him. I did not dance, but I might as well have.

We left the bay, then raced along the open ocean for a mile or so to a place where the shoreline gave way to broad, saltwater marsh. Griffin turned the boat into a narrow channel between a sea of water and green grass. He leapt onto the bow deck and expertly furled the various sails. I pivoted to watch him work, drinking in the long-legged, broad-shouldered grace with which he moved. He was recovering from his injuries well, and the scar on his face had become a ruddy decoration, curved from cheek to jaw like a crescent moon.

"We'll use the motor from here on," he said, looking down at me with a background of blue sky and white clouds behind him.

I nodded, gazing up at him, hypnotized, pouring out reckless waves of arousal and resistance submerged in my old childhood fear of abuse.

God help me. He heard that plaintive song before I realized I was singing it. He went very still, frowning, searching my eyes for more clues, absorbing my bleak music too quickly for me to draw back in silence. Sorrow and surprise crossed his face, ending in a gaze so hard it would have chilled me, except that I felt his anger wrapping around me like a protective cloak. He was mad *for* me, not at me.

Without touching me, he took me in his arms. *I wish I had been there when they hurt you.*

Deborah Smith

I shut my eyes, luxuriated in his vow, sank down in the depths of that extraordinary moment, then cautioned myself and rose for air, trembling. "I didn't know how to help myself," I said, "and I didn't know how to call for help."

"Is that what we're doing, Ali? Calling each other for help?"

Ali. He named me by his own shorthand, as if I had always been some special person, known to him but unknown to myself. I couldn't speak. I was overwhelmed with gratitude and adoration. My emotions affected him deeply—I could see the tortured discipline in his face, hear the desperate restraint humming inside his mind. "You'd best keep away," I whispered. He nodded.

He went back to the ketch's controls, cranked the engine, and we motored quietly onward. I clenched my hands in my lap and faced the far side of the marsh, where our small waterway disappeared into deep forest. When we reached that place, we were suddenly in a new world, shaded by oaks and maples, bald cypress and magnolias, traveling on a small, sandy river with water as dark as tea. Tall herons waded in the shallows, fishing. Around a wooded bend, the forest opened. A lovely little dock appeared at the edge of broad lawns and stately oaks. I put a hand to my heart as I saw low, simple but handsome buildings of gray coquina with old terracotta roofs. Several dozen small cabins lined winding walkways of crushed shells. A pavilion overlooked the river and a beautiful little chapel.

My heart twisted. So this was the church retreat where my mother had spent her summers working as a counselor at a children's camp. Where she and eighty-five-year old Orion Bonavendier had met when she was seventeen, and where she, at least, had fallen in love. And where now, as Griffin slipped the sailboat into a berth beside the docks, I stared at a weathered brass plaque fixed to the dock's pilings.

Sweetwater Haven. Dedicated by Griffin Randolph to the memory of his parents, Porter and Undiline Randolph.

I turned and looked at Griffin, stunned. "I own the whole place," he said.

∾∾∾

Griffin and I sat on a bench before the chapel. He told me this church camp is a Randolph legacy, one of many charitable projects the family owns or controls along the Georgia coast. Undiline Randolph doted on it and spent a considerable amount of her time here, supervising the construction of the pavilion and the docks, among other projects, and charming the children with her Scottish accent and her fairy tales about the ocean. He opened a mysterious little folder he'd carried from the sailboat. "This is for you," he said and handed me a small photograph. "It was taken the year before the *Calm Meridian* sank."

I uttered a soft cry of surprise. Sitting on this same bench was his mother, Undiline—a tall, smiling redhead surging with sexuality even in a demure 1960s swimsuit, and Griffin—a stalwart, black-haired child, already muscular and lean in swimtrunks, grinning as he clasped her hand—and *my own mother*, laughing, beautiful, an auburn-haired young woman looking wholesome and strong in light shorts and a white blouse with the camp's name over her right breast. Griffin held her hand, too. He was safe between his own mother—and mine.

"You *knew* my mother. You *met* my mother. Look at her. Oh, look at her," I whispered, huddling over the photograph.

"I don't remember her. I remember playing here, though. My mother brought me here a lot while my father was away in Savannah, working. I loved this camp."

I raised my head and gave him a tearful smile, then returned to gazing at the picture. "You touched my mother. You held her hand. I know I'm being maudlin, but that connection— I'm glad for it—and I envy it."

He held out his hand. "It was this simple."

I laid my hand inside his, and he closed his fingers over mine. Across all those years, sitting on the same spot as my mother, I held Griffin Randolph's hand, too. *Mother, look what you've given me.*

Griffin looked down at our linked fingers.

He drew the pad of his thumb along the back of my hand, tracing the course of a tender blue vein. "I'm trying to make you so grateful you'll do anything for me," he admitted.

I looked at him sadly. "I know."

"Hello, I didn't realize you were here yet!" a woman called from the door of the main building. "I'm coming right now!"

Griffin and I sat back and slipped our hands apart.

～～～

"Your mother was always willing to listen. She opened her heart and never turned anyone away, and I believe, if she'd lived, that she would have bucked the system and become a minister, as I did. Your mother told me once that she'd been raised to take what God gave her and never question the rules of man, but she was *full* of questions, Alice, and I admired her for asking them—and for listening for answers the rest of us might miss."

Dr. Lucille Abernathy, minister of the gospel and president of Sweetwater Haven's board of directors, had become good friends with my mother during several summers they worked together as counselors. Now a stocky and energetic southern grandmother who wore a clerical collar with her white Camp Sweetwater T-shirt, she spoke to me kindly over iced tea and crisp gingersnaps at a picnic table under the oaks as Griffin listened.

"She was crazy about children, and they

loved her back," Dr. Abernathy went on,
breaking cookies with ecumenical briskness,
feeding half to a flock of wild mallards that
crowded around my feet. She gave the ducks
bewildered glances as they rubbed their bills on
my bare legs. I stroked their heads and curled my
webbed toes under. Griffin watched the strange
alchemy between the ducks and me with somber
interest, cataloging yet another bit of evidence
in his quest to catalog me as well.

I gathered my courage and asked a hard
question. "How well did you know my father?"

"He'd come by regularly as a favor to Mrs.
Randolph—"a nod to Griffin indicated his
mother—"to teach swimming lessons. I don't
care how frightened of water a child was, if we
turned him over to Orion Bonavendier, before
long that child would be swimming like a fish."
She smiled. "All of us were in love with him—
every female at the camp, including little girls
and old women. He had a Rhett Butler voice,
hypnotic green eyes, and beautiful silver hair—
not to mention, excuse me, but a fine, hmmm,
physique. He was old, but there was nothing old
about him. He was an amazing man to look at,
to listen to, to watch."

"Did my mother ever say anything to you
about their relationship?'

"Not much. I suspect they were only
together one time."

"Once? One night?"

Dr. Abernathy nodded. "We took a

boatload of children to Sainte's Point for a day at the beach. Mrs. Randolph—Undiline—used to host beach parties for the camp's children there. A storm came up and we spent the night. Bunked the children in various bedrooms at that incredible mansion, and your mother and I shared a room." Dr. Abernathy paused. "I woke up in the middle of the night and she was gone. When we came back here the next day, she was different. Distracted, happy, sad, excited, depressed. But not . . . hurt . . . you understand. Just changed. Mr. Bonavendier came to see her that day, and they went for a walk. He was obviously worried about her. After he left, I found her sitting in the chapel. She looked peaceful. Radiant. She said at the end of the summer she was going to find a job in Bellemeade and a place to live. That she was never going back to the mountains, and she was breaking off her engagement to the young man she intended to marry up there. That she was in love with Orion Bonavendier, and she expected to love him forever. I said, 'Have you lost your mind? What has he done to you?' She just looked at me and said, 'He's taught me how to breathe and hear voices in the water.'"

Dr. Abernathy looked at me sadly. "She was so fanciful that way, speaking in metaphors. She was only seventeen, and nothing and no one was going to stop her from staying near the man she loved. Orion Bonavendier." Dr. Abernathy touched my hand. "A week later, he drowned during a swim off the shores of the island."

"My sisters told me he drowned, but I had no idea it was so soon after he . . . he knew my mother."

"No one knows what happened. He was an incredible swimmer. Maybe he had a heart attack. When she heard the news about his death, your mother collapsed. We found her in her cabin. She had a pair of scissors. She'd cut off all her hair, and . . . bound it in a tight braid, about a foot long. 'I'm giving this to Orion,' she kept saying. 'I have to. It's a tradition in his family. I have to.' She was out of her mind. Her family had to come get her. That was the last time I saw her, Alice. When they took her back to the mountains." Dr. Abernathy couched my hands in both of hers. "I wish I had known she was pregnant. I'm sorry you grew up not knowing how wonderful she was."

After a moment I found my voice. "I feel that I do now. Thank you." I didn't understand what my mother had meant about her hair, about some Bonavendier tradition none of the sisters had yet described. But I knew what it meant to shear yourself in mourning for the person you wanted to be.

"You look like her, around the mouth, and in the shape of your face," Dr. Abernathy went on kindly. "And the soul in your eyes. You're a beautiful young woman."

"I wish I'd had a chance to look into her eyes."

"Look in the mirror. You'll see her. And your father, too."

A chapel bell began to chime. Dr. Abernathy exhaled. "Sorry. I have to go."

"Thank you for speaking with me."

"Words are easy."

We rose and walked toward the docks. Griffin had said nothing during all this, and he kept discreetly at a distance beside Dr. Abernathy and me. When we stopped at the docks, she held out a plump, strong hand to him and smiled when he took it, bowed over it, and kissed it. I knew what he made her think and feel because I felt it, too. *Scars and all, this man can make women fall in love with him as easily as he wants to.* I pushed that thought aside.

"Charmer," she accused. "But bless you for the money to build the new gym."

He nodded and shrugged off the admiring look she gave him. "My mother loved this place." As if nullifying his own good works, he pivoted toward me and said quietly, "So now you realize *my* mother introduced *your* mother to your father. For better or worse, it was her doing."

A small breath froze inside me. "Better or worse remains to be seen, but if you're wondering if I might blame your mother for something, what would it be? The circum-stances that led to my own birth? No. I'm glad to be alive." That stunned me, and I had to think about it a moment. I was actually glad to be alive.

He absorbed my bittersweet look of wonder and scowled. "That's the one thing that makes it all worthwhile," he said. "You."

I lost my heart just looking at him, and him at me.

Dr. Abernathy broke the spell by tossing the remnants of gingersnaps to the ducks. I twisted away from Griffin in self-defense. A tingle went up my spine, and a gift of love, clear and pure, came to me. "Dr. Abernathy, about your grandson, the one who has the tumor."

Her mouth popped open. "How did you know about him?"

I shook my head. "I'm just telling you. He'll be fine after the surgery."

Her eyes filled with tears. I avoided Griffin's intense scrutiny, which felt like fire on my skin. Red-faced, I climbed into Griffin's sailboat without another word, sat down on the bow, and faced forward. After a moment, Griffin cranked the engine, and we began to ease away from the weathered docks of beautiful Sweetwater Haven.

"Alice!" Dr. Abernathy called to me, and I looked back at her. She stood at the dock's end, stubby and T-shirted, with fat little knees showing beneath old khaki walking shorts and her face flushed with tearful conviction above her white clerical collar, a huggable speaker of the gospel, as wise as an old choir melody. My mother's friend and now mine. "People say the

Lord speaks to Bonavendiers in mysterious ways," she called. "Just be sure to keep listening!"

I waved to her, neither confirming nor denying.

And not daring to look back at Griffin.

～'～'～

She trusts me. Either I believe in her or I don't, but she trusts me with the choice.

Griffin told himself he should feel victorious—he had her wrapped up; he could use her against her sisters and their secrets. But instead he felt dirty and depressed. *No time like the present for a little tough conversation.*

He turned the *Sea Princess* toward open water and set a course that would curve out beyond the shoals of Sainte's Point, where the ocean floor dropped suddenly into starker depths.

Alice studied him hard, then made her way gracefully to the cockpit and stepped down beside him. "If you're going to take me someplace I won't like," she said, "then at least give me a fighting chance to learn the way."

He stepped back from the wheel. "Take it. I'll show you how."

She slipped between him and the wheel, faced forward, and lightly rested her hands on the wooden spokes. He stood close behind her, not quite touching her. She cleared her throat. "I know a lot about boats from reading. I've sailed

every kind of boat on every kind of waterway—
at least in my imagination."

He bent his head next to hers. Her auburn
hair caressed his scarred cheek. He lifted a hand,
tucked her hair aside, then moved his lips close
to her ear. "Bear away before the wind."

"Aye-aye, captain." She turned the wheel.

"Keep the sail full. No sudden moves. If
you do it right, you can use just your fingertips."

She spread her hands on the spokes so
only the pads of her fingers rested against the
polished wood. Her breathing seemed to merge
with the rhythm of the sailboat, rising and
falling. Griffin inhaled with her, inhaled her
scent, imagined the warmth of her back and hips
against his chest and thighs, and did not lift a
hand to stop it when her hair curled in soft
waves across his face again. "That's it," he said.
"You're a natural."

"Except I don't know where we're going."

"If you're afraid, I'll take you back."

"Nothing on the water frightens me."

There was a clear challenge in her voice.
He moved closer to her, chest to back. "Then I
envy you," he said. The ketch surged unevenly.
He placed his hands over hers and fitted his
arms along her arms. "Steady. Dead ahead."

She shuddered and pulled her hands from
his, twisting inside the cusp he made with his
arms, almost frantic. But when she looked up at
him, she wasn't asking for escape. What had
been cased in defiance became surrender.

"I've never," she said.

"I know."

She kissed him. She fitted her untested mouth to his gently, as if he might break, something a woman had never suspected of him before. She tasted him, opened him, held him still with that kiss, as the ocean passed beneath their feet without any threat at all. He found himself trembling against her. She clenched her hands together against his chest. The kiss deepened. He touched his tongue to her lips, then between them, and she returned the caress, the stroking so quick it was like her breath licking him, and nearly brought him to his knees.

Her hands unfurled against his chest, then slid up to cup his face. Griffin gave up all control and wound one arm around her waist. She bent willingly, and with a measured tug he fitted her to him, hard against soft, a couching intimacy. The ketch turned into the wind, slowed, and stopped of its own accord.

Alice looked up at him, her eyes clear and calm. "You are more like a Bonavendier than you think. How else can you explain what happens between us?"

He should have said something sardonic in his own defense, but the song she and he shared was a miraculous thing, a gift, and now that he'd accepted it for whatever it was, he wouldn't desecrate it. "There are very few things I'm willing to take on faith," he said quietly, "but what happens between you and me is a blessing, no matter where it comes from."

"I'll take you on faith, too," she said softly. She slipped from his arms, then stepped up on the ketch's narrow side deck and gazed out over the water. Suddenly, she sank her hands into the flowing dress she wore. With one graceful swoop, she pulled it over her head and let it drop behind her. She wore only pale silk panties beneath it.

Griffin caught his breath at the sight of her. Her bare back was a fluid river of soft flesh and muscle pooling in taut, heart-shaped hips. She turned her head, her auburn hair fanning out along the perfect line of her strong shoulders, that mane seeming to grow longer even as he looked at her. Long strands curtained over her right eye as she looked back at him. The unplanned allure was staggering.

"Follow me," she whispered. She dived over the side in a smooth bow of motion, piercing the ocean's surface with one of her nearly soundless entrances into the world he feared so much.

Griffin swayed as he stepped up on the deck.

She surfaced a few yards out, and looked up at him, waiting. His hands shook. He pulled his sweater over his head, kicked off his shoes, then halted, standing there in only his trousers, looking at the water, looking at her. The fear sang through him along with desire and courage and sheer pride. And trust. Alice would either destroy him gently or save his soul. It was now or never.

He swung his arms over his head, then, springing off the balls of his feet, plunged into the ocean. At first immersion, his ribs seemed to squeeze his lungs into airless fists, and his heart convulsed. As he shot down into the dark depths above the *Calm Meridian*, he was a child again, lost and terrified, broken and searching.

Alice touched him. In the darkness, her warm hands met his outstretched fingers. She linked her fingers through his, and he righted himself. They faced each other, treading water a dozen feet below the surface, holding hands as if dancing slowly, rising. Sunlight began to cascade around them, pale green and gold.

Feel me all around you, she whispered in his mind. I'm holding you in my arms, and you're floating inside me.

Take me up, Ali.

She nodded, her expression somber and flushed, her eyes worried, glowing, aroused, tender. She put her hands on his shoulders, then drew them down his chest, stroking, exploring. She kissed him, slid close, ran her hands around his waist and up his back, and for the first time since the accident in Spain he began to feel healed, as if her touch could loosen the scars on his skin.

Looking into his eyes, she pressed herself

to him. Her breasts, high and firm, fit softly against his chest, and the treading motion of her legs stroked him. He forced himself to stop fighting the water, to hold onto the line and the look in her eyes. His legs relaxed, parted a little, and her thighs pressed into the center of his body, massaging him with each languid undulation.

She took his face between her hands and sank her mouth onto his. His hands flexed on the anchor line above them. Her eyes never leaving his, she unfastened his trousers, curled her hands inside them and then inside the waist of his briefs, and slowly eased the clothing down his legs—sinking with it. Her upturned eyes were poignant one instant before the water covered them, and then she was at his thighs, and at his knees, and at his ankles, and the trousers and the briefs slid away.

Griffin shut his eyes as her hands explored upwards on his bare legs and groaned when she touched her lips to first one thigh and then the other, and then, very gently, on the tip of the hard erection thrusting helplessly out from his body.

She crested the surface with a deep blush and a look of uncertain pride on her face. "I've never," she whispered.

"Neither have I. Not like this. Not the way it is right now, with you."

The last vestige of her shyness vanished. A moment later, she let her pale panties float to the surface, making a strange, pretty flower riding the ocean's currents. She enfolded him, wrapping him in the cloak of her naked body, and with her eyes on his, watched him move just so, and then she moved, too, and he found her.

She kissed him. "I don't know who I am or who you've turned me into, but don't stop."

"You're not alone," he answered.

They moved together like waves on the shore.

And certain stars shot madly from their
spheres to hear the sea-maid's music.
—Shakespeare

Eighteen

⁓

Golden sunrises over Pacific palms. The
glimmer of an ancient Grecian coin. The taste of
curried fruit aboard an Indian freighter filled
with Hindu pilgrims. I lay in Griffin's arms in
the dark of his bed at Randolph Cottage, hearing
the images of his life on the sea, the song he
shared to let me know him. Rain slipped down
the night sky in a steady wash of silver, hiding
Sainte's Point across the bay, raising cool fog,
filling the darkness. We were warm and
cocooned; he'd built a fire in the room's
fireplace. Its light was the only lamp in the room,
flickering on our naked bodies. We lay facing
each other, still dancers, legs and arms lightly
entwined. We looked into each other's eyes,
speaking in metaphors and symbols, flashes of
emotion, the quiet lull between the irresistible
desires, all our silent songs. I shared mine in
return.

The sweet coo of birds in the Riley Pet Shoppe.
The cold beauty of my mountain lake. The safe solitude
in my cabin. Loneliness. How odd I am. Taste the

butter I mound on my chintz saucers. I eat butter like a pudding. Like ice cream. In big bowls. Embarrassing.

He touched one of my nipples with the back of his fingers. *I like butter that way, too. Damn strange. I don't eat it in front of normal people.*

Astonishment. Delight. A purr of appreciation.

The smooth cream of small secrets became my fingers tracing his lips in wonder, became his hand caressing my breasts, became my thigh easing over his, became his hand sliding down my side, curving over and then behind the crest of my hip, reaching between my legs from back there, finally coming to rest where his forefinger can stroke soft folds of skin and the silky opening that welcomed him.

And we made love again.

Whatever I should have done, should have thought, should have worried over or resisted has been washed away along with thirty-four years of virginity.

As I fell asleep for a few minutes with his head cradled on my stomach, I called out to Lilith. *Did you expect this?*

Of course, she answered.

He is a good man. Whatever worries you, I'll make it right. I need to tell him that he's one of our kind. Help him believe somehow.

My dear Alice. You can't tell him yet. You don't quite believe in our kind yourself. When you truly know who you are, he'll see your soul and have no doubt you exist.

What should I do for now?

Just do what you're doing. Love him. Let him love you. Keep singing.

Easy, I hummed.

∼∼∼

"She's with him," Lilith told her sisters that night. "It's meant to be."

Pearl clasped her heart in hopeful support, but Mara turned away, shaking her head. "We're doomed."

∼∼∼

The next morning I left Griffin sleeping and slipped from the cottage naked in the bright spring sunshine. I glanced around the cottage's isolated sand dunes and pine forest, then walked to the dock and dully studied a sinister, dark barge tethered there next to a sleek speedboat and the classic *Sea Princess.* I noted the barge's wenches and scoops, diving gear and buckets. I went into the cabin and gazed at a large console of electronics and computer screens. This was a vessel for hunting beneath the water, for clawing up the ocean's secrets, Bonavendier secrets.

The *Calm Meridian.* Something about my sisters.

My family, I thought for the first time.

Oh, Griffin. I could not bear to wait for the explanation of my use in his larger plan. I dived into the bay, met up with my dolphin friends a few minutes later, and swam for the open Atlantic.

Griffin could find me when he awoke.

He wouldn't need help for that.

∼∾∼

I clasped the bow of the ruined yacht again, spreading my arms out along it, trying to hug the memories it stored, the truth it could confess. How could such a terrible accident have taken Porter Randolph—an experienced yachtsman—and Undiline, who was, to say the least, at home in the sea. A sense of prescient horror suddenly washed over me. My right hand curled spasmodically, gripping an invisible item, wanting to form an outline around a mystery hinted at but only shadowed in my senses.

There was something important inside the bow.

I slid down on my stomach and felt along the bottom, where for more than three decades the current had pushed sand high around the bow's broken end. When I reached the area where the slope of the Point Trench began, I found a washed-out place. There, the water had tunneled beneath the nose of the yacht. I got close to that small black maw, that aperture into the heart of the trapped world inside the old bow. I measured the opening with my hands. Big enough for me to slither through.

The thought curdled my nerves. Go into the bow of the yacht where Griffin's parents had died? Their bodies had never been recovered. I thought of bones. I began to shake. I crept closer, my heart pounding. With a rush of conviction, I shoved both arms inside the opening, pawed away a hummock of sand, and began to squirm through into the grotesque void. I sang nervously, a vibrato of silent sound, and many small shapes came back to me.

My hand closed around one of them, just as it had instinctively imagined the outline before. I froze. Encrusted with sediment, bulky and no longer sleek, the shape still carried a meaning, a history, a song. My mind filled with the storm of that autumn day in 1967. Wind, rain, the crash of thunder, the bellow of waves breaking over the *Calm Meridian's* sleek bow. The yacht tilted wildly, everything in chaos. And then, unmistakably, I heard a sharp crack, and then another.

The sound of gunshots.

I had a pistol in my hand. *Oh, no, no. What? Tell me. What does this mean? Who was the last person to touch this weapon before me? Why was it fired?*

At that moment, behind me in the open water, the softest of hands stroked my bare feet.

I dropped the pistol, jerked my arms from inside the bow, then twisted wildly and drew my legs up. I strained to see in water too dark for even a glimmer of light. I sang out loudly, but no sonic shapes echoed back to me. Whoever—or whatever—had glided away—or had only existed in my overwrought mind.

Sing to me, Ali.

Griffin's voice. Not behind me but up there, in the bright, ordinary world.

I'm here. I'm down here. I rose to the surface,

making myself move slowly, having more dignity than sense. The water paled and warmed. Bright spring sunlight streaked it. I sent out songs but marked nothing except fish and dolphins, which swirled around me with urgent or perhaps excited noises. Had they seen someone down there with me, or were they just reacting to my panic? I had imagined the hands.

But not the gun. That had been very real.

I propelled myself to the border between water and sky and raised my face into the air. Instantly, my ears filled with the rumble of an engine. I pirouetted in the water as Griffin brought a speedboat to an idle not more than a few yards from me. He looked harried, tousled, but infinitely competent above the water. Salt spray had splashed his khaki trousers and the soft brown sweater he wore. The air was cool; just the slightest steam rose from his body.

With a great swoop of one strong arm, he threw an anchor over the side. He expertly flipped a soft ladder over the diving platform protruding from the boat's stern. Then he knelt on the boat's stern and thrust out one hand to me. "Out of the water. Right now. Come here." His expression was a mixture of tense emotions. I felt his fear—fear for me—and his relief at finding me. And his anger.

I shook my head. I was sad and tired, shaken and despondent. "Tell me why you brought me here yesterday. Tell me what you really want from me."

"I want you to stay away from this wreckage. It's dangerous."

"Most of our deepest memories and strongest passions are dangerous." I gave him a sad look, which he returned. "If I intended to avoid all danger in my new life, I wouldn't have been with you yesterday and last night."

"You know I'd never hurt you."

"I know you want something from me, and you're tearing yourself apart inside because of it."

"I want you . . ." he paused, his throat working, his face grim. He calmed himself and went on with a rueful smile, "I want you to teach me not to fear the goddamned water. So I can bring up every piece of the *Calm Meridian* by myself."

My blood chilled. "What do you hope to find?"

He lowered the hand he had continued to hold out to me, as if knowing I wouldn't touch him after he spoke. "I'm looking for proof," he said, "that your sisters killed my parents."

~·~·~

"I don't remember much about that day on the *Calm Meridian*," Griffin admitted. Alice sat in the well of his speedboat, wearing his long sweater and nothing else, her green eyes tragic, her hands bunching the hem of the sweater in her lap. Griffin stood on the bow, bare-chested, staring out at the ocean to avoid looking at her eyes. "I was only four years old. I know what I've been told and what I've pieced together. And I know what I feel."

"Small evidence for such a terrible accusation," she said quietly.

"Lilith and her sisters have never offered anything to dispute it."

"I see," she said in a small voice.

"I don't know why my parents were at Sainte's Point that day. My father *never* went to the island. He didn't like the Bonavendiers, and they didn't like him. Everyone knew Lilith and her sisters always tried to lure Mother away from him. Lilith told the police he and my mother brought me there for a polite visit. That doesn't make sense. Not just because of the storm. Not anytime."

"You've asked your cousin C.A. to tell you what he knows?"

"C.A. accepts the police report: An accident caused by weather. He doesn't deal well with Bonavendiers. He won't talk about them if he can help it."

"You were so afraid that day. And so confused. I feel that memory."

"Something must have happened at Sainte's Point—something that made my father so angry he'd put Mother and me on that sailboat and leave in the middle of a storm. He was an expert sailor. It makes no sense. The ocean was a roller coaster. I remember Mother locking me in the cabin. She went up on deck to help Father. The yacht started to buck. I got tossed around. I screamed. I heard the sound of the mast snapping—two sharp cracks—and then the yacht capsized."

Alice stood up. "Two noises like gunshots." Her face paled.

"Yes. The mast snapping. Then the yacht rolled. I remember being trapped upside down in the dark, and I remember the cabin filling with water as the yacht sank. When it hit the ocean floor, the hull broke in two. I was badly hurt. I was drowning."

He stopped, breathing hard, and looked at Alice for a long time. She kept her eyes riveted to his, hypnotizing him with her concern, her ethereal face just as he'd imagined it as he floated after the explosion, redeeming the ocean with its sorrows, her gray-green eyes a window into the soul of the sea as he'd never imagined it—loving, and redemptive. "I remember being pulled out and carried to the surface by your sisters," he said slowly.

"I see."

"Before I met you, I always told myself it was impossible. No human beings could have survived in open water during that storm, diving without any scuba gear, without any help. But now I'm convinced they *were* there." He paused. "They know more about my parents' deaths than they've ever admitted. They've got something to hide."

Alice bowed her head. He watched her struggle with her arguments and doubts, and he struggled along with her. "I have to find out the truth. And you do, too. You don't know them very well. You can't be sure. You're asking yourself if they're capable of murder. You're telling yourself they *are*."

"I have to go," she said. Before he could stop her, she dived over the side. She surfaced a few feet away from the boat and looked up at him as if he'd broken her heart. "I have to be alone and think."

"If you want to believe in them, you have to risk destroying them."

"I want to believe in them. I want to believe in you, too. And in me. I insist on finding islands of faith in my life."

"You will, I promise you. Help me."

She raised a hand, let it fall. Swore testimony. An answer. She *would* help him find the truth if it could be found, but at the moment she wished they'd never met. She disappeared beneath the water.

Griffin watched for a long time, tracking the arching progress of several dolphins that followed her. She went toward Sainte's Point.

His heart sank.

She was going back to her sisters.

～～～

Speak to the dead and the dead shall awake and listen. Memory is life.

As a girl I read that sentiment in some frayed novel of gothic philosophy I checked out of the Riley library. But I spoke to my mother

often as I swam in the town's lake, and if she
heard a single word, I never knew. I finally
decided because I had no memories of her she
would never answer, and I quit trying. Now I
wondered if she hadn't waited all these years to
speak through my heart, in choices and
moralities and complex longings and extraordinary family bonds she had bequeathed me when
she took an extraordinary man, Orion
Bonavendier, into her young body.

*I have given you your father's family. Don't
turn away from them.*

I stayed out in the ocean for a long while,
watching from a distance as Griffin sailed back
to Bellemeade Bay. If he felt me nearby, he let
me own my privacy, but I think he knew. He
fears I hate him for threatening my idyllic new
life and the women who have done so much for
me. The dishonor is that I will search for the
truth beside him, but I won't stay by his side if
he tries to condemn them. But if they are guilty,
I cannot stay by them, either.

For the first time in my life, I understand
the true bonds of kinship. Its oaths are universal;
nations have usurped them. *Liberty, justice, all for
one, and one for all.* Like healers, I search for
simplicity in the most profound sentiments. *But
first, do no harm.*

I want desperately to do no harm.

I swam to the island's bay side and
climbed out of the water at a calm inlet hooded
by forest. I still wore Griffin's sweater, a heavy,

soaking weight I could not bear to take off. I stumbled along a well-kept path until I suddenly stepped upon a beautiful marble dais, easily ten feet in diameter, set flat atop a knoll. I pirouetted in wonder, studying that strange marker in the edge of the woods. Abruptly, I faced the mainland and halted with a moan. The dais made a perfect viewing spot for Randolph Cottage. With my unusual eyesight, I could make out the cottage's peaked, shingled roof easily, far across the placid bay, and even see Griffin's white-trimmed sailboat at the docks.

Oh, Griffin. Griffin. You think you're ugly, and you believe I'm beautiful, and neither is true.

As if in response, the cool, rose-carved stone brought a shiver inside me, forlorn in its loveliness, kind in its encouragement. I moved off quickly, as if I might be lured to stay and talk about him if I weren't vigilant. *Talk to whom?* As I hurried away, I glanced back with the peculiar sense that I could almost hear a woman's whisper, a voice I didn't know.

Was it Melasine, a human creature beyond belief, echoing through the stone as she made her lonely, aged treks God knew where?

Was it Undiline, betrayed by her own kind, her own family?

Was it my own mother, begging me to avoid her doom?

Had the voice touched me with her hands when I was at the *Calm Meridian? Whoever you are, I don't want to hear you. I only want witnesses, not more advice.* I raced through the lush forest to a shady glen I had already come to know well. An enchanted place. The Bonavendier cemetery. There the giant oaks drape their mossy arms over fine mausoleums and monuments engraved with the Bonavendier crest. The interment of my kind—I have begun to think of them that way—is one of the most beautiful sites on the island. Water bubbles from a natural spring enshrined in a gray coquina fountain. The sunlight seeps, like luminescent freckles, through oak limbs wider than my body. Short, squat palms rattle their fronds in the slightest salt-stung ocean breeze. A mist rises from the fountain as the spring air cools the day; in the late afternoon, the quiet blue light of the gloaming sets the place apart in time. One sandy path leads back through the woods a quarter of a mile to the island's bayside banks, from which I had come. Another leads to the ocean and the mansion. The souls of Bonavendiers rest, not between heaven and earth, but between heaven and water.

Where do I fit in? Who has seduced me more, my sisters, or Griffin? I sat down on a marble bench upheld by pediments of web-footed men, dusted sand from the webbing of my feet, tucked the tail of the thick sweater around my thighs, then waited with my head up, my back squared, and my hands clenched together in my lap.

My sisters came as quickly as I expected.

Half-sisters, I reminded myself.

"I should pull out your recently unmown hair, you precocious brat," Mara said in a filthy tone, and as no idle threat. She strode from the forest along the path that went up-island to the mansion. Her dark hair was tangled amongst rich silver combs atop her head, and a snugly fitting suit of rose silk gave her an almost Asian look. Her eyes were the ocean on a cold day, and she poured off waves of fury. "How dare you call Lilith to come here as if she's your servant? Now that you've shed your dewy virginity, are you convinced you're the new queen?"

"That's enough," Lilith said, arriving with a calm stride, her silver hair plaited in interwoven circles around her shoulders, her lithe body outlined in a smooth periwinkle-blue shift with a gold belt around her waist. Pearl rushed up behind her, huffing and disheveled, red hair dangling in wavy streamers from a thickly bound knot, a dark-green maillot hugging her torso, a scarf of delicate hues fluttering like a skirt around her hips.

My half-sisters, as always, made a stunning sight. I stood and faced them, using every ounce of the courage I'd garnered in my life. "I have a very simple question, and I thought it best to ask it among the souls you honor." I hesitated, then added quietly, "Did you kill Griffin's parents?"

Mara and Pearl gasped. For a moment, I could have sworn the wind rose and a chorus of shocked Bonavendier spirits sang protests to me. But Lilith regarded me with calm resignation. "That," she said quietly, "is for you to decide."

Pearl began to cry. "Does it have to be this way, Lilith? Can't we just tell her what a terrible tragedy it was?"

"No. This is a test we all must face if we are to be true sisters beneath the skin. I could tell you the facts, Alice, but telling is only telling. I want you to decide it for yourself. You have the power to do that—and to help Griffin do it, as well."

I gave her a begging look. "If there were extenuating circumstances, old feuds, a rash decision, an accident—I can forgive any of that. If you want me to be a full part of this family, then trust me."

"It's not a matter of trusting you, my dear. It's you, trusting us. And trusting what your own heart will tell you about us. And about Griffin."

Mara found her voice and lunged at me, shaking both hands. "Ingrate! Weakling! Troublemaker!"

Pearl grabbed her arm. "Don't hurt her! She's just a child! She still thinks she has to defend herself against the world, and that includes even us."

Mara shook her off and glared at me. "You expect us to live by the ridiculous rules of your dirt-poor ideas! You're not one of us, and you never will be. You have the talents but not the spirit. And Griffin is no better."

I gave her a look that stopped her in her tracks. "My expectations, Mara," I said evenly, "are of honesty, integrity, and a fair hearing, just as I'm giving to you-all. If my kin have killed people, I deserve to know it. And since you are distant kin to Griffin, as well, he deserves to know it, too."

"He deserves? You *deserve*? What have you ever done to deserve anyone's respect? Whine and hide and run and sneak up on people. Take gifts and kindness but give back treachery." She whipped toward Lilith. "*Now* is there any doubt why you couldn't hear this timid little bastard singing to you all these years?"

Lilith slapped her hard. Mara stepped back, laying a hand along her assaulted cheek, giving Lilith a look of utter shock, grief, and humiliation. None of the sisters had struck one another before.

Pearl sobbed, "Oh, it hurts me, too," and covered her face.

Silence stretched out. Birds had stopped singing, and even the distant surf seemed to whisper. I waited to no avail. I felt as if I'd been led to the edge of a cliff. I bowed my head. I felt bereft, outcast, alone already. "I cannot in good conscience continue to live here while I collaborate with Griffin, or expect you to extend your hospitality to me any longer. You've been most kind. I would like my old clothes back, please, and if Barret will take me and my belongings to Bellemeade, I'll—"

"Do you *wish* to leave us?" Lilith asked. I looked at her for a moment, saying nothing but speaking volumes. She heard me and nodded. "Then please, dear Alice, don't go. I am not angry with you in the least."

"I don't want to betray your hospitality."

"You won't. You haven't."

"I'll throw you to the sharks if you do," Mara said.

"Oh, Mara, hush," Pearl cried. Then, to me, "I don't want you to go, either. We've only just found you. We want to believe in you as much as you want to believe in us." Pearl began to sob dramatically.

"Stop that wailing," Lilith ordered.

The harsh words might as well have been another slap. Pearl's head jerked up. Both she and Mara stared at their older sister in clear surprise.

"We've indulged ourselves for far too long," Lilith told them. "Believing we can keep the outside world away, that the old feuds have honor and the old sorrows must continue to define us. But the world is changing, my dears. Alice and Griffin are the future. And I intend to *give* them that future."

She turned her back to them and looked at me. "If you are one of us at heart, you'll learn the truth out there." Lilith nodded toward the ocean. "You and Griffin, together."

I felt my heart fall through my chest. I couldn't imagine how any of us were going to escape without pain.

"Don't make any mistake about it, I want Alice to stay here, too." Mara gave me a sharkish smile. "Where I can watch you. Or are you too much a coward to stand up under my scrutiny?"

That settled it and saved enough face for us all to agree. I was not sure whether I was being coerced or seduced by Bonavendier spirits who might or might not have my best interests at heart. My mother's memory told me to stay, but, then, she had died for loving the Bonavendiers. "I'll survive," I said.

My own oath.

≈≈≈

I was with Griffin tonight. Not in words so much, but in the deep current that carries passion, that reflects living shapes and sensations, that outlines life and calls life to it. I lay in my sumptuous bed at Sainte's Point, my hands going over my bare body with feverish want, touching myself for him, lifting myself to him, spreading and softening and soaking the sheet beneath my thighs with the fluid of desire. I was guilty and angry and manipulative, but, then, so was he. I could feel every move of his body, every tortured emotion.

His back arched.

I'll make you believe what I know is right, I whispered.

You can't. Don't try. Yet, he sent back

waves of arousal.

I felt his startled reaction, then gave him my agonized pleasure. *I won't betray my sisters.*

You're mine. I'm yours. Don't betray us.

The image of my fingertips over his face came to me. In the air just above his skin, I traced his jaw, touched the scar on his cheek, floated my forefinger lightly above his lips. He shut his eyes, groaned again, and our sorrowful desire merged us. I halted my hand, trembling. *It's no use. Leave me be, and I'll leave you be, too.*

I wish it were that simple.

Then I have to touch you. I have to try.

For Gods sake. Please.

I cried and seduced him.

~ ~ ~

I am ashamed, so shaken of what I've done with Griffin and to Griffin—who is a threat to my new family and new life--that I lie here at Sainte's Point, still crying.

He whispers inside me, *I'm only sorry for your tears.*

Leave me alone with them, is all I can manage.

And he kisses me goodbye.

~ ~ ~

Mysteries made worried songs in Lilith's mind, unspooling old fears and sorrows, old mistakes, bitterness, regret, the deepest loves and losses. She felt immeasurably sunken by concern over Alice and Griffin as she wrote in her journal. *Forces have been set in motion. Strong currents are merging.*

Alice asked her in private, "Were you out at the *Calm Meridian* with me? Was Mara? Was Pearl?"

"No, none of us," Lilith answered. "Why?"

But Alice only shook her head.

Lilith went down to the beaches and stood gazing out beyond the surf, singing. *Are you out there?*

Tell me what to do to save my family.
Your family, Melasine.

At the risk of insulting those Water People who believe Landers cannot possibly share our legacy, I must point out that if the sea is the mother of us all, then we must all be, at heart, both Water People and Land People.

—*Lilith*

Nineteen
∼

Honor, kindness, and revenge. And I will always take revenge, Mara thought grimly, as she exited a private car driven by one of the Tanglewoods, then made her way down a cobblestoned alley behind a street of Savannah's most exquisite historic mansions. Moving with stealth and confidence, she fitted a stolen key into the lock of an elaborate courtyard gate and let herself inside C. A. Randolph's private garden.

She had never claimed to be anything other than her family's enforcer. She stood in C.A.'s garden and began to sing to him softly, her voice perfect and haunting. He walked into the garden.

Mara posed as deliberately as a geisha beneath the flowering dogwoods and old jasmine vines of a house so fine General Sherman had commandeered it for himself and his favorite colonels during the occupation of the Civil War. The house stood in the midst of the city's historic residential district, on a boulevard hooded by oaks and washed in the murmurs of fountains.

C.A. had never been able to put aside the whisper of water, and Mara's effect flooded his veins now. He hid a tremor behind clenched fists. "All these years," he said, "I've pictured you standing here, and I've pictured myself telling you to get the hell out. How did you get a key?"

"I have keys to most of these old homes. I'm a welcome guest in certain circles."

"A pickpocket. Sad."

"You made me swear to stay away from you. I always have. But you never said a thing about leaving your *house* alone. I've slipped into your home on many occasions. Studied your books, your belongings, the things you use to mollify the emptiness in your life. I've lain naked on your bedsheets, and I think you know it. Haven't you made love to your lady friends with my perfume in your senses? Oh, those must have been glorious nights for the poor, ordinary Landers."

His silence and the look on his face confirmed every word she said. His expression turned to stone. "I can't imagine why you've gone to the trouble of watching me since I'm one of many you've used and deserted."

"I do have a certain curiosity about you— and a certain admiration for your refusal to settle for the ordinary, after me. I find it fascinating that you've never married."

"Is your own life so full of happiness that you have the gall to pity mine? You fell in love with me, and you never counted on that. You wouldn't lower yourself to admit it. So you ran. Ran to New York—and married some web-footed bastard you never loved."

"How dare you. How dare you." She raised a trembling hand to her throat.

"You didn't love him," C.A. repeated. "And he knew it. That's why he was always trying to prove himself. You didn't want him to buy his own small plane and learn to fly, but he did it anyway. Flying—the one thing that frightens you—that's what he did, to impress you. And when the two of you had children, as soon as they were old enough he took them up, too, because he—"

"Do not speak of my children! Do not! I would never stoop to torment you with such private and dear—"

"I *grieved* for your children." C.A. put a fist over his heart. "When the plane went down with your husband and children, I *hurt* as if they were my *own* children, Mara."

She swayed, struggling to maintain the facades that protected her. "Lilith told me you wanted to help. But it's not my way to accept—"

"So you secluded yourself at the island and wanted no one to care about you. And you've gotten worse every decade since."

"We Bonavendiers grieve for our losses in the water, alone. I have my own brand of honor." Her voice broke. "And kindness."

"Then what do you want from me now?" He kept the courtyard's centerpiece between them. It was an anchor from a long-lost Randolph ship, one the Bonavendiers had been accused of sinking. Tendrils of spring grapevine had begun to wrap their delicate fingers around the iron, as if the earth, not the water, claimed all Randolph vessels.

Mara became so somber he felt alarmed. "I want your promise that you'll tell Griffin the truth when he asks you about Porter and Undiline."

"I don't want my godson ruined the way Porter was."

"You know what happens when a Bonavendier is determined to find something in the water. Alice will help him dredge up the *truth*, C.A. And when that happens, you had better be there with us, for Griffin's sake, because that is where he will be *ruined*—by the ugly truth. And you'll have to admit what you know about his father and mother."

Slowly, C.A. walked to a teakwood bench weathered oyster gray. He sat down with a bowed head. "God help us all," he said.

Mara hesitated, breaking down inside, telling herself to go, now that she'd made her point. But she moved helplessly toward C.A., trembling, sat down just as slowly beside him, and fought an urge to cry. Controlling him was her second nature. Her first, unfortunately, was loving him. *I'm going to take him to bed tonight. He'll never turn away from me then.* "I'm sorry," she whispered sincerely, and then laid a warm, stroking hand on his. "Maybe this time God will care."

~~~

Soon, we will learn whether our kind can survive into new centuries, Lilith wrote in her journal. Everything they were, everything Bonavendiers had fashioned of themselves on Sainte's Point, defying the accepted course of nature, hung in the balance between facts and faith.

Pearl went to Bellemeade with Barret, nervously frittering at management of their shops to distract her worries. The sales clerks adored Pearl and listened politely to her suggestions. Even the most ordinary people sensed her sweet songs and were lured into the Bonavendier enterprises. Pearl was very good for business, and she needed something to keep from wringing her hands over the growing drama of their lives.

Mara had not returned from Savannah, where Lilith knew she was manipulating C.A. Randolph's assistance against all of Lilith's counsel. Only Alice and Griffin would determine the outcome of this old heartache. In a matter so fundamental, peace would come from the wellspring of Alice's and Griffin's souls, or not at all.

"Yes, my dear Judith Beth?" Lilith said, without turning from her writing desk.

"Lady Lilith, hurry. You have a visitor. Oh, my. Oh, my." The Tanglewood sister fluttered her hands. Her blond hair looked electrified, and her plump face was flushed deep pink with excitement. "It's *him*, Lady Lilith."

Lilith frowned and left the room at a quick walk, striding down the main hallway and out of the mansion. Immediately, she saw the large white sailboat slipping into the cove's docks. A crew of several lithe men, all dressed in white, altered the tall sails and threw heavy ropes around the dock's pilings. She gathered her dignity and walked down the path with her head up and her hands swinging calmly by her sides. A simple white top moved smoothly on her breasts, and a long, pale skirt whispered about her jeweled feet. She lifted a hand to a long onyx comb at the crown of her head, and her silver hair tumbled down her back.

Suddenly, she saw him.

A tall, olive-skinned man dressed in dark trousers and a flowing white shirt stood on the bow of the yacht. His thick silver hair flowed to his shoulders. He stood with his hands by his sides, his dark eyes never leaving her.

A flood of shock and emotion lifted Lilith's senses like a tide. She couldn't believe it, couldn't imagine him here. Her stride slowed.

Dazed, she picked out the last few steps to the edge of the dock as his crew lowered a gangway. Her visitor walked from the luxurious vessel onto the very boards of her own home. His face, lean and handsome, creviced with lines at the eyes and mouth, could still steal her breath. His full name, a lengthy and traditional Arabic one, was far too formal.

"Riyad," she whispered.

He slid off soft leather slippers in the tradition of their kind and stood barefoot before her. "Lilith," he answered in the voice of pharaohs.

The spring sun haloed him, reflecting off the water and casting his shadows across her face, then flashing its brilliance into her eyes. She sheltered her gaze. "The sunlight," she protested and smoothed tears from her lower lids. "It has a voice of its own."

He nodded, unable to say more himself. She held out her arm. He took it, and she escorted him up the path toward the house. Alice stepped onto the veranda. Lilith studied her expression, a look of bittersweet understanding. And Lilith realized the amazing truth.

My dear young sister, have you learned to sing for love? Did you call him here for me?

Alice nodded.

～．～．～

I sang a song for my sister, and the song was heard.

I realize how afraid I've been to send my

voice into the world. And how much I want to believe in my family.

"Where is Lilith's and Riyad's son buried?" I asked Pearl that night.

"In Mother and Father's crypt, alongside Mara's two children. Their bodies lie in small marble coffins with just their precious names etched on them." Pearl looked at me wistfully. "There's something you should know. Lilith named her baby son *Griffin*."

I stared at Pearl. She nodded. "And years later, Undiline named *her* son Griffin, too, in honor of Lilith's lost boy. Lilith was so pleased. Undiline asked Lilith, Mara, and me to be Griffin's godmothers. We accepted with true joy." Pearl pressed a hand to her heart. "So do you understand what Griffin means to us? He is, in so many respects, our only son." She paused. "Just as you, darling Alice, are like a daughter."

"Does Riyad know about his and Lilith's child?" I asked Pearl wearily.

Pearl sighed. "He will soon. She's telling him tonight."

~~~

Lilith and Riyad stood before the crypt in the moonlight. Her heart rose in her voice. She struggled to put the story of their son into spoken words. Riyad riveted his gaze to her face. Lilith moaned. Her legendary discipline deserted her. The truth poured in psychic waves of grief and regret. Riyad stepped back as if struck. He bent his head into his hands, then dropped to one knee before the crypt.

Lilith cried out as she sank down beside him. "I've never doubted that you would have loved our son."

Riyad dragged his hands from his face and tilted his head back. He shut his eyes as if even the moonlight were too bright. "All these years I've sensed a secret between us, but I shut it from my mind. I tried not to imagine what it might be." He shuddered and looked at her with tears on his face. His expression was tortured and tender. "Please, forgive me."

Lilith hugged herself. "I'm the one who must ask for forgiveness. You had a right to know."

He held out his hands. "Let us mourn together."

She took his hands and bowed her head to his. They grieved for their lost son and lost love without sound, without pride, without artifice. Slowly, they slipped their arms around each other and clung tightly.

The tide made a low murmur in the distance. Out in the depths, the souls of all the knowing creatures listened and sighed with relief. Mercy was fluid. Sorrow ebbed and flowed.

Love returned with the moon.

〜〜〜

I sat outside in the deep curve of the tree limb in my dark garden. My heart twisted when I glimpsed Lilith and Riyad in the moonlight.

They walked side by side, their hands tightly clasped, along the path out of the forest. They had made peace over the body of their son, the first Griffin.

Griffin, I sang urgently to that child's namesake. *Do you realize what you mean to Lilith? She and her sisters couldn't possibly have harmed you or anyone you loved. Griffin, please listen. Please talk to me. We can't hurt them. Where are you?*

Silence.

Stalwart and true, by Ta-Mera's princesses enslaved
Devoted lovers, bound to earth yet fulfilled in water,
We shall whisper their mortal names on shores
Kissed by eternal tides,
And forget them not in fluid rhyme:
Beckrith, Padrian, and Salasime.

Ode To Mermaids And Men
Emilene Merrimac Revere
Victorian poetess and singer

Twenty
~

"I found him this way when I came by to check my menus for a dinner he's givin' tomorrow," the stalwart housekeeper told Griffin as she led him up the dark marble stairs of C.A.'s home that night. She dabbed tears from her face. "Lord, I've never seen Mr. Randolph drink himself into such a state. I know he thinks the world of you, and I figured you'd come see if he's all right."

"Thank you. I'll take care of him." Griffin stepped ahead of the woman as they reached a landing. He halted, shocked. The marble floor was strewn with broken liquor bottles. Paintings and nautical charts had been ripped from the walls.

"He did all this damage," the housekeeper

237

moaned. "His hands are all tore up from hittin' things and rippin' his own house apart."

"Don't tell anyone. We'll get this cleaned up tonight."

"Yessir."

Griffin held his breath as the housekeeper led him into C.A.'s large bedroom, which was equally destroyed. His elder cousin was stretched out among the jumbled dark sheets of a tall mahogany bedstead. C.A. was naked, though he'd had the presence of mind to pull the end of the bed's comforter over his belly and thighs. He lay on his back, his eyes shut, his bloody fists unfurled by his sides.

"Some woman was here with him," the housekeeper whispered. "When I picked up his clothes I could smell fine perfume, and there was lipstick on his shirt . . . *on his shirt front, down low,* Mr. Griffin." The housekeeper blushed. "I don't know what that woman did to him, but I hope she never does it again."

"You can leave us alone now. I'll try to talk to him."

"God bless you. He sure does love you. You're like a son to him."

She left the room. Griffin slowly picked his way through broken lamps, tossed chairs, and ripped paintings, to C.A.'s side. Griffin set a small bedside lamp upright and flicked its switch. As he bent over C.A. and pressed fingertips to the pulse in his throat, Griffin inhaled the scent of liquor—and more. The raw scent of sex.

C.A. stirred lethargically, opened blood-shot eyes, and recognized Griffin. C.A. groaned. "What are you doing here?" He slurred the words.

"What happened, C.A.?"

"My own weakness. Goddamn furious . . . with myself. No one hurt but me. That's all I want. No one hurt but me. Leave me the hell alone."

"Who was the woman?"

"My business, not yours."

"You didn't tear up the house in front of her, did you?"

"No. After she left."

Griffin reached past him, staring at mounds of hair twisted in the sheets, a river of tresses. His hand shook a little as he pulled it free. It filled his hands and spilled over, dark, luxurious, reddish brown, wavy, and nearly six feet long. *Mara Bonavendier.* "What was Mara doing here? Why did she do this to you—and to herself?"

"You own her heart when she gives you her hair. Not that she'll stay with you. Not that you own *her*."

Griffin straightened. "You get some sleep. Tomorrow you and I have to have a talk. I don't want you involved in my problems with the Bonavendiers. You can't handle whatever goes on between you and Mara. That makes it my business, C.A. Not just yours." Griffin pulled more covers over him. "I'll be here all night. Get some rest." He turned to go.

"Griffin."

"Yes?"

"You have no idea . . . what you've gotten into. With them. With Alice."

"C.A., take a break. I said we'll talk in the morning."

"Your father didn't know, either. But I know. I accept what they are. But your father couldn't.   I tried to tell him.   I loved your father . . . like a brother. But he was stubborn."

"What are you saying?"

"He was as strong as any Randolph can be. Strong-minded. A hard man, sometimes. Your mother almost convinced him . . . anything is possible. He loved her like his life. But there was no room for imagination in him. Or . . . faith."

"What are you trying to tell me, C.A.?"

"I don't want you to hate . . . your father for what he did to your mother."

After a stunned moment Griffin said evenly, "What did he do to her?"

But C.A. turned on one side, groaned, and fell asleep. Griffin stared at him a long time, then finally turned out the light and left him alone. Griffin sat in a downstairs library in the dark the rest of the night. He heard Alice calling to him but didn't answer. She would feel the worry and confusion around him. She would know it involved her family and some connection to his mother he didn't understand.

He rose and paced. What had his father done to his mother?

In the morning, bandaged and sober and ashen, C.A. sat across from Griffin in the tall leather chairs of the dining room, drinking coffee. C.A. only shook his head when Griffin asked him what had happened between him and Mara. Griffin said with strained patience, "All right, let's pretend you don't owe me that explanation. But you do owe me something else. Tell me what you meant about my parents."

C.A. laid his head against the chair's high back and looked at him through slitted, resigned eyes. Griffin's stomach twisted as C.A. gave him a bleak smile, as if expecting Griffin's reaction already. "Porter realized your mother was a mermaid, *and he lost his mind.*"

"A mermaid." Griffin stared at him, got up slowly, and bent over C.A. until their faces were close. "If you can't tell me a better lie than that," Griffin said softly, "then stay the hell out of my life."

C.A. said nothing else but held Griffin's gaze with unrelenting sorrow and that same, chilling smile.

Griffin slammed a hand on the table. "If that's how you want it, then." He walked out of the house.

C.A. shut his eyes. Mara was right. All he could do was be there when Griffin and Alice learned the truth in their own way. And believed it.

∼‿∼

Lilith and Riyad lay together at the edge of a quiet cove at dawn. "Why is this all happening now?" she whispered. "How can we go along for years, decades, sometimes even centuries, and then suddenly everything converges? Those years—when I returned here, when our child died, then Mara returned, heartbroken, widowed, her children dead. And Pearl, of course, refusing to leave Barret, spending her life here as she lost one child after another. All those things make no sense, Riyad."

"Because random sorrows never do." He stroked her hair. "Our lives are drops of water. Yet each helps fill the ocean. I quote some dusty cleric writing in thirsty sand. To be blunt, Lilith? Perhaps we bring many of our sorrows on ourselves. The talent lies in bringing many joys on ourselves, as well."

"If there is an answer beyond any hard journey, it is joy."

"The answer may lie in children yet to come. Children that would never be born without your guidance, my love."

Alice and Griffin's children, she thought. She lay back with Riyad in the water, placing her head on his chest, as he took her in his arms.

To sing is to charm the soul with illicit lures, said the churchmen of old. And so the songs of Water People, male and female, were designated a form of witchcraft. How sad, to silence love.
—*Lilith*

Twenty-One

~

Chaos. This morning the Tanglewood brother who drove Mara to Savannah is in tears because she hasn't returned or contacted us. He is convinced, with cherubic devotion, that the evil denizens of that city have had the nerve to harm her. This despite the fact she's more than capable of terrorizing any urban miscreant short of Godzilla. Riyad and Lilith have cloistered themselves somewhere in the ocean to mourn their son together, and Pearl is frantic over it all. Barret has tried to soothe her by heading to Savannah in search of Mara. I find myself in an unsettling position of leadership, as Pearl and the Tanglewoods are suddenly asking me, *The Alice*, what to do.

"Mara is more than a match for any city on the face of the earth," I told them with feigned certainty, "and Lilith requires a period of time in prayer and meditation with the father of her child. Her solitude is very understandable. Both Mara and Lilith will return home when they are ready. I have no doubt." And since I could think of nothing better to offer, I added, "Now let us make some creamed shrimp with sherry for breakfast, drink a tall vodka, and be calm."

After a moment spent in staring at me, Pearl and the Tanglewoods exhaled as one. "Oh, good. All right, then," Pearl said.

"The Alice is wise," a Tanglewood proclaimed.

They went off to prepare breakfast, leaving me stunned by their faith in my command.

Because I am so afraid of every new moment, and Griffin is still silent.

∼

You'll know when it's time to open your mother's keepsake box, Lilith had said.

It was time.

Griffin carried the box upstairs and out onto a captain's walk. The narrow balcony looked over Bellemeade Bay, its boards worn by wind and weather. He had loved playing there as a child. He sat down on a weathered bench with the box on his knees under a sun-washed blue sky. The lock clicked easily when he inserted the slender, feminine brass key into it. He laid the key aside and opened the box's lid. His heart pounded. On top were yellowed handkerchiefs with his mother's maiden initials embroidered on them, as if she'd put away all symbolic evidence of her family's name when she married his father. His throat tight, Griffin gently laid the items beside the key. He curled his callused fingers beneath a stack of aged albums and dried flowers from his parents' wedding. When he removed them, he saw what was his mother had stored carefully beneath.

Memories flooded him.

Mother, why do you and me have to cut our hair every day?

Oh, we McEvers are known for our hair growing as fast as seaflax in a strong current. Mother laughed as she spoke in her gentle Scottish brogue and continued to snip several inches of new growth from her shoulder-length mane. Griffin sat in the floor or her dressing room, watching her, fascinated by the flow of her, the way her silk robe clung to her soft, strong body, the salty scent of her skin after one of her morning swims, the soft, golden slippers she loved to wear. Once he crawled beneath the tasseled bridge of her vanity chair and deftly, playing, snatched a slipper from her foot. She gasped and curled her toes tightly together, but not before he glimpsed the terrible scars that lined their insides. *Mother, what's wrong with your feet?*

Nothing, my wee love; my feet are just a little peculiar, hmmm? Nothing wrong with that.

He examined one of his own feet, prying apart his toes. *I have lines inside my toes, too, but they're not so bad.*

Well see, then, we're alike—only your feet are

much nicer than mine.

But Father doesn't have lines inside his toes.

Not everyone is as lucky as you and I are. Smiling, she lifted him quickly into her lap and slid her foot back into the slipper. *I say you've got fine, handsome feet. So much the better for you. Now don't you be telling other people about my secrets, promise?*

I promise.

She went back to her hair. The snipping of her scissors accompanied the soft copper fluffs as they fell into Griffin's outstretched hands. *I'm giving you my heart, every time,* she told him. *Just as I gave my whole heart to your father on the day we wed. You take care of my heart, promise? Just as you must care for all the lovely gifts of the sea, but do no' forget you're a Randolph, and you live on the land.*

I promise, Mother.

Now, as a grown man, Griffin reached into the box. The memories suddenly had new meanings, possible and impossible. He lifted out a thick coil of copper-red hair bound with white ribbon at the cut end. He unwound it with trembling hands, held the ribboned end as high as his head, and let the stunning hair unfurl. It draped sensuously toward the floor, more than six feet long.

Mother's hair.

His hands shaking a little, he carefully laid the long swath across his knees, then reached back into the box. He picked up a slender silver case about the size of a wallet, heavily figured and tarnished almost black. He closed the box, set the silver case atop the lid, and gently popped a tiny latch.

Inside was a folded note on fine, yellowed stationary, and beneath that, a mysterious silk bag. He opened the note and read in his mother's hand:

My darling son, forgive me for what I did to you when you were a baby. You never knew, you never remembered. Your father accepted the idea that you had a harmless deformity, and a surgeon snipped it away before anyone else knew. If you are reading this, it is because Lilith feels you have no heart without the truth. Never forget your father loved you, and that I sacrificed small pieces of your soul because I loved you, too, and wanted you to be what you could never be.

Ordinary.
All my sorrows, and all my love,
Mother.

Griffin slowly picked up the small silk bag, which felt bulky but light. He untied its drawstring and poured its contents into his palm. Eight small, dark, curled bits of leather fell out. He frowned, touched them with his fingertips, and a jolt of understanding went through him with sick shock.

These had been part of him when he was born. A delicate part of his feet, soft and tender, like Alice's, no doubt easy for a doctor to cut away without leaving a trace.

Webbing.

～～～

Hair, you see, contains potent magic, I had read in one of Lilith's books, *and was believed by some to contain the person's soul. Thus the ancients thought the sensual celebration of it could release the most evil and passionate forces. They were right about the passion.*

"What have you done? What have you done to your *hair*?" Pearl cried.

Mara staggered, naked and shorn, from the cove's edge. Standing a few paces above her and Pearl on the pathway to the docks, I tried not to stare at her in horror and pity, but I felt both. What was left of her dark hair hung in blunt rags around her face, chopped off, ruined. Her face was wan, her eyes swollen from tears. She looked up at me with terrible exhaustion and pain and anger. "Love a Randolph and you'll give up all dignity, Alice. He'll own you more than any other Lander ever could."

"You gave your *hair* to C.A. Randolph?" Pearl whispered. "Did you tell him what that means?"

"Leave me be. I had a moment of blind impulse. I left him immediately after I did it. I was a fool. He seduced me. We won't talk about him anymore."

"But—" Pearl gazed from her to me in tearful awe. "Among our kind, giving your hair to someone is a symbolic vow of eternal love."

"Vows are ludicrous with a Lander—and especially with a Lander who's a Randolph. It's only hair. It will grow back." Mara slumped at the water's edge, then pointed a sharp finger up at me. "You see the lesson I'm teaching you? Stay away from Griffin. Give up this plan to betray us. You're bringing misery to us. This is all your fault."

I bowed my head. "Please, don't say that. I've never wanted to—"

"If you don't care about us or yourself, think of Griffin at least. You're going to destroy him. *Destroy him.* You'll destroy him as well as us." Mara searched my face with her devastated eyes. "You believe me. I see it. And I *hear* it, in your pathetic little worried humming."

I went silent, struggling for defensive words that wouldn't come.

Mara crept in for the kill. "Do you want to know what really happened to your father—our father—because of your mother?"

"Oh, no, no, it's too cruel. It wasn't her mother's fault," Pearl cried. "She was seduced. Father dishonored himself. He did what he felt was right. He did it to set her free."

I stared at Mara. "What are you implying?"

"Your mother—the fool—told him she'd never leave him, never love another man, never give up loving him. *He drowned himself to escape her.*"

I reeled. Now I understood what Dr. Abernathy's strange story really meant. My mother had given Orion her hair. My mother wanted so badly to be one of the Water People, and my father knew that she wasn't just mimicking their customs, she was giving him her devotion forever.

Mara saw the understanding in my face, laughed bitterly, and got to her feet. "Live with it," she said, then dived back into the water.

Pearl ran to me, threw her arms around my shoulders, and hugged me hard. "Please, don't feel bad, Alice. We love you, anyway."

"He killed himself because he thought that was the only way to give my mother a future without him?"

She took my face between her hands and made a dolphin-like click of sorrow. "Darling Alice, when someone ordinary loves one of our beautiful kind, the love is all-consuming. Father knew that. Your mother fell in love with him— that was his fault, not hers. He didn't want to bind her to him—he didn't want to trap her in his aging life. He did an honorable thing— painful though it was to us. He had no idea your mother was pregnant, or he surely wouldn't have left her. Lilith doesn't blame her for his death, just as you have found it in your heart not to blame him for your mother's death. Haven't you? It was love, Alice. Love. Among our kind, love can either keep us afloat or drown us."

I staggered.

Pearl kissed my cheek. "Darling Alice, please don't look like it's the end of the world. When Lilith comes back, she'll make it all make sense." Pearl looked frantically at the cove, where Mara reappeared briefly, shoving at dolphins that tried to nuzzle her like anxious pets. "I have to go. I've never seen Mara so upset over a man. She shouldn't swim alone right now—she'll hurt the dolphins' feelings." Pearl shucked a soft silk lounging outfit and followed her sister into the cove. They disappeared like matched nudes in a water show, beneath the spring tide.

I stood there utterly alone on the shores of Sainte's Point.

And quietly, very quietly, I began to sing a mourning song to myself, understanding what I had to do.

The child displays remarkable calm despite the trauma of the near-drowning incident in the ocean. Her fantasy remains intact. She continues to assert that a white-finned mermaid saved her.

Psychiatric counselor's journal
Somewhere on the East Coast
1976

Twenty-Two

~

Alice had never been afraid in the water until she went back down to the *Calm Meridian*. She felt its sorrows around her, the physical wreckage as well as the heart's, as she sank down next to the bow. Her skin flinched at every hint of movement. A sting ray fluttered along the bottom, and she jerked up her feet as it grazed them. Despite all admonitions to herself, at any moment she expected to feel the mysterious hands again. She sang out, received no images or vibrations in return, and told herself to hurry.

She had come there to take the gun.

And then to disappear.

She saw no other choice. The gun was the key to a tragedy of deliberate violence. *Someone* had pulled its trigger. Could Mara's dislike for Randolphs have justified killing a cousin who married one? Was Lilith protecting Mara's crime? Or had Lilith pulled the trigger, equating honor with death, a tradition Bonavendiers clearly enshrined? Had she decided Griffin would be better off without his own parents? Alice groaned, not wanting to picture Lilith performing some horrible act of matricidal execution, nor even Mara stooping so low. As for Pearl—unfathomable. Pearl would have been harmless, blameless, a horrified bystander.

Griffin deserved to know the truth about the sisters—whatever it was. He deserved to punish anyone who had deliberately caused his parents' deaths. He deserved to put his grief and fears to rest. But would the truth do it? No. The truth rarely changed minds and only sometimes provided peace. All the answers were imperfect, caught between two worlds.

Alice had no good solution, nothing that would heal anyone, no side she would willingly sacrifice. *I brought this on*, she thought. *I let Griffin see my abilities, and he realized the sisters really could have been out here, doing the impossible during the storm. And I gave Griffin the idea to search this wreckage when I found the little sculpture. I caused this misery, just as my mother caused misery for the Bonavendiers.*

She bowed her head to the ruined bow of the *Calm Meridian* and cried. For the first time she realized her transformation. She'd gained a lover and a family, a home, a new idea of herself, and poignant truths about her beginnings. Her father had been a flawed man but ultimately a man of honor, and her mother had innocently ruined him as much as he ruined her. Alice had her own debts of honor to pay.

So she would take the gun, and no one but her would ever know about it, ever touch it, ever hear its terrible, incriminating song. On the south end of the island, near the lighthouse, she'd left a waterproof bag stuffed with a few clothes and some money. She planned to swim back for those belongings, then head down the coast into Florida. From there she thought she might make her way to the Caribbean, or anywhere. The irony was that she had the courage and know-how to consider such a journey without flinching, and that the strongest emotion she felt was not fear, but the pain of losing the sisters she had come to cherish and the man she loved dearly.

She slid down to the sandy bottom and felt her way around the bow. When she reached the gap where she'd attempted to enter before, her feet floated where the slope dropped off. She turned and sang into the Point Trench. *Ancient riverbed, that's what you are, flowing to an ancient sea. Green trees grew on this hill once. The sky met you at the borders of your shores. I remember you, and so you still live.*

Nothing died, not love, not honor, not the memory of water. She would always remember the love. She shut her eyes for a moment. Then she turned, shoved her arms into the small black tunnel beneath the ruined bow of the *Calm Meridian*, and squirmed inside.

How still it was, and darker even than the ocean outside it. She spread her hands, moved around, was tickled by small fish that had sought refuge inside there. The width was easily ten feet. She tilted her head toward the sandy bottom and hummed. Shapes came back to her. She got down on her hands and knees, touched bits of debris, rivets, and then, the barnacle-encrusted gun.

No, please, don't do it, please, think of Griffin. . .

She heard Undiline's begging, windswept plea as if she were standing beside her. Alice lurched back and slammed into the bow's inner wall.

The bow trembled, tilted, then began to slide down the ancient slope of the Point Trench.

Alice grabbed for a handhold but couldn't find any. The bow's lurching movement threw her forward, and the side of her head struck an outcropping of the yacht's ribs. A snap of pain flashed away every specific thought. She floated, unconscious, as the bow settled on the slope, twenty feet below its former spot, mired hopelessly in deep sand with no escape route.

A tomb.

It is quite likely the fabulous worlds of Melasine and her kind had been in ruins for millennia when Neptune began paddling around Grecian male fantasies with his nubile nymphs and phallic trident.
—Lilith

Twenty-Three

~

Griffin knelt on the dock at Randolph Cottage, sitting back on his heels with his hands on his thighs, his gaze on the water of Bellemeade Bay, his manner utterly still. Once again he remembered the sight of dolphins circling his laughing mother as she swam—but also circling him when he swam as a child, too. Now he recalled that Mother had been careful to take him swimming with her only when Father wasn't there to watch.

Dolphins. Circling them.

Circling Alice, the day she had arrived.

Recognizing a branch of the family tree a helluva lot closer to their kind than the average human being?

He thought of evolutionary biology, of ancient history, of sailors' dirty jokes and fanatics' theories and mystics' mythologies and a thousand other doctrines to explain the unexplainable. If there were seeds of truth in all the world's fabulous mysteries, then anything was possible.

Even himself.

He spread his hands, the hands of any man, as if webbing might begin to grow between his fingers. He touched the sides of his neck. No gills. He thought of horror movies. *The Creature from the Black Lagoon.*

This was what Alice had grown up believing, that she was different, alone, impossible. And all the time he'd been out there in the world, feeling the same way. Lilith had tried to tell him, but he had hidden that part of himself.

He stumbled to his feet. The singing. *God, it's another element of what we can do. Like sonar, like telepathy, who knows? Ali, talk to me. Meet me anywhere out in the water. I know how to find you, if you'll only sing. I'm listening.*

But she didn't answer.

He stared at the bay, clenching and unclenching his hands. *Dive in. Try it. Let go of the fear and see what happens.* Sweat broke on his brow. He called out to Alice again, and heard nothing again. He wasn't sure how long he stood there, but the slam of a car door broke into his thoughts.

"C.A.," he said, without turning to look.

C.A. walked up behind him. "I want to apologize—"

"How much did my father know about my mother and me?" Griffin pivoted and searched the older man's startled eyes. "Did he know we were . . . something different?"

Sorrow filled C.A.'s face. His shoulders slumped. "He knew there were some odd traits. But your mother hid a lot from him."

"I had webbed feet when I was born."

C.A. sagged. "She told your father they were a common deformity in her family. They had your feet surgically altered, and no one in our family ever knew. Except me."

"Did he think I was a freak?"

"Griffin, he loved you, and he loved your mother. For years, he pretended there was nothing seriously different about you or her, and, as I said, until the last she hid a lot from him."

Until the last? rose to the tip of Griffin's tongue but vanished as a tremor went through him like a high-pitched chime. He gasped. His bones echoed, his skull filled with the most potent vibrato of a lyrical feminine voice he'd never heard before, wordless but swollen with urgent information. *Out to the sea, to the dying place, to her, to her.*

"Griffin. Griffin." C.A. had him by the shoulders, staring into his blind eyes. "What is it?"

"Ali's in trouble." Griffin shoved him aside and ran for the speedboat.

C.A. followed, jumping down into the well of the fast boat just as Griffin slung off the dock lines, then sent the boat flying across the bay, heading around the tip of Sainte's Point, toward the open Atlantic.

Toward the *Calm Meridian*.

~~~~~~

The water is the womb and all our children flow from it. Go to her before you lose her, too.

Lilith awoke on the secluded cove's beach with the singing voice in her mind. She slid from Riyad's sleeping embrace and stood quickly, her disheveled silver hair cloaking her in matted sand and dried tears, her hands rising to her throat as she pivoted like a compass, searching for the direction, finding it, halting with a soft cry.

Riyad woke and bounded to his feet like a young man. He clasped one olive-skinned hand on her white shoulder. "Who is this voice, and why is she calling you?" he asked gently.

"*Melasine*," Lilith whispered. And then, in answer to his second question, "*Alice*."

~~~~~~

"When did Alice leave?" Pearl asked the Tanglewoods. She and Mara had just wrapped themselves in robes after climbing from the water at dockside on Sainte's Point. The Tanglewoods peered at Pearl and Mara anxiously from the island's dock. Pearl regarded them as three middle-aged blond dodo birds, asexual and wingless, as sweet as cherubs.

"We've seen no sign of *the Alice* for over an hour." Kasen moaned. "She just swam away. Oh, woe is us. The world is turning upset down and will pour dirt on us. We're so worried."

Mara threw up her hands. "Did she say where she was going?"

"No! And she took a small travel bag with some of her belongings in it."

Pearl gasped.

"Relax," Mara ordered. She scowled as she strangled droplets of water from her chopped hair. "We can't get rid of her that easily."

Pearl whirled toward her sister. "You vicious sea creature! You've driven her away!"

"That was my intention. I'm surprised it happened so soon." But even Mara frowned and glanced toward the ocean. "Anyway, she's too cowardly to go far. She'll be back by nightfall. Like a sea slug creeping back to its shell."

No, a foreign voice whispered. *She is dying for love of you all. Just like her mother. And just like Undiline.*

The sisters went very still. Pearl uttered a cry. She saw a look of frightened wonder come over Mara's face. Without a word, they dived back into the water and swam for the *Calm Meridian*.

～～～

Water. Smooth. Life. Flow.
How do I find it?
How will I know?

When you love someone else more than yourself, that love makes you the person you ought to be, and you've found the flow of life. Alice had the answer now, but too late. She floated in and out of consciousness inside the mired bow of the *Calm Meridian*. She could taste her own blood in the dark water. Her head throbbed. She gagged, spit out the mercurial fluid, and drew on her lungs' deep reserves of air. Dizzy and disoriented, she sang out weakly, then stopped herself. She would not draw Griffin and her sisters to a place that might endanger them, too.

Moving lethargically, she dug along the sand at the base of the old hull, hoping to find a space like before. When that didn't work, she felt along the rough interior walls and ribbing with her fingertips until she found the porthole. Alice stroked its thick, smooth glass, wishing she could see through the darkness into the open water of freedom. She flattened her hand on the glass for a moment.

When she removed it, it left a ghostly negative of itself.

Alice shut her eyes, waiting for the illusion to vanish. But when she looked again, the ethereal white hand was still there. Alice eased closer. The movement shot pains through her skull, even as wonder filled her. The hand remained, shimmering, the spread fingers merging in phosphorescent arcs, webbings of light.

A pale, webbed hand.

Now you believe, a voice whispered.

Then the hand was gone.

Alice made a dazed, prayerful gesture,

steepling her fingers to her lips, bowing her head. The weight of the ocean seemed to compress her skull. Stars wandered in her vision, and her stomach convulsed. That internal night sky remained when she closed her eyes. She fought the pain in her temple as the darkness veiled her thoughts. *I believe in mysteries and miracles. I believe in myself.*

That was her death knell, and she knew it. If she sank into unconsciousness again, she would forget to breathe. But she would never forget to love. *Griffin. Lilith. Pearl. Even Mara. Sainte's Point. My father, my mother. Melasine.*

How I love you all.

Almost all the stories of Water People are preposterous and insulting. They say we lure people into the sea and steal their souls. What a terrible stereotype. Our souls are in the water, not theirs.
—*Lilith*

Twenty-Four
~

"Take the wheel," Griffin told C.A., as their speedboat skimmed the ocean's surface beneath a spring sky turning gray with rainclouds. Griffin stripped off his shirt and kicked his shoes aside, then leapt to the boat's bow. C.A. grabbed the wheel. "Anchor there," Griffin said and pointed to the waters above the *Calm Meridian.* "I'll go get her."

"What the—Griffin, you can't go down to that wreck without help!" C.A. throttled back on the engine, and the speedboat began to slow. "You can't—without scuba gear, wait—you can't just dive down there—"

Griffin turned for just a moment, looking back at C.A. quietly. "I think you know what I'm capable of. And so do I now." He faced forward and dived straight down. His powerful, aquiline plunge left C.A. staring after him in wonder.

The water closed around him. He left the light of the surface behind with a few deep strokes. For a moment, he panicked in the black depths, lost. Then the mysterious voice filled his mind with a pulse of sensation. *Sing to the water. Listen with your heart.* He sang out without a sound, channeling the strange vibrato and reeling inside as images echoed back to him. Suddenly, the ocean was a teeming, visible landscape of shapes. He *felt* the bow of the *Calm Meridian* below him and groaned when he realized it now rested farther down the steep slope of the Point Trench.

What had Alice been hunting that was worth that risk? Why had she come here in secret and alone?

He plunged downward, sweeping the ocean behind him as his body knifed into the cold darkness. He called out to Alice but heard nothing. When he reached the bow, he flattened both hands on its rough surface and explored swiftly. *She's inside somehow. She's trapped inside.* He pounded the rough surface until his hands were raw. *Ali. Breathe.*

No answer.

Griffin braced his bare feet on the treacherously angled slope, then levered himself against the bow and pushed downhill with all his strength. The bow shifted slightly but refused to topple. He got down on his knees and dug in the sand at its ragged base, then slid his upturned hands beneath the edge and tried to lift it. The bow shifted again, then settled heavily. He tried again, air bursting in bubbles from his lips and nose as he strained. *She'll die in there. Something's wrong; she would be calling to me if she could.* And he did something he'd never thought he would do. He filled the world with a deep, urgent song of need.

Calling his mother's kind— and his own.

Calling Lilith and her sisters.

Now you know who you are, the voice whispered.

He lunged at the bow furiously, shoving, clawing, silently cursing it. *I'm Ali's kind,* he yelled inside himself, *I'm her kind, and she's mine. Ali. Breathe.*

Suddenly, new hands were around him, touching him lightly on his bare shoulders and back. *Griffin, we're here.*

That was Lilith's voice, and with her came Mara's grim song and the frantic hum of Pearl, joining with the strong presence of a man whose name came to Griffin in a quick flash. Riyad. The five of them surrounded the bow. *Push.*

This time it tilted, fell away, and Griffin plunged beneath it. He closed his hands around Alice's shoulders and snatched her limp body into his arms. The bow of the *Calm Meridian* tumbled down the slope, lifting clouds of sand and silt into the water.

Up, Lilith cried, and everyone pulled at Griffin, urging him away from the choking sediment. Griffin vaulted upward, kicking with his legs as he cradled Ali to his chest. He shielded her face with one hand.

When he surfaced he saw Barret steering the *Lorelei* close to C.A. and the speedboat.

"Take her to Barret," Pearl called. "He can pull her out the easiest."

Griffin held Alice up to Barret's strong clasp, and he lifted her aboard the ferryboat's wide bow deck. Her head lolled, and blood quickly stained her face at the right temple.

Griffin hoisted himself onto the deck. Lilith, Mara, and Pearl climbed aboard *the Lorelei* and huddled around Alice with their hands on her limp body.

Pearl was crying, Mara looked troubled, but Lilith spoke with quiet conviction, "Teach her to breathe again, Griffin."

Alice's simple black maillot hugged her breasts like a thin sheath, and Griffin saw no movement in her chest. He dropped to his knees beside her and laid his hand on her ribcage. He felt her slow heartbeat. Griffin hunched over her, sank his hands into her hair, tilted her head back, and covered her parted lips with his.

Alice shivered, sighed into his mouth, and kissed him.

Griffin drew back from her just enough to see her eyes open, wistful but alive, greener than usual, glowing. Victory and sorrow mingled in her. Griffin stroked the hair from her face, then cupped her head roughly in relief. "You could hear me," he said hoarsely. "Why didn't you answer me?"

"I believed I should go away."

"Why?" When she didn't answer, he helped her sit up, then wrapped her in his arms, rocking her a little, cradling her head to his shoulder.

Alice looked at her sisters, then shut her eyes and turned her face away from both them and Griffin.

"Ali?" he insisted gruffly. "Just tell me."

Lilith moaned. "She feared what she'd found in the wreckage. She didn't want the truth to hurt any of us. She was willing to risk her own life to protect us all."

Griffin took Alice by the chin and gently turned her face to his. He smoothed a trickle of blood from her temple, then touched his fingertips to his mouth. *A blood oath. Tell me.*

Griffin, I don't know enough. Only pieces of the past.

He looked at Lilith. "Whatever it is, I don't want revenge anymore. If this is what it does to her—I don't want her hurt."

C.A. spoke suddenly. He stood in the speedboat, staring at its diving platform. "Who put this here?"

Everyone turned quickly to look at the platform. Near the waterline lay a rough thing, at first bewildering, a grayish form covered in barnacles and muck, an answer some unseen hand had brought up and placed before them.

The gun.

It takes a brave Lander to love one of our kind.

—Member of the British royal family 1898

Twenty-Five

~

It has been the darkest of years on Sainte's Point, Lilith wrote in her journal that autumn of 1967. Father's suicide was still a raw wound, and young Joan Riley, devastated and emotionally ruined, had left under the grim auspices of her stern mountain family, borne a child, and died with that child. Pearl was bedridden, barely coping with grief over Father's death and her third miscarriage.

"No more babies," Barret said, tears on his face. "It kills another part of her heart each time."

Mara had returned from New York for Father's funeral only to have her husband and children die in the plane crash days later. She spent most of her time roaming the island's wilds and the ocean beyond like a lost soul, keening in the wind and waves.

Lilith settled in wearily as matriarch of the despairing family. Her own losses lay inside her like stones. She still sang sometimes, but the music was growing dimmer. She no longer spoke of Riyad or their dead son. She prayed as she swam every day, seeking to know why such a spiral of misery, a cycle of converging bad fortune or the mistakes of hubris, sheer fate or bad luck had taken over hers and her sisters' lives.

Does even God see us as outside the grace of nature and man? Lilith remembered a frightening story from her childhood, one she would never include in any book. A small cult of fanatical, self-hating Water People bitterly insisted that their kind had defied God's natural laws and thus been condemned to the shadows between ocean and shore, outside the understanding of humans, never to be accepted in either the realms of earth or water.

"We've been cursed since Undiline married Porter Randolph," Mara claimed instead, with bitter pragmatism. Lilith feared Mara was right. Undiline's marriage to Porter Randolph had caused nothing but misery for the Bonavendiers. Despite all of Undiline's efforts to pass for an ordinary wife and mother, that autumn Porter discovered the truth about her and Griffin.

It was the eve of the worst storm in decades, not quite a hurricane, yet aimed directly at their section of the Georgia coast. Heavy winds gathered and moved toward the land. Undiline had driven down from Savannah with Griffin the week before, taking one of their sojourns at the cottage at Bellemeade Bay.

Porter disliked her visits to her Bonavendier relatives and rarely went to the cottage with her. He ordered her home the moment the storm began brewing in the Caribbean hundreds of miles southward, and she was due to drive herself and Griffin back up the coast that evening.

"Still time for one last outing in the *Sea Princess*," she told her husband over the phone.

A Coast Guard cutter found the *Sea Princess* in choppy waters miles from shore but no sign of Undiline or Griffin. Since Undiline was an expert swimmer and could handle the small ketch like a seasoned sailor, Porter feared the worst. He flew into Bellemeade in a small private plane, then sped to the site of the *Sea Princess* in a fast motorboat. By then, the Coast Guard had abandoned the sailboat's area to search for Undiline's and Griffin's bodies. The *Sea Princess* rocked like a cradle on the rough Atlantic.

Porter anchored his motorboat and began yelling Undiline's and Griffin's names, knowing such calling was futile and pathetic, but he was helpless to do otherwise. To his amazement, both his wife and son suddenly surfaced. Undiline had taken Griffin on his first deep-water swim. She moaned when she realized they'd been discovered.

"Porter, my darling," she called out. "What are you—" The look on his face halted her. He stared incredulously at her and their son in the cold, rolling water. Wild dolphins surrounded them as playfully as pet cats. Both she and Griffin were naked despite the whipping wind and the chill. Neither shivered, though they'd been in the water for hours.

Griffin smiled up at his father proudly. "I can swim like a fish, Father. Mother says it's a secret, but she can, too. We went all the way to the bottom of the Point Trench. I can hold my breath forever."

Undiline saw the horror and revulsion on Porter's face mingle with fear. She moaned again. What he'd discovered about her and their son was unexplainable. Impossible. Beyond the laws of nature. Inhuman. "My love, please, let's talk," Undiline hugged a bewildered Griffin to her in the water. Porter remained frozen in place, dazed. He said nothing and made no move at all.

"Father, it's all right. I really can swim like a fish," Griffin called out again. "And I sing to the dolphins, and they sing back. I even know their names. Mother says they're our family, too. Like the Bonavendiers. We're Water People."

His father flinched.

"Into the *Princess*," Undiline whispered to Griffin. "Your father's worried about us being gone so long, and we'll talk to him later."

Griffin slid from her arms, dived innocently beneath the water, and reappeared with startling speed beside the nearby ketch.

Several wild dolphins gathered around him like protective aunts. "See, Father?" he called again. "I'm a dolphin with legs."

His father stared down at him, ashen, then tracked Undiline's equally swift swim to the ketch. She lifted Griffin to the deck, then climbed up naked after him. Quickly, she dressed him and herself in the white shorts and T-shirts they'd worn before swimming. Tears slid down her face, and she barely took her gaze from her stunned husband, who steadied himself like a sleepwalker in the well of his motorboat. "Porter, I'm taking Griffin to Sainte's Point. Will you follow, please? Please, my darling. Do no' look at us that way. We're flesh and blood, not monsters. Come and talk to me. Come and try to understand."

"Stay away from me." He cranked the speedboat's engine, gunned it, and left them there.

～～～

The storm drew closer. Rain whipped Sainte's Point, pouring from the mansion's slate roofs and turrets into pipes that fed a freshwater storage tank. The ocean surged over the beaches and cast white spray as high as the dunes. Even the sheltered cove beat against the island's docks. Life-giving water was everywhere, and yet nothing could soothe Undiline. Porter had deserted her.

"The bastard broke her heart," Mara said. "I always knew he would. Randolphs are the antithesis of everything our kind represent. Undiline's known their marriage was doomed all along. She hated hiding her true nature from him." Mara clasped a locket to her soft white sweater. Her children's pictures were inside. "She stayed with an unworthy husband for the sake of a child."

Didn't you, as well? Lilith thought, but said nothing.

"A child is love," Pearl countered sadly. Then only twenty-seven, she looked like a red-haired teenager playing Ophelia in a school production of *Hamlet*. Her long hair streamed over a flowing white nightgown. Her face, pale and ethereal, mirrored her agony. "Anyone capable of love knows that pure love is a child." Her face crumpled. "And when children die . . . when they die, all love dies with them."

"Back to bed," Lilith ordered gently, and Barret, who had been watching with grim misery, carefully picked Pearl up and carried her from the parlor where they had gathered.

"Say no more," Lilith told Mara.

"Nothing's left worth arguing about," Mara said dully. "Nothing's left worth caring about."

Lilith went down a hall to the bedroom suite where Undiline paced and sobbed, a long silk robe trailing her, her shoulder-length hair in matted streams around her swollen face. Griffin played in another part of the rain-swept old mansion, distracted by adoring Tanglewoods who called him *The Griffin*.

"Are we not meant to have husbands and children?" Undiline asked brokenly, as Lilith grasped her hands. "Is it beyond the hope of our kind to be a part of the greater world?"

"If I say you should have fallen in love with a man made in the image of our own special God, what good does it do? That is no guarantee of happiness, as you can well see in the case of my sisters and me. We have to love whomever we love and accept the consequences. When the weather clears, I'll go with you to Savannah. We'll plead your case to Porter. This façade is over, my dear. Either he'll accept your mysteries and make peace with the knowledge that there are far more unusual people in a world he thinks he knows so well, or he won't."

Undiline bowed her head. "When Griffin was born, Porter ordered the doctor and nurses to tell no one about his webbed feet and to keep his wee toes covered in booties so no Randolph could see them either. I saw the humiliation in Porter's face. He told me, 'Well, it's not as bad as a cleft palate or a clubfoot. It's just a small deformity. I'll get a good surgeon to fix him, not like the hack who sliced your feet when you were a baby.'" She groaned. "He thought my own parents had me 'fixed' as a child. Freed of a *deformity*, Lilith. And he clearly could no' accept even the smallest 'deformity' in his son. That's when I knew I could never tell him the rest about myself. Oh, but he's such a fine man in other ways, and I love him so!"

"Undiline, regardless of your love for him, you couldn't go on hiding your true self from him. Or Griffin's."

"Yes, yes, I could! I wanted my son to be one of his father's kind, one of 'Them.' It's so much easier that way. Just to be a full and plain human being."

Lilith grasped her hands hard, almost shaking her. "We see worlds they can never see. We travel where they can never go; we hear music they only wish they could hear. We are not less human, Undiline. We are *more*."

"Without him, I'm nothing."

"Without you, *he* is nothing."

Undiline shook her head, pulled away, and buried her face in her hands. Lilith watched her with pity but also firm resolve. "I am the head of this family now. My sisters and I will never have more children of our own—I feel that judgment in my soul. If worse comes to worst and Porter can't be reasoned with, you have a home here, and so does Griffin. We adore him, and we need a child to raise. But I swear to you, if there is any way to mend this breach between you and Porter, I'll help you. I swear it."

A soft knock came at the room's doors. "Mother?" Griffin called. "Don't you want to come and eat? Kasen is making a butter pudding with oysters in it."

Undiline stretched out on the room's broad, canopied bed and flung an arm across her eyes. "Please don't let him see me this way. Tell him I'm sleeping. I want him to know as little as possible about this upset. And, yes, I know hiding the truth from him is as hopeless as the rest of it. But I love him too much not to try. Our kind can live in secrecy, Lilith, but no' in despair."

Lilith stroked her hair, then turned out the room's light. Standing in the darkness beside Undiline, she whispered, "I do understand."

~~~

The sound of a ship's horn blasting drew Lilith, Mara, and Undiline to the windows early the next morning. The oaks were bent in the wind; rain fell in silver sheets. In the cove sat the *Calm Meridian,* a forty-foot sailboat Porter proudly swore he could command in full winds with only Undiline as his mate. The two of them had sailed the tall-masted yacht to South America and back for their honeymoon.

Porter stood on the *Calm Meridian's* deck, his black hair plastered to his skull, a yellow slicker slung open carelessly over his khakis and sweater. He swayed as the yacht rocked in the cove's protected waters. Its sails were furled; the mast probed the rain and mist with barren command.

"Keep Griffin inside," Undiline cried. He was still asleep in a small bedroom off her suite. She ran from the mansion and down the pathway to the docks. The downpour clamped her white silk robe and nightgown to her tall body. Her coppery hair curled in soaked tendrils down her back. "Porter!" she screamed.

"Stay here," Lilith said to Mara. "I'll follow her."

Mara scowled out the window at the reckless sight Porter Randolph made. "He's drunk or out of his mind. Be careful."

Lilith slung a soft cashmere cape around the shoulders of her gold robe. Her hair, the color of rich chocolate then, burst from tortoise-shell combs. As she strode from the mansion's veranda, the wind and rain took her breath away, and she stared in dismay at Undiline on the dock. Undiline held out both hands to Porter. His handsome face contorted. He shook his head, then placed a fist over his heart.

"No, my darling, no," Undiline sobbed.

He turned to the yacht's wheel. The motor made the slightest throbbing in the wind. He guided the sleek sailboat toward the cove's mouth and the deadly, open Atlantic beyond.

Lilith took Undiline by the shoulders from behind.

Undiline shook. "He thinks he married a demon or such. He does no' know how to comprehend it. So he's going out there to die."

"Sing to him. Sing with all your heart."

"He does no' want to hear what he can't believe!" Undiline pulled away from her and dived into the cove's churning water. Lilith lunged to a piling and held on as a gust of wind raked her body. She screamed for Undiline to come back, knowing it was useless.

As the *Calm Meridian* slid into the open water, Lilith saw Undiline reach up from the water and snare a docking line. She climbed aboard and lay on the yacht's aft deck, then got to her feet and made her way toward Porter. Fog and rain closed around the yacht like a curtain, and Lilith strained hopelessly to see more. They disappeared into the mists.

Pearl and Mara were waiting when Lilith made her way back up the path to the mansion's veranda. Pearl clung tearfully to Mara's staunch arm. Both were like windswept butterflies, hair and nightgowns floating in the air. They gazed at her in distress. Lilith waved a hand.

"I'll go after them alone. If anything happens, you two must care for Griffin."

"Even you shouldn't brave this storm," Mara said.

"Oh, you can't," Pearl cried.

"I'll take the *Aqua*. It's strong and fast." The *Aqua* was the island's small cabin cruiser. "Go inside, Mara. Tell Barret to bring me the engine keys."

But before Mara could go, Judith Beth ran onto the veranda, wringing her hands, her soft blond hair flying. "The Griffin saw his mama and papa from the upstairs window, and he's gone. He's gone after them!"

Lilith and her sisters traded quiet looks. This was one child they could save. "We'll all go find him," Lilith said.

~~~

Lilith's heart sank when they spotted the *Calm Meridian* tossing on the deep swells of the open ocean. The mast had snapped and toppled, dragging sails and ropes in the water. The yacht dipped heavily to its starboard side.

Drenched with rain, Undiline was slumped beside the broken boom on the yacht's foredeck, her arms twined in the rigging. There was no sign of Porter or Griffin. Lilith shielded her eyes in the whipping torrent as she, Mara, and Pearl leaned over the *Aqua*'s bow.

Barret cut the engine. "I can't bring us any closer!" he yelled from the cruiser's small cabin. "Too dangerous!"

Lilith threw off her soaked, clinging cape and nightgown, and sang out grimly. *Into the water, my sisters.*

Yes, into the water.

Yes.

Mara and Pearl stripped their gowns off. They plunged into the churning ocean after Lilith.

When the three of them reached the *Calm Meridian*, they grasped the tangled rigging and held on as the yacht lurched and bucked. *It will roll over at any moment*, Lilith thought. She sang out. *Griffin, Griffin, where are you?*

She and the others heard a faint, wounded hum in return.

He's locked below, in the cabin. Dear God,

what has happened here? Undiline, can you hear me?

Save my son, came the weakest reply.

Pearl and Mara moaned aloud, and Lilith bowed her head. *She's dying.*

"Wait here," Lilith told Mara and Pearl. Lilith climbed through the ruined rigging and the torn mast. When she looked over the side of the yacht, she saw Porter lying across Undiline's folded legs, his head in her lap, his eyes open in death. Blood streamed from a gaping wound at the center of his chest.

Lilith clawed her way across the rainswept deck and knelt beside the collapsed Undiline, who was also covered in blood down the front of her body. *Oh, my dear, my dear doomed cousin.* Lilith cried out at the sight of the equally horrific wound just below Undiline's ribcage. Lilith took Undiline's face in her hands and lifted her head.

Undiline opened her dreaming, dying eyes. Lilith, crying, bent her head to Undiline's and saw everything Undiline had seen.

Mother, why are you and Father leaving me?

Oh, Griffin! How brave you are! We weren't leaving you. Never. She pulled him from the churning water at the bow of the yacht.

Where's Father taking us?

Home, of course. Now into the cabin with you, where you'll be safe.

I want to stay up here with you and Father.

Into the cabin.

She shoved him below and shut the door tightly, then made her way back to the wheel.

Porter, my darling, no. Please, no.

Porter Randolph stood on the yawing deck, a heavy-barreled revolver in his hand. *I can't live without you, and I can't live with what I know about you. I don't know what you are. Or what our son is. You can't be real. And I can't go on if you're not.* He raised the pistol to his heart. She lunged at him, caught his hands, and twisted them away from his target. A tall swell broke over the yacht, flinging them down. The mast snapped. The gun fired.

Undiline felt the bullet tear through her body and fell back, arching, gasping. Porter yelled her name, and suddenly his arms went around her. He knelt on the tilting deck, gathering her to him, trying to staunch the rush of blood from the wound, failing.

How human he saw she was then, dying in such an ordinary way. He begged her forgiveness, he told her he loved her, he raised his face to the wind and rain, he sobbed. And then he grasped the pistol as it slid across the deck near him, put it to his heart again, and pulled the trigger.

Lilith shivered as that sight came to her and held Undiline closer. Undiline sighed her last breath. *Save my son, Lilith. And never let him know how this was. Only let him know there was love.*

Lilith rocked Undiline in her arms, crying. *I swear to you. Only the love.*

Mara and Pearl screamed as the ocean suddenly rose up like a hand. The *Calm Meridian* capsized in a terrible crash of water and ripping wood. Undiline's body was torn from Lilith's arms. Lilith plunged as deeply as she could, kicking aside a tangle of rigging, singing out to her sisters.

Here, yes, we're here, they answered.

She linked hands with them deep beneath the rolling ocean and watched in horror as the yacht sank past them. They trailed it to the bottom. It struck with a sickening collapse, tearing apart at the midsection.

Lilith pointed. *There. There he is.*

They pried torn planks aside and reached into the ruined cabin. Griffin floated inside, bleeding and badly hurt, yet faintly moving his broken arms. His dark young eyes looked straight at Lilith, and he pleaded with her to save his parents. She and her sisters cradled him in their arms and hushed him.

Remember only the love, Lilith whispered in his mind.

And he began to forget everything else.

∾∾∾

C.A. was nearly thirty years old then, rough and ruined and elegant, roaming the waters bitterly, drinking, chasing illusions that could never match the affair he'd had with Mara as a college student. He mourned Porter's death like a brother and spent days after the storm searching the wreckage for Porter's and Undiline's bodies, to no avail. Other Randolphs openly accused Lilith and her sisters of hiding something, *something* that would have explained the reckless journey that had killed the family's brightest scion and put his heir, four-year-old Griffin, in a Savannah hospital. Griffin had been found by fishermen on the shores of Bellemeade. He could remember almost nothing about the storm or his parents' reasons for sailing in it. Nor could he remember having visited Sainte's Point, or why.

Submerged in grief, Lilith and her sisters revealed nothing, ignored the accusations, and refused to answer the questions.

C.A. roared into the cove at Sainte's Point alone in a speedboat one cold autumn afternoon and strode up the pathway from the docks. Dark-haired, dressed in rough-weather wool and rubber boots, a beard shadow darkening his harsh expression and haunted dark eyes, he looked dangerous.

"He's my problem," Mara said quietly, and went out to meet him alone. It was the first time they'd spoken face to face in years. He halted before her, and the look they traded seethed with agonized defenses. "Where are Porter's and Undiline's bodies?" he demanded.

Mara exhaled slowly. "You accuse us as well? Are you no smarter than your relatives?"

"Don't play your goddamn games with me. I'm not a kid, anymore."

"Don't stand here hating me and my sisters for miseries your cousin brought on mine." In a rush of anger and pain, she leaned close. *"Porter killed her."* C.A.'s shoulders sagged. Mara put a trembling hand to her heart as he bowed his head.

He suspected the truth, and he believed her. C.A.'s eyes gleamed with tears. "She should never have lied to him about what she was."

"What should she have said about herself, C.A.? What should she have called herself? What was she—what am I and my sisters? Circus freaks? A figment of decent, ordinary human beings' imaginations? No. We're a wonder. We're a marvel. Porter saw her as she really was, and he couldn't accept her, so he destroyed her." Mara stepped closer. Tears slid down her face. "There are many ways to exist, C.A. Many ways to love and be loved. Many ways to have your heart broken. Do I horrify you? Do you consider me a monster, a circus freak, too?"

"I consider you a miracle at heart and a monster in your soul."

"Would you kill me if you could?"

"No." He looked down at her with a furious love that tore her apart. "I'd kill myself."

She shivered. When words came, she said softly, "If you ever do that, I shall hate you for eternity." He reached for her but she pulled away. "You need to know exactly what happened between Porter and Undiline." She told him everything, and when she finished, they swayed together for one brief moment of tenderness. She clutched his shoulders and whispered brokenly in his ear. "Do you ever want your family to know how they really died? Do you want some heavy-fingered coroner to pry the bullets out of their bodies? Do you want Griffin to grow up knowing his father shot his mother and then killed himself?"

"No." C.A.'s voice was a guttural rasp of emotion.

She stepped back from him. He looked as ruined as she. "Then that is a secret you must help us keep."

"*Where are their bodies?*"

Mara gazed up at him with quiet resolve. "By the water."

～～～

Lilith, Mara, Pearl, and C.A. stood beside the dais of Italian marble facing Bellemeade Bay and the mainland. The faint outline of Randolph Cottage could be seen on the spit of sand where the continent seemed to turn a corner away from the world. The sky was blue, as if a storm had never occurred, but the island's forest seeped its grief, and the earth around the dais had been churned into sandy mud.

"We wrapped them in lace duvets and gold silk before we buried them," Pearl said tearfully.

C.A. dropped to one knee and laid a hand on the large dais. The sisters turned their heads as he prayed silently. But when he stood, his face was hard. "Stay away from Griffin."

"Oh, please, no—" Pearl began.

"That's not fair," Mara said, then bit her tongue.

"Stay away from him, or I swear to God I'll take him to the other side of the world and never bring him back."

Lilith said as calmly as she could, "Please let us help raise him. You know he's not like ordinary children. Without us, he'll forget who he really is. That's never what I intended."

"His own mother wanted him to be *normal*. I'll make sure he grows up thinking he's like anyone else."

"That's impossible."

"I said, *Stay away from him*."

Lilith searched his face but saw only bitter devotion.

Mara asked hoarsely, "Is this the pound of flesh you have to take? Then punish me, not my sisters."

"I just want Griffin to forget you all," C.A. said between gritted teeth. "I want to forget you myself." He and Mara traded bitter looks. He walked into the forest.

The sisters stood there by Undiline and Porter's secret grave. The past closed over them, and the future became a dull vision. In the grave, they had also buried their own youth, the memories of children who would never be, their father's charm, their mother's smile, Griffin's magic, Joan Riley's innocence, and the dead baby daughter they believed she had borne, yet another lost child.

"We saved Griffin, and only Griffin," Pearl whispered. "How will we ever tell him?"

In that moment, Lilith lost the ability to sing.

"Without a miracle, we won't," she said.

They say there are tragic water spirits who sing to passing boatmen. Yet as anyone who has heard one of us singing can tell you, there is nothing tragic about the music of the water. It is the singing, not the silence, that matters.

—*Lilith*

Twenty-Six

~

Thirty-five years later, Griffin bowed his head over the gun, which he held on his cupped palms, like an offering, listening to its terrible song. I saw the resignation on his face. He did not doubt the story Lilith had told us. Neither did I. My head ached, and my body was sore and bruised. I watched Griffin with a quiet mewl of devotion inside me. We were like children, comforting each other in the sharing of grief.

Hurts me.

Hurts me, too.

Lilith laid a hand on his bare shoulder. He looked like a lost wayfarer in drying trousers, the scars on his body blue in the sunlight, his dark eyes haunted. "All these years we didn't know how to tell you," she said, "or how you'd react. We feared the truth might destroy you. Without Alice's influence, I think it would have."

He nodded and raised those dark eyes to

hers, then to C.A.'s face.

"I never wanted you to know how they died," C.A. admitted hoarsely. "I thought it'd be better if you forgot everything—including how different you were."

"I see now," Lilith added, "that our silence did you no good. Alice opened us all to our fate again. Whatever that may be—to love and love passionately and risk the truth is what we must do. What you must do, too."

Griffin slid an arm around me, and I kissed him. Lilith touched my face, then stroked a fingertip over the white gauze that covered my temple. "You, my dear Alice, are our miracle."

Everything I might have said to apologize to her and the sisters was locked inside me. Happiness and sorrow, shock and relief, the deepest love for Lilith, Mara, Pearl, and Griffin. I had done the right thing. Something larger than me existed, but I could not name it yet.

"I don't know. . ." I attempted, then stopped. "I don't know," I could only conclude. I huddled beside Griffin with my feet curled and a soft mauve blanket wrapped around me.

My sisters, along with Riyad, C.A., and Barret, sat around us on the stern deck of the *Lorelei*, wrapped in other light blankets brought out by anxious Tanglewoods. My sisters were still naked beneath their blankets, and so was Riyad, silver-haired and regal with his blanket discreetly wound around his hips. He stood behind Lilith on the deck and kept the fingers of one hand entwined lightly in the long drying curls at the top of her head. A maroon sunset washed over the ocean and the somber faces around me. I looked from Lilith to Griffin. *How do I help him?*

Patience.

Pearl clutched Barret's hand and said tearfully, "We saved the only child we could that day."

Mara met my gaze with a troubled frown. "The only one we *knew* about. You do understand that we would have helped you, too?"

I inclined my head. "I have no doubt you'd have terrorized all the Rileys and taken me."

Mara nodded. She drew a little closer to C.A., who had assumed a position just behind her, close enough for her to lean back into his embrace, which she did. Her chopped hair fluttered around her face, and there was nothing vain or decorous about her at the moment. She seemed to have landed like a bedraggled butterfly inside C.A.'s arms, and he barely breathed as he held her.

We make a special and beautiful kind of people, I thought, and suddenly I knew what to do. I knelt in front of Griffin and rested my hands atop the gun on his palms. I searched his eyes and saw the understanding there. *The people who loved us then and love us now all want us to live in peace and joy.*

He nodded. We stood and walked to the bow of the boat.

He held the gun up for a moment, then dropped it into the ocean.

We watched it disappear.

That night the house at Sainte's Point mourned with renewed passion. Lilith and Riyad, Pearl and Barret, Mara and C.A., Griffin and me. I woke in the darkness of my suite and listened to the soft songs of redemption, forgiveness, poignant acceptance, and change. The pillow beside me was empty. I rose gingerly on one elbow.

In the moonlight, I saw the open French doors to the private garden. Griffin leaned there, his somber face turned up to the moonlight. I slid from the big bed and went to him. He welcomed me within the curve of his arm, and we stood together in the moonlight, naked and close.

"I still have to learn how to forgive and forget," he said.

"You have to learn how to sing and remember," I replied.

He touched my face. We walked outside and through the forest, past the Bonavendier cemetery streaked in pale golden moonshine to the island's bayside shore, where the marble dais glistened in the ethereal white light. We sat down beside it.

"I *want* to forgive him," he said finally.

"But, it'll take time." He let tears come then, and I leaned against him with one hand tucked inside his elbow and the other laid flat on the cool stone, alongside his.

Sing to your man. Soothe him and be soothed, a soft voice whispered to me, growing fainter as it traveled out beyond the Point Trench, into the abyss, back into fantasy.

I bowed my head. Yes, Melasine.

The more pragmatic among Water People insist that no finned ancestors ever existed and certainly don't exist now, and that variations in our skills and physiology are mere vagaries, easily explained by random intermingling among our kind. I will not get into any wilder claims, here.
    —*Lilith*

Twenty-Seven

~

We sat in the sunroom with Lilith. I read from a book some Bonavendier, long having disappeared into another kind of sea, had written. "It is not necessary," I recited, "to prove where we Water People began, or whether we owe our origins to beings as gossamer as Angels. No more than a grain of sand can comprehend the earth that birthed it, nor a single drop of water imagine its place in a summer cloud. It is simple enough to cherish the special shore we inhabit and to return the rain as a gift to the land. To celebrate the Belonging of both."

Griffin turned his somber gaze from Melasine's portrait to me. "What would you think of marrying a merman who's a pirate?"

I closed the book, got up, took his face between my hands, bent down, and kissed him. "A merman who's a *privateer*," I corrected.

Lilith smiled.

∾⸝∾⸝∾

Lilith stood on the beach of Sainte's Point with her sisters, Mara, Pearl, and Alice. Bright, warm sunshine streamed over them, their pale silks rippled in the breeze, their bare feet were sunk into the sand. All gazed at the ocean. "Melasine is out there, somewhere," Lilith said. "She and the other Old Ones. Their legacy to us is real. There is so much more to tell you about our kind, Alice."

Alice faced Lilith and the others. "I'm ready to listen, if you believe in me as much as I believe in you." Her eyes glowed with tears, and she struggled to say more. Lilith felt every word. Apologies, devotion, regrets. Love.

"Don't make me cry, too," Mara warned.

"Hush, you sentimental shark," Pearl ordered, sniffling.

Lilith took Alice by the shoulders. "It's this simple, my dear." She paused. "Tell us your name."

Alice studied her face for a moment, then began to smile through the tears.

"Ali Bonavendier," she said.

∾⸝∾⸝∾

The Greeks and Romans were quite enamored with us, Lilith wrote. *They filled their temples with shape-shifting water deities, lusty gods and goddesses of the sea, Nereid's and nymphs. I'm rather fond of their view of our kind. Quite romantic.*

We sailed for several months, Griffin and I. We took the *Sea Princess* and went exploring down the southern slip of the planet, past palm islands and Latin coasts, across Caribbean inlets and old pirate coves. Days passed in which we spoke few words aloud but said volumes in our quiet language and through the merging of our bodies. A whole lifetime of healing can come in small moments of simple fulfillment, the whisper of a kiss on intimate skin, the promise in a loyal gaze.

It was late summer when we returned to Sainte's Point. Lilith and Riyad had gone to visit Undiline's relatives in Scotland. C.A. and Mara were in the Gulf of Mexico, sipping margaritas. Pearl and Barret had taken a slow boat to China. But we had all vowed to return for the autumn solstice, so I expected them soon. We were a family.

Griffin and I walked the island in quiet contemplation, holding hands, making love in the coves, and sitting quietly beside the marble dais where his father and mother were buried. One day we went to Bellemeade to sip vodkas on the veranda of Water Lilies, looking over the bay. The same little girl who had greeted me when I arrived months earlier saw me and ran up the veranda steps with a gaze of wonder.

"Oh, your hair is so pretty now," she said and stroked the auburn locks which curled to my waist. She touched the slender silk sundress I wore and grinned at my bare, bejeweled feet. I wore the emerald ankle bracelet Lilith had given me in the mountains. I also wore a finely woven ankle bracelet of Griffin's hair. On one of his ankles, hidden beneath his trousers, he wore a bracelet of mine.

The little girl looked at my feet carefully. "Now, I'm *sure* you're a mermaid."

I thought for a moment, then cupped my hands around her face. "So are you," I assured her. "We all are, at heart."

She looked at Griffin with wide eyes, studying his bare feet. "Him, too?"

"Yes."

Griffin touched his fingers in a water glass on our table, then smoothed the moisture on the child's nose, admitting just a little bit of the magic our kind can endow. She smiled widely, a believer.

After she left, Griffin held out a hand to me, and I took it. We sat there together contentedly, looking out over the bay with quiet wisdom and devotion, the sorrow of hard-earned faith, but much joy. The water called us to keep its secrets, to listen and know, to love and remember. To sing.

And we answered.

A Note From Lilith Bonavendier

Dear Readers:

Surely you want to believe in us now. Surely you know, deep in your hearts, that Water People have always existed alongside Land People ("Landers"), and that the veil between us is as soft as the sand of a shifting beach. Will you ever look at the great, mysterious oceans with the same casual reverence again? Examine the soft skin between your toes. Hold a deep breath inside the blue cloak of your swimming pool. Sing out to the goldfish in your aquarium. Now you understand. The world floats in a far more fluid reality than you ever imagined.

We two peoples—Land and Water—must rise from the dark divisions and wild rumors of our past. I believe Melasine sent a message when she appeared in our midst out at the Point Trench on the day of Alice's rescue. She called for mercy, and for unity. I intend to promote those ideals by helping other outcast souls discover their true nature, as Alice did. By helping you, dear readers. Let me start by offering the following excerpt from one of the humble records I've kept of Water People legend and lore. I pray you will soon cherish the uncharted waters of our shared souls as much as I do.

Let us begin the long voyage together.

Lilith

HIDDEN BETWEEN WATER AND EARTH AWAIT MIRACLES

The Legend Of Ta-Mera

Excerpted From *Fables of the Water People*

In some ancient time of great honor and noble deeds, some millenium thousands of years before our own, Once Upon A Time, as they say in fairy tales, Melasine and the other Old Ones, male and female, ruled a great empire of extraordinary beings such as themselves, half human but also half aquatic.

Whether this mythical empire existed in the blue waters of the Aegean, as is usually coined by fervent fans of the Atlantis legends, or in some totally unconsidered ocean realm, is unknown. Certain scientists among our kind have quietly removed incredible statues of the Old Ones from sunken ports in every ancient coastal city of the world.

Their findings suggest an amazing civilization existed long before the first Greeks erected temples to sea gods and goddesses. It is quite likely the fabulous worlds of Melasine and her kind had been in ruins for millennia when Neptune began paddling around Grecian male fantasies with his nubile nymphs and phallic trident.

Water is life, water is love, water is the womb. All the great religions believe so. Water People say the earth formed as an afterthought inside the glorious depths of great seas, hardening like the dull, dry pit of a luscious fruit.

At the risk of insulting those Water People who believe Landers cannot possibly share our legacy, I must point out that if the sea is the mother of us all, then we must all be, at heart, both Water People and Land People. Do not all children float first in the womb as female beings? Thus all men begin in fluid, as women. Similarly, all Landers began as Water People. And all Water People began as the Old Ones.

Mermaids.

I rarely use that cartoonish term, but it does prove convenient for first impressions. Whether fact or fancy, the portrait of Melasine at Sainte's Point indicates she is far more surreal and complex than a simple, popular name can surmise. I have no doubt she exists—an ancient, ageless, female being, isolated and reclusive, lonely and yet seductive.

My own grandmother, Deirdre Bonavendier, told me about meeting Melasine and learning, directly from her, the Water People's mythological Ta-Mera legend. Deirdre was born in the mid-1800s, not many years after the passing of her grandfather, Simon Sainte Bonavendier, that heroic French Lander who captured Melasine's heart.

"Melasine had long since disappeared from our family's circle by then," Grandmother Deirdre said. "She was not a doting grandmother in the traditional sense."

Indeed, neither Melasine nor her children were destined to stay at Sainte's Point. The

three halflings Melasine and Simon birthed
together during the late 1700s and early 1800s
eventually left to roam the abyss. By nature they
were loners, like their mother. (Dear Readers:
Please see my addendum about genealogical
clans for more information on volatile first-
generation halflings.)

At any rate, Grandmother Deirdre
insisted that as a child (during the Civil War)
she met her Grandmother Melasine while
attempting to lure a Union gunship into the
shallows near Bellemeade Bay. The encounter
occurred more than ten years after her
Grandfather Simon's death (he had lived to a
manfully gracious Lander age of ninety.)

"Grandmother Melasine saved me from
being captured by the Union navy," Grandmother Deirdre told me. "I was about to be fired
upon in the water when suddenly someone
whisked me down deep and held me safely. I
turned in those strange arms and gaped. I
recognized Grandmother Melasine from her
portrait as well as by sheer instinct, of course.
Her skin glowed pale white, like the finest
creamy silk, and her golden hair floated in trails
as long as her body, swirling around her from
head to fins. She was terrifying and beautiful; I
settled with her on the bay's bottom and
couldn't move or look away. She stroked my
face with her long, webbed hands and sang to me
without words. She was crying, still grieving for
Grandpapa, though she had always known that

he would grow old and die. 'Such is the curse of my kind when we love Landers,' she sang to me. 'But it was not always so.'

'Please tell me your story, Grandmama,' I sang back.

'Yes, brave child, I will give you that gift,' she answered.

"And so Grandmother Melasine shared her memories with me. I saw an ancient alabaster city beneath the bluest water. I saw visions of all that Grandmother Melasine had known and been many centuries before she gave her heart to Grandpapa. And that is how I know that Ta-Mera really existed."

Here is what my grandmother, and her grandmother—a mermaid—said about the beginning of our kind. And yours.

~·~·~

When Melasine and the others like her–both male and female–were young, they called themselves Tamerians, after their greatest city. The Tamerians openly ruled the coasts of the ancient world, creating amazing palaces in the waters, traveling across land via rivers and inlets and fantastically engineered channels which connected the great seas and freshwater lakes. Landers—pathetic, two-legged, short-lived humans—were deemed inferior and treated as servants or were driven to the wild interiors of the continents, where their shuffling, land-trapped ways could be ignored by the elegant and handsomely finned Tamerians.

Ta-Mera was built more in the water than on the land, with submerged temples and fluid passageways, fine promontories of marble for sunning in the warm air, and broad canals of the most beautiful stonework. (Dear Readers: You might want to look for an article from the magazine *Strange Science,* circa May of 1997, titled "The Mysterious Lost Alleys of the Ancient Coasts." It's inaccurate but fascinating, especially to those of us who know why those "alleys" truly existed.) The Tamerians were a far older race than the plodding Landers. They considered themselves a far more brilliant kind, far more talented, far more *evolved.*

There is always a "pride goeth before the fall" theme in mythology, and the Ta-Mera story may be just such an instructional tale: Perhaps the Tamerians abused their hold over the Landers, treating them as a lesser tributary of the familial sea, and the Landers finally rebelled. Or the Tamerians worshiped inconstant gods who smote them for frivolous injustices. Or they were doomed by the ordinary afflictions of both Land and Water Kind—greed, envy, lust, and jealousy.

Whatever the curse that descended upon them, it inspired all the great fables of the world since. Is it not true that in the storytelling traditions of every major culture we find tales of unthinkable disasters, which cleansed the world and restored order? Of course, among Water People these tales have a certain irony. For example, in our version of Noah's Ark, the world was destroyed by a great drought.

Be that as it may. Some terrible cataclysm abruptly destroyed Ta-Mera and the vast empire it anchored, along with all the Landers—except three young men—and the Tamerians—except Melasine and two others—young mermaids named Acarinth and Leirdrela.

In some accounts the three surviving Landers are described by Water People as barbaric and low (typical Landers, some insist) and are assigned names commiserate with such an unpleasant portrayal. A web-footed priest writing in fourteenth century England named the Landers Gumaldin, Fray Daval, and Altenhop--names from the classic storytellers' lexicon of bumbling demons and clownish villains.

Even modern Water People coax their children to sleep with disparaging comic tales about the three Landers. In many bedtime stories the trio become drooling lechers named Squat, Frag, and Goop, and children are assured that our finned foremothers nobly consorted with them only for purposes of repopulating the ocean with Water People.

Most Water People, however, prefer a more romantic and sympathetic image of the three legendary Landers—who are, after all, our mythological ancestors. They call the threesome by handsome names that were assigned to them in a classic eighteenth century narrative written

by a Bonavendier relative, the infamous Victorian singer and poetess Emilene Merrimac Revere, of Boston, Massachusetts. To quote a verse:
Stalwart and true, by Ta-Mera's princesses enslaved
Devoted lovers, bound to earth yet fulfilled in water,
We shall whisper their mortal names on shores kissed by eternal tides,
And forget them not in fluid rhyme:
Beckrith, Padrian, and Salasime.

Beckrith, Padrian, and Salasime. The mates of the three Tamerians and the mythological founding fathers of all Water People. They were two-legged, ordinary Landers. After the great cataclysm nothing was left of either Land People or Water People except those three gentlemen and our three ladies. A classic dilemma.

Even if you were the only man left on Earth or in water . . .

Melasine, Acarinth, and Leirdrela fell in love with the men. But after many years their devoted Landers died, and also their halfling children and grandchildren and great-grandchildren—all mortal.

As the centuries passed, every lover and every child left them. Melasine, Acarinth, and Leirdrela realized it would always be so. Thus they began to harden their hearts against

Landers and even halflings, to stay alone, until some rare man lured them into love again or some halfling descendent earned their sympathy.

They cannot resist loving us. In their souls they cherish their mingled descendents, neither Lander nor Tamerian, neither earth nor water, but the best of both.

And that is a truth I believe.

Every time I recount Grandmother Deirdre's story I feel a bit defensive. The more pragmatic among Water People insist that no such finned ancestors ever existed and certainly don't exist now, and that variations in our skills and physiology are mere vagaries, easily explained by random intermingling among our kind. (Dear Readers: I will not get into any wilder claims here, but do please read my addendum about clans.)

Many Water People claim (as, in fact, we Bonavendiers do) to be only a few generations removed from either Melasine, Acarinth, or Leirdrela. We engage in endless debates over reported sightings and encounters with the three. A certain snobbery demands that one not only claim a member of the trio as near kin but also show proof that the link actually exists.

The portrait of Melasine at Sainte's Point has generated spirited controversy among Water People for two hundred years. Some fervently accuse us of fraud. Did she actually pose for the artist, or was her image merely conjured up by social climbing eighteenth century Bonavendiers? (I assure you, dear readers, she posed.)

Regardless, let us all be proud of whatever talents we have inherited, however and whenever, at every level of clan and kinship. I fully admit that my native Southern fascination with family history is as strong as my devotion to my kind. And thus I am calling, as I said to begin with, for pride and unity.

Like Deirdre, I do believe in legends.

And I do believe, Dear Readers, that we are all One People, only separated by fluid degrees.

Land People fight and struggle and yearn to find magic in their lives. Water People hide behind that magic but realize the loneliness of it. As for Bonavendiers, add to our psyche the spoiled attitudes of a silver-spoon upbringing in the deep, coastal South, and you have that most dangerous of all combinations (and here I stoop to use two common stereotypes.)

Southern belles who are also mermaids.

Gilding the magnolia, to say the least.

Now you know.

Notes

"**Halfling**" is an all-purpose term, which refers to all mixed-blood descendents of the Old Ones and Landers. More specific distinctions are made through the use of generational prefixes—"first-generation halfling, second-generation halfling," etc.—and by clan names. (See the addendum.) However, some Water People use the word "halfling" as a slur when someone exhibits Lander-like traits, as Mara did once in speaking of Alice. That usage, however, is generally considered both inaccurate and ill mannered.

Ta-Mera is an ancient Egyptian place name meaning, "Land of the Waters" or "Land of the Great Mothers," depending upon interpretation. In the interest of accuracy I must point out that Grandmother Deirdre sometimes embroidered even everyday stories with classical allusions, whimsical imaginings, and outright untruths. After all, she was a Healer, (see the addendum on clans) and Healers are notoriously fey.

As given names, **Beckrith, Padrian**, and **Salasime** are without discernible origins in any known language. Emilene Revere may well have made the names up entirely. She was a Singer (her clan as well as her career) and Singers are sometimes prone to improvisation. (For the record, we modern-day Bonavendiers are also classified as Singers, a fact I tell you at risk to my own reputation for veracity.)

Addendum—Clans of the Water People

Introduction

As I have already stated, both Land and Water People are descended from three couples in ancient mythology: Melasine and Beckrith, Acarinth and Padrian, Leirdrela and Salasime. Most of the world's Lander population is so far removed from those origins that they have no hint of the fabulous traits left in them. But because Melasine, Acarinth, and Leirdrela still exist, still occasionally fall in love with men, and still bear children, we Water People are only a few generations removed from their original ancestry, and our talents are strong.

A more scientific explanation? Historically, some clans of Water People have shunned Landers and intermarried only with other Water People, thus re-enforcing certain special traits. Some of our kind is even so strong in bloodline that very, very amazing talents are reported. Most such reports are suspect and very hard to believe, however.

For example, neither I nor anyone I know have ever encountered a Swimmer (see the clan description, below.) A Swimmer—if, indeed, the Swimmer clan is more than rumor—is, by nature and circumstance, a recluse and loner, even among Water People. The more closely a person is related to one of the original three "Old Ones" (Melasine, Acarinth, and Leirdrela), the less like we two-legged folk he or she is, either in body or soul, and so will not risk love and affection. I have even heard rumors of Swimmers who are shapeshifters, but I refuse to indulge such an idea. The fantastic abilities of Water People are rooted in the physical laws of nature, not fairy tales.

I say that quite seriously.

The terms I've listed below to categorize our clans are, at best, fluid and capricious, often leading to prejudices and foolish judgments among Water People, who can be quite smug. That is why I forbade Mara and Pearl to mention such a hierarchy to Alice, though Pearl, naturally, couldn't resist hinting at it. Oh, all right, neither can I, at this point. As I said earlier, we Bonavendiers are Singers. One of the more highly evolved clans.

But enough discussion or I shall digress into vanities. Here, in simple terms, are our clans and their most basic descriptions, in descending order.

Clans of the Water People

The Old Ones

Melasine, Acarinth, and Leirdrela. Our real or imagined half-human, half-aquatic progenitors, also known as The Tamerians, who, according to legend, mated with three Landers after the ruin of Ta-Mera. They have continued to mate with men in all the centuries since. They are assumed to be immortal and extremely reclusive, yet also extremely seductive. No absolute proof of their existence has ever been produced.

Swimmers

Swimmers, if they exist at all, are either first-generation halflings (the immediate descendents of a Tamerian and a Lander), or simply Water People of extraordinary and rare abilities. Claims of encounters and matings between Swimmers and Water People of other clans abound, but may simply be a fanciful way to cover up reckless romances or to further gild the reputations of children with unusual abilities. Example: A pregnant woman with no husband may insist she was seduced by a

Swimmer—who, of course, left the scene immediately afterward. Swimmers are variously described as predatory, irresistible, incorrigible loners, and terrifyingly possessive shapeshifters. They cannot or will not live among either Land People or Water People. They do not look quite human.

I recently received disturbing word about a young Scottish relative of ours—a brilliant and beautiful young woman of impeccable honor, whose reputation I have no reason to doubt. She was found murdered in waters off the Isle of Skye only hours after confiding to her brother that a volatile Swimmer fathered her three remarkable young daughters. Her murder remains a mystery, and her brother has hidden her daughters for fear their father—if indeed a Swimmer—may be the killer.

Swimmers are said to be acutely psychic (much more than other Water People) and possess extraordinary powers in the use of sonar and sonic vibration, which can be used as a weapon. Their lifespans are impossible to calculate, but according to anecdote and speculation they may live several hundred years.

I cannot say more about the current family situation in Scotland at this time, but I am involved in resolving it.

Healers

Healers are a small population among us.

They quite often exhibit the best qualities of both Landers and Tamerians. Some are born with lightly webbed hands as well as feet and other unusual physical traits, which makes them avoid Lander society, but nonetheless they tend to be moderate souls, and, as their clan name suggests, they exhibit a marked talent for healing others. Some scientists among the Water People believe their healing abilities are related to our prevalent talent for sonar and sonic vibration, which has been shown to have a marked effect on cellular regeneration.

One might say that if Swimmers represent the dark side of Water People, then Healers are the light. (Dear Readers: The daughters of the murdered woman are Healers.)

Singers

Singers represent the largest clan of Water People and are by far the most successful at coexisting in the Lander world. We are categorized by webbed feet, remarkable swimming abilities, and an average lifespan of ninety to one-hundred-ten years, among other traits. Our prevailing talent is indicated by our clan name: we are psychic "singers," with the ability to lure, enthrall, and communicate in wordless vibratros of emotion. Virtually all of us also have extraordinary singing voices in the more conventional sense of "singing." In fact, a notable percentage of the world's popular entertainers and operatic stars are Water People of the Singer clan.

Good manners and common sense prevent me, of course, from naming celebrity names.

Floaters

Many of you, dear readers, are Floaters, though you don't know it and probably think of yourself as just a Lander. Your Tamerian ancestry is hidden at least a few generations past, and your feet, I'm sorry to say, are indeed the feet of a plain Lander. But you have a marked love for the waters of the world, whether fresh or salt, and you can often be found on some sunny coast or shady lakeside. You may be a sea captain or an oceanographer, or simply a land-bound devotee of the water. Regardless, you revel in fluid whimsy and daydreams, you are drawn to the great marine mammals and the colorful fish, and you are quite elegant in style, in purpose, and in thought. You sense something different about yourself, something that sets you apart from the Landers—an urge, perhaps, to take a long ocean voyage and settle in some exotic cove, or to swim beneath the surface of life's illusions and breathe against all odds.

I firmly believe that most of the great sailors and ocean adventurers of the world are, at the very least, Floaters. Though we often refer to him as a Lander, Simon Sainte-Bonavendier belonged to the Floater clan.

Landers

Land people. They make up the vast bulk of the earth's population, good and decent and special in their own way, yet so far removed from their glorious beginnings in the seas that they fear the water and try to conquer it. They are to be treated kindly and welcomed into our midst and, dare I insist, respected for their love of the earth, no matter how stubborn they are in their dominance. I intend to reform them.

There is no more to say about them than that.

~~~

And so, Dear Readers, I bid you adieu, for now. I hope you cherish all you've learned about my kind—and your own—and I promise to tell you more. But first I have a wedding to plan for Alice and Griffin, and I must address the tragic situation with my Scottish relatives.

There is another matter as well, one involving a descendent of Emilene Revere. A truly exceptional young Floater, who needs to embrace her true legacy before it's too late.

Her name is Molly.

I'm singing to her, even now.

And though she may not know it yet, she's listening.

About the cover painting...

Maxfield Parrish
"Stars," 1926, oil on board, 35-1/8" x 21-3/4"
Private collection
Photo from the archives of Alma Gilbert, Cornish, NH

The Artist: Born in Philadelphia, Maxfield Parrish (1870-1966) studied at Haverford College and the Pennsylvania Academy of the Fine Arts. He worked as an illustrator in Philadelphia until 1898, when he settled in Plainfield, New Hampshire. He lived and painted at his beloved estate, "The Oaks," until he died at the age of ninety-one. His famous works were created in the studio building located in the rear of the main house.
Parrish's work is in the permanent collections of a number of museums, including the Metropolitan Museum of Art, the Detroit Art Institute, and the M. H. DeYoung Museum in San Francisco.

Discover more of Parrish's work:
The Cornish Colony Museum is considered to house the largest collection of original works by Maxfield Parrish of any museum open regularly to the public. Alma Gilbert, curator and author of thirteen books on Parrish, is considered the living authority on his work. She has owned most of the major originals in the past thirty years.

Cornish Colony Museum
Rt. 12-A, Box 292
Cornish, NH 03745
Open to the public: Memorial Day through October
            10:00 a.m. - 5:00 p.m. EDT
            (603) 675-6000
            www.Almagilbert.com

THE STONE FLOWER GARDEN
Deborah Smith

Deborah Smith, the New York Times bestselling author of A PLACE TO CALL HOME and ON BEAR MOUNTAIN, sets her next novel inside the glamorous lives of a wealthy North Carolina family beset by tragedy and secrets. THE STONE FLOWER GARDEN will be available in hardcover from Little, Brown, & Company in February, 2002.

⌒⌒⌒⌒

On a dark spring night twenty-five years after I helped bury my Great Aunt Clara Hardigree, I found myself digging her up. I felt as if I was playing the lead in a scene from some grotesque southern soap opera. Scarlett O'Hara does the gravesite scene in Hamlet.

Alas, poor Clara, I knew her well.

A propane camp lantern hissed and flickered among the ferns by my feet. I dug for my great aunt's bones as quickly as I could in the moonlit woods. A huge marble urn loomed over me, its cascading marble flowers and marble vines poking my shoulders and head like hard fingers. The Stone Flower Garden was as much a part of the forest, as much a Hardigree symbol, as Clara's hidden grave. I shivered. Appalachian

mountains as old as the earth looked down on my shame, and beyond the deep glen with the bones and the marble urn, the lights of Burnt Stand, North Carolina, my sleeping hometown, winked knowingly at me.

We always suspected you weren't cut from the strongest Hardigree stone. The Hardigree name stood for unbreakable women and unbreakable marble. But I, Darl Union, granddaughter of Swan Hardigree Samples, great-granddaughter of Esta Hardigree, had cracked.

And it was all because of a man. I looked up at Eli Wade, the man whose trust I'd betrayed, just as my silence had betrayed his wrongfully accused father, twenty-five years earlier. Eli watched me with no understanding of what I was about to show him.

I finally found Clara's skeleton no more than an arm's length down in the loamy forest sod. When I was a child, watching my Grandmother Swan dig the grave, it had seemed like a mile. Now Clara was just dirty bones waiting to be pulled up one at a time. Perhaps I should have brought one of Swan's finest linen tablecloths to wrap her in. A monogrammed one. We Hardigrees set a nice table.

The only thing that startled me was a necklace I plucked from the grave soil. When I wiped its small pendant and held it to the lantern light, I saw the twinkle of a diamond set in a tiny, polished chip of milk-white Hardigree marble.

Grandmother had one just like it. So did I. It was a tradition in our family. Not a family crest, but the next best thing: Hard stone on hard stone, tinged with the soil of our ambitions.

I shivered again. *Done, then.* Every piece of infamous misery lay exposed. Nausea rose in my throat and I sat back on my heels with Clara's pendant clasped in my fist, my head bowed, my eyes shut. As a child I never meant to help Grandmother murder her and blame it on someone else. Like all the unforeseen fates -- hate and true love and success and failure -- it just happened.

"Your father didn't kill Clara," I told Eli. "Swan and I did."

Eli looked at the grave in shock, and then, slowly, back at me. Ineffable sadness and anger began to crowd the night air between us. I believed at that moment that he could never forgive me, and I could never forgive myself. "How could you do this to me?" he asked.

"Family," I whispered.

Children lose their innocence piece by piece. The layers are carved away until our hearts have been exposed and polished into an unnatural gloss. We spend the rest of our lives trying to remember why we ever loved so passionately and how we dreamed so simply, before life chiseled us down to the core.